The Road Is Nev(

Copyright © Jeff

The right of Jeffrey Brett to be ident
been asserted by him in accordanc
Patents Act 1988.

All rights are reserved. No part of this publication may be reproduced,
stored in a data base or introduced into a retrieval system, or transmitted
in any form, or by any means (electronic, mechanical, photocopying,
recording or otherwise) without the prior written permission of the
author.

Any person who commits any breach of these rights in relation to this
publication may be liable to criminal prosecution and civil claims for
damages.

This book is a work of fiction, references to names and characters, places
and incidents are products of the author's imagination. Any resemblance
to actual events, places or persons, living or dead is purely coincidental.

For more information, please contact: magic79.jb@outlook.com

First Published January 2019

Introduction

Aimlessly I wandered along the high street with no real intention in mind other than to be amongst the crowd absorbing the interaction of passers-by quietly studying their faces wondering what each was thinking as I shuffled left then right moving my feet in a somewhat awkward tango. Every so often I would intentionally rub against the arm of a female going by catching the scent of her perfume as she looked back over her shoulder with indignation contemptuously sneering my way that I had violated her space instantly dismissing the notion that our coming together had meant something.

Into the third week of December it was gaining momentum as Christmas loomed as fast as the grey skies overhead started to turn a greyish white threatening an imminent downfall that night. The afternoon however was awash with bargain hunters seeking out a knock-down gift to save hard earned cash although some were beginning to make their way home heavily laden down with brand named bags their day exhaustingly done and ready for tea.

As for me I wasn't here to shop only observe. Coursing my way between the oncoming pedestrians I hated Christmas, detested the hype and the expectation that others put upon you to enjoy the event. All that loving and giving, drinking and eating, a time to be kind. I wondered what was so different any other time of the year. If truth were known for every one that like it another nine despised the festive season.

Looking around I saw the normal stalls selling hot roasted chestnuts, greasy burgers and fried donuts the vendors eagerly rubbing their gloved hands together to stave off the cold. What was it with the modern trends of today and were people too afraid to rock the boat, conform to tradition or had commercial exploitation sucked us down a never ending chasm of hesitant indecision.

Beneath the overhanging glass canopy to the entrance of a large department store I sighted the well-stuffed and bearded Santa standing on the first step up. His presence as had days before set my teeth together and had the sinews of my body tense. The closer I stepped in his direction he seemed to see me coming, immediately ringing the small brass handled bell that he held in his right hand where with desperate jerks he incessantly bellowed his customary 'ho-ho-ho' to the annoyance of all around. He was as contemptible in his delivery as when I had first set eyes on him.

Dropping by several degrees the temperature had passers-by exhaling small clouds of exhausted oxygen bringing out a flurry of scarves, hats and gloves. In the air the inviting odours of a coffee filter permeated our senses and I for one was sold on the idea of grabbing a hot chocolate accompanied by a warm mine pie. I would joined the others heading towards the coffee shop had I not been thwarted by the voices in my head demanding that I accomplish my mission that afternoon.

Almost on top of my quarry the bell continued to ring to the sound of coins as they filled the red coloured plastic buckets held aloft by two young women who stood either side of the overweight Santa desperately dancing on the spot to keep their limbs from collapsing. Dressed in a green and red outfit they had little protection from the elements evident by the taller woman whose nipples I could see through her tunic.

The louder the bell echoed in my head the more intense my memory became descending over my eyes like a nightmare and through the haze I saw a vision of a defiant young boy who had been sent to his room without any supper or love as the church bell in the distance chimed incessantly to announce the call for evensong. Like Christmas I hated bells.

Standing there watching I recalled the evenings that I had been forced to read and repeat back the scriptures reading from the only book in the cottage the bible, asking that god would forgive me my sins. What sins I would ask myself, was it so wrong to love someone. Was it so wrong to want them there with you? I despised god as I did the fat oaf ringing his little bell. If I had seen a reindeer pulling a sleigh I would have snapped its neck.

3

For days I had been walking the streets observing the people, families inside their homes, watching them prepare for the festivities ahead. At the weekends people had gathered and partied into the small hours forgetting the week that had just gone past, trying desperately to dismiss the hardships. I had lay witness to couple arguing over seemingly pointless matters and others wondering how they could afford all the presents that the children demanded. Looking up at Santa I wondered why he deemed it necessary to smile.

On either side of the stepped entrance the window display had been created in two parts, first the journey made by the magi and on the opposite side the nativity. They had been crafted beautifully by somebody skilled at their art. Mary looked on lovingly as she cradled the baby Jesus, watched over by Joseph and the three kings, a donkey, several lambs, a goat and even small children. I had lost count how many times I had prayed wanting to be one of those children. In bed at nights under the stars I had shivered and begged that somebody help my mother and me, asking the good lord to be merciful but not once had he listened.

More recently my dreams had been evolving as nightmares, frightening visions of a man walking along a long road slowly travelling towards a darkness, where beyond lie hope and peace. Waking in a sweat I had never worked out whether the place beyond was hell or paradise as the road had never seemed long enough. Last night's nightmare however had been the worst this week.

Moving first left towards the magi then right at the nativity I caught sight of myself in the reflection of the glass seeing the faceless demon that looked back at me beneath my hood. Moments later I felt the trickle of sweat as it ran from between my shoulder blades and down my spine. Somewhere between seven that morning and four in the afternoon Satan had told me what needed to be done.

Despite my disapprobation of religion I had visited a church to dispel the evil from my mind but my salvation had already been stolen and my salvation lost to the voices. I did not pray and I did kneel but I did see an angel descend from the stained glass window. Like me she wore a hood and although I could not see her face I knew that it was my mother. We

4

sat and talked until she had to leave. Sometime after that propping myself up against a headstone I vowed to take revenge.

I was reliving the moment that we had talked when a voice nearby shrieked loudly in my ear *'Want something for Christmas, come on in and bring the children, come people join the queue!'*

Instinctively I wanted to lash out there and then, wrap my hands around his throat and throttle the life from his lungs. I was desperate to hear the fat imposter beg for mercy as his bladder lost control and his knees gave way realising that his end had come. With a look of contempt I glared back.

'The only thing that I'd want from you is a couple of hours with the taller of the two elves, otherwise fuck off you contemptible bastard!'

Momentarily shocked he stepped forward to protect the two young women and realising where my eyes were focused the taller elf suddenly crossed her arms to protect and hide her chest. I grinned when I saw the shorter elf shrink from sight and hide herself behind Santa's cumbersome bulk. His initial indignation was soon replaced by anger.

'Over my dead body,' he retaliated 'now be off with you asshole before I call the police!'

With senses and nerves strung tight I considered cutting him there on the step but there were far too many witnesses. Inside my head I could hear them all laughing, I wondered why everybody had always considered me as worthless.

Dropping my right hand down to the inside of my trench coat I caressed the cold steel of the knife. The metal blade felt reassuring, even comforting. I smiled, it would only take a swift lunge and sideways slash to end the man's life it was that easy. Accepting that it was not the right time nor the moment I turned away.

'Merry Christmas you fat fuck, I'll be seeing you around!'

Winking at the taller elf she snubbed her nose in the air at me reacting with indifference as though I did not exist, that somehow pleased me. If time permitted later I might seek out her interest as well.

Walking to where I was no longer visible I crossed the road dropping discreetly into a convenient unlit alleyway which at one time had been the service passage around the rear of the shops. Using the shadows as cover I took advantage of my position to watch Santa and his elves.

Soon after our brief encounter the trio went back inside the store where the welcome heat from the overhead blowers was a stark reminder of how cold it was outside. At the other end of the shopping precinct the church clock chimed three times announcing to the last of the shoppers that they had a quarter of an hour left until closing time.

Shuffling my feet the cold was beginning to numb my toes, I had to keep the circulation moving about my body so blowing between my cupped hands I stepped back under the cover of darkness until I was virtually invisible. The weather had changed quicker than I had anticipated.

I focused my attention on the staff exit hearing the continuous thump of the metal bar as it slammed against the timber panel of the emergency door watching members of the store staff leave in two's and three's, some by themselves. After five minutes of the store closing the two elves appeared much more suitably attired. They walked away arm in arm and I considered following but their souls were saved that day when moments behind Santa exited through the same door. Waving at the young women he headed in my direction as I knew he would.

Without his ridiculous outfit to pad out his torso he was still way too fat. Following close behind the knife slapped against the outside of my leg. I was surprised although satisfied that so many shoppers had left the area and keeping my head low under my hood I prevented any closed circuit security cameras from recording my face.

Taking a left or right turn at various junctions we crossed going between parked cars until eventually we entered a quiet unlit street where despite the sudden loss of artificial light I could tell that the houses were well maintained, expensive. This was a nice area the likes of which I had never seen, would never see for myself.

I let the overweight fraud reach his front door and go inside before I sauntered down the garden path acting out my part as though I was an expectant visitor should I have been observed by a neighbour. Inside the hall light was left on moments before the landing above was flooded with light as well. Waiting patiently I knew instinctively that he would come back down having used the bathroom. Standing under the porch I heard his footfalls descend the wooden stairs as I reached forward and depressed the bell taking the knife from the side of my leg as he reached for the door. This was the season of surprise and he was about to get his.

With the hood of my long coat riding low over my face and covering my eyes I gave a confident whoop of *'ho-ho-ho'* as he pulled the door back. The surprise of my standing on his doorstop caught his breath as I forced myself inside and shut the door. With the tip of the knife against the underside of his chin we went through the kitchen. The kitchen diner had been tastefully designed with clean lines and beige coloured units.

With his eyes bugling above his nose he stammered to ask *'you... you, what do... do you want?'*

I had considered laughing but this was no laughing matter, it never had been.

'Why you of course, you fat fuck.'

We stood there for several seconds in silence as I listened to the voices in my head before I made him sit on one of the dining chairs. Lashing his wrists to the uprights of the chair I added *'come to think of it, you and others like you have been on my Christmas list for a long time!'*

Frozen in fear like the bushes outside as the beast from the east descended he started to babble like a baby offering me money, jewels anything that I wanted although had I been so generous to tell him I doubted that he would have had the time left to understand.

Beyond the kitchen window the stars had all come out watch.

Part One

Chapter One

Nine months later

The call was received by Southport Police early Thursday morning where the female reporting the incident sounded breathless as the blood coursed erratically through her veins, she had not been running. There was a slight hesitancy, trembling in her voice as she introduced herself not quite sure how to begin. For the call taker this was the last shift of a tedious four day rota and come two o'clock that afternoon Carole Hawkes wanted nothing more than to get her head down and make up for lost sleep.

'Take your time ma'am and breath slowly, I will listen and record whatever you say. Do you understand caller?'

Emma Crandon forced her mouth shut and breathed in deep through her nose inflating her lungs several until she felt the tension ebb from her brow. Opening her eyes once again she turned around to make sure not wanting to be accused of wasting police time.

'He's dead…' she blurted out 'cold as a lifeless kipper fresh from the ice sheds down by the harbour!'

Carole Hawkes looked up at the digital clock on the wall thinking to herself it was a little early for a crank call. Bottom right of her monitor the automated clock registered eighteen minutes past seven. Sat beside Carole her colleague had stopped threading the needle through the sleeve of her granddaughter's jumper. She adjusted the volume of the headset.

'Have you called an ambulance or the doctor?' Hawkes asked.

'Why… why would I do that,' replied Crandon wondering if she should have called them first before alerting the police. 'Mr Benson is lying on the kitchen table and from the way that he's lying there it's bloody obvious that he's dead!' Doubt had quickly changed to frustration.

'Are you sure, have you checked his airway?' Hawkes felt it was pertinent to ask to make sure.

'No I have not checked his airway, that's a little bit difficult with his fucking nuts and meat sticking out the side of his mouth!' Frustration had become anger.

Immediately raising her hand Sue Jenkins alerted the attention of Sergeant Johnson, the control room supervisor making him aware of the call.

'I am sorry caller but I missed the last part of what you said, could you please repeat it again!'

Emma Crandon sighed emphatically, the fucking police were all the same whenever you called them, always so bloody suspicious and forever asking stupid inane questions. Filling her lungs again with fresh air she repeated herself.

'I said love that if you had your bollocks sticking out the side of your mouth, you would probably want to come down here and have a look wouldn't you!'

Behind where she was stood at the end of the hallway Emma Crandon sensed that her employee was in no position to help, but that she needed help more than him. If the police didn't come soon she was liable to lose control and not just of her mind but her bladder as well.

Making his way around the bank of consoles Sergeant Johnson headed towards where Carole Hawkins was doing her best to placate the caller. Plugging his headset into her console he took over, his soft, yet influentially calming.

'Good morning ma'am. My name is Sergeant Johnson and I am from the Southport Control Room, how may we help you today?'

That was much better Emma Crandon thought, she had always preferred talking to men.

'I came round to do a bit of cleaning at Mr Benson's house this morning, only I found him lying on the kitchen table minus his wedding tackle. Somebody has murdered him.'

'I see… have you touched anything?' asked Johnson.

'No… nothing, I promise!'

'That's very good,' replied Johnson 'now if you would just confirm the details of the address that you are calling from we will get a mobile patrol to you within minutes.'

With the address verified on screen he whispered to Hawkes and Jenkins to check it out on voters and then check the addresses either side in case it was neighbourly dispute.

'You promise that you won't be long,' Emma pleaded 'it really is awful… really awful and I don't want to be in the house any longer than I have too!'

'I assure you that a unit has been dispatched ma'am and it is already on its way to you. Now why don't you go out front and await their arrival. Sit down if you need to, and remember to inhale long and hard, it will make you feel better!'

Emma Crandon did as suggested. She did like talking to men unlike the silly bitch before him, only men had an inner strength that she found alluring. Sitting on the front steps she could hear sirens in the distance. One thing was for sure, she would never ever go back inside.

.....

Several weeks in after passing her final exams at the central training academy Amanda Jones was sat in the passenger seat of the patrol car when dispatch radioed through that they were to attend the report of a suspicious incident at seventy two Parkway Drive. Amanda wrote down the address and the name of the caller.

'And there are no further details other than that?' she asked mentally preparing herself for an early start to the day. Suspicious incident could mean anything from a cat in the attic to a stiff.

Accelerating hard with his foot down on the pedal Simon Preston flicked on the roof lights and two tones.

'Control have to be cautious as to what details they give over the airwaves mainly because of radio hams. Very often they'll turn up at an address just to see what we've got.'

Jones disapproved of their hobby. 'You would think that they'd find better things to occupy their free time.'

Turning at the junction they saw the woman wave from the steps at the property two thirds down from the corner shop where a group of teenagers with hoodies had already gathered.

'They're early,' said Jones.

'They never sleep,' was all Preston wanted to commit himself to.

With three years in Simon Preston recognised the expression on the woman's face as he pulled the car in alongside where she was waiting.

'Grab your cap and your gloves, we'll need both.'

'Why?'

Removing the keys from the ignition Jones handed him his cap.

'Gut feeling that well be needing them,'

Relieved that the police had arrived Emma Crandon felt she was no longer responsible for the scene inside. Holding onto the female officer's arm as she pushed the door of the patrol car shut Emma advised that she wait for her colleague.

'It's not good darling. He's in there... in the kitchen only I ain't going back in, not for all the tea in china!'

Amanda Jones pulled clear as Simon Preston locked the car.

'That's alright ma'am, you stay outside and wait here. We'll go inside and see what's occurring!'

Wanting to prove to her older colleague that she had the pluck to be in a front line response unit Amanda Jones headed up the short flight of stone steps and pushed open the unlocked door. Looking back at the junction Simon Preston was suspicious of the youths who were still watching. He double checked that the car was secure knowing that this wasn't the sort of area where you took any chances.

Jones cautiously waited until the door was right back before she went inside as Emma Crandon witnessed the young officer's trepidation. She had a niece roughly the same age. She wondered why anybody that pretty and young want to compete in such a violent, unpredictable occupation. To be spat at, verbally and physically abused when they could be safe working in a shop or office. And like she had warned Amanda Jones she did the same with Simon Preston.

'I'd be getting in there if I was you because your colleague is going to need help when she find's what's lying on the kitchen table!

A minute later Amanda Jones came back clutching her stomach before disgorging the contents of her breakfast over the small lawn. Removing a bottle of water from her handbag Emma Crandon offered a drink. 'Here love, sip this it will make you feel better!'

Standing in the doorway of the kitchen Simon Preston could do nothing but stare his focus going between the dead man's vaulted groin up to the mouth. He had never seen anything so distasteful. With his thumb depressed he radioed for help. 'Alpha Bravo One to control...' the walls however inside the house were strong Victorian, well built and affecting his transmission. He tried again. *'Come on control answer the bloody radio... Alpha Bravo One calling!'*

Sergeant Johnson was the first to pick up the call.

'Tell me what you've found Preston?'

'It's not good sergeant... not good at all. The lady was right and we will need help, Supervisory, CID and CSI.'

Johnson instructed that the two officers were to make sure Emma Crandon didn't leave the scene and that everything from the front gate to the rear yard was to be contained until back up arrived. Up at the shop some of the youths had disappeared.

A father in his own right and a police sergeant second, Johnson asked. 'Is Jones alright?'

Preston looked down along that short passage and to where the two women were talking. Amanda Jones was sat alongside Emma Crandon sipping from a plastic bottle.

'She's fine sarge, she was the first in!'

The unwritten rule was that colleagues however green would back one another in the learning curve of professional protocol. Everybody had to start at the bottom and work their way up. Without moral support a shift could be a very lonely place. Preston decided that there was nothing he could in the kitchen so he went back outside to erect a cordon as a few of the neighbours were beginning to open windows and front doors.

'Feeling any better?' he asked.

Amanda Jones managed a half-hearted smile 'yeah, I'm okay, it's just my pride that has let me down!'

Emma Crandon put her arm around the young female and gave her a quick hug.

'Hopefully we'll never have to see anything like that ever again love.'

'And you...Mrs Crandon,' Simon Preston asked 'are you alright?'

Emma Crandon looked up at the young man, the police were all young these days. Preston was unusually calm and in control with an air of authority in his voice like that of the sergeant in the control room.

'I will be when I get a cup of tea inside me, then I'll stop my heart from leaping about my chest.' She looked at the open door although she could not see the kitchen beyond. 'It's not every day that you come round first thing in the morning and see your employer lying naked on the kitchen table.' Taking a deep breath she breathed in through her nose and hug Jones again giving her a wink 'ordinarily men are only ever naked for one thing!'

Amanda Jones responded with a wry smile, she was no virgin.

Looking back up the road to the shop Preston observed that all the youths had disappeared, it wasn't a good omen. As the crowd gathered the other side of his taped cordon a lonely figure in a long coat and hood hung low watched as the events of the morning began to unfold. Soon other vehicles with flashing lights turned the corner and came down adding additional resources to the relief of Jones and Preston.

When a familiar blue Saab arrived the officers gathered to receive instruction.

.....

Recently promoted to Detective Sergeant and based at Southport Central, Daniel Atherton had travelling into work when he had taken the call from Neil Johnson in the control room. Collecting Pete Byrne on route from his home they had made their way direct to the address on the east side of the town.

'It can kick up rough around here sometimes,' Byrne warned as he released the lock from the seatbelt of the Saab 'only last week a patrol had bottles thrown at them on night duty!'

Atherton nodded appreciative of the advice, he had worked similar areas, respectful of the tension that had divided police and residents opinion. Locking the car door he asked. 'How are Anne and the girls?'

'Good... thanks.'

They slipped under the crime scene cordon and approached Preston where he gave an account of what he and Jones had found upon arrival. Preston concluded stating that the scene was unique.

'And who's the witness?' asked Atherton.

Pointing at his marked car he told them that Amanda Jones was grabbing a quick statement from Emma Crandon. Atherton was pleased with how the scene had been preserved, the young crew had done well.

'Neil Johnson told me that she was the cleaner, is that right?'

Preston agreed 'Emma Crandon has her own key, a private arrangement with the owner of the house. She arrived around seven, knocked but getting reply let herself in. What's inside is what she found. Nothing's been touched.

'A bit early to be cleaning isn't it and especially if she expected the occupier to be in?'

Preston looked over to the car where his colleague was still gathering details.

'Mrs Crandon told us that she likes to get in early on a Thursday finishing around lunchtime, after which it's a quick flit down to the shops before settling down in time for the afternoon soaps.'

'What's it like, inside?' asked Atherton. He wanted to appreciate what Simon Preston had felt when he had first come across the scene as initial reactions could help the investigation.

'It's not at all good sarge and I would be lying if I didn't say that it hadn't turned my stomach when I first saw the dead man but it needed calling in. Whoever did this can't be all right in the head!'

Byrne sucked in air through his teeth. 'That good eh.'

Daniel Atherton glanced up then either side of number seventy. Most of the properties were the same, in need of attention, double glazed windows and new roofs. It was abundantly obvious that the council did not consider the street or its residents a priority.

Ascending the short flight of steps Atherton turned and asked 'Did you check upstairs?'

Preston shook his head wondering if they should have 'We didn't want to contaminate any evidence that might be on the stairs or upper landing.'

Atherton smiled accepting the reason why. Standing in the kitchen doorway they stood in silence absorbing the impact of the brutal and extreme scene in front of them. Beneath the table supporting the deceased a pool of blood had reservoired like an abstract painting and above both testes and penis belonging to the deceased hung limply from the side of his like the disgorged innards of an octopus.

'That's put me off going to the fish market this weekend,' Byrne remarked as he reached for a stick of chewing gum. He offered Atherton a stick but the detective sergeant declined. Byrne had seen reform, changes and restructure throughout the force and an influx of new personnel many with university degrees like Daniel Atherton but in almost fifteen years of police work he had never come across anything as bizarre.

'Crime never changes Pete, only the offenders.' Atherton walked around the table sensing what Byrne had been thinking. Nowadays violence had become the norm and was part and parcel of life.

'Well somebody was certainly pissed with our victim.'

Careful where he placed his feet Atherton crouched down to visually examine the hands and fingers of the deceased. The fingertips especially were blooded.

'You think he knew?' asked Byrne.

'Knew what Pete?'

'That his bits had just been removed.' He also had seen the stained fingers.

Atherton momentarily looked up and nodded. 'That would be my initial thought... yes. And I'd say that he was possibly drugged only there's a familiar odour lingering about.' He sniffed 'possibly pentobarbital.'

Byrne continued searching through the eyelevel cupboard as he sniffed the air detecting nothing.

'And you can tell that just by sniffing the air.' He asked.

'Up until last year I had a pet Labrador only during her life she had contracted rheumatism and a failing kidney. In the end the vet and I agreed the humane thing to do was give her a lethal dose and put her to sleep. He used pentobarbital. Up close it has a distinctive smell.'

Byrne tried again but reached the same result. He sniffed as something had irritated his sinuses. 'And it can be used on humans too?'

'Sure Anaesthetist's use it to safely put a patient under before they go in to have surgery.'

'So with the administration of a narcotic we could possibly be looking at some weirdo sex game that went horribly wrong!'

Atherton looked from the groin to the bits hanging from the deceased's mouth. 'No I don't believe so. This has the hallmarks of a straightforward torture and execution.'

Byrne was somewhat relieved. He didn't mind dragging in screaming, plea bargaining queers he just couldn't abide the waste of good police time.

'Well I know this... drugs or no drugs, if some bastard tried to remove my tackle and shove in my mouth I'd fight back like rabid dog from hell.'

Atherton appeared dubious 'That might not have been possible only pentobarbital is a muscle relaxant!'

Sniffing and rubbing the underside of his nose where it was still affected by an airborne irritant Pete Byrne sensed a presence walking down the short hallway to the kitchen, looking he saw a woman feeling his resolve disappear.

'If you have a cold detective please take it elsewhere only I would prefer that my crime scene wasn't contaminated.'

Putting her bags of trick in the doorway the head of forensic investigation, Marjorie Matthews stood her ground glaring at the older detective. It was no secret that they didn't get along.

'I doubt the stiff will object!' replied Byrne.

Marjorie however was ready for a fight 'Obviously not but with open wounds any airborne germ can easily contaminate and affect a biopsy result. Gathering evidence has to be undertaken in the most sterile of circumstances available.'

Byrne conceded the point vacating the room raising his palms in her direction to help placate any further verbal exchange aware that Atherton was trying to find a solution to their hostility.

'I'll go see if Jones is finished with the informant.'

Atherton felt the tension in the air dissipate.

'Are you okay sergeant only you seem a little distracted?' Marjorie asked.

Atherton smiled although the scene did not warrant any sign of facial expression.

'I'm fine Marjorie. It's good to see you. I was just running through a scenario in my mind, that's all.'

Marjorie liked the young sergeant. Since he had been promoted heading up the criminal investigative department things had changed dramatically, good things and now crime scenes were being respected in a different light. His university degree had also brought a fresh approach to her work as Daniel Atherton had on many occasions shown a keen interest in forensic investigation.

'This is brutally bizarre.' She replied.

'That's what we were thinking.'

Extracting several instruments from her bag she placed several plastic makers about the table.

'This is almost certainly as cold-hearted as what I have seen before today. I'm used to limbless cadavers but not without the genitals. There's a sense of barbarism in what took place here.'

Circling the table she began her investigation by taking photographs numbering the marker and starting a chronological sequence. Beneath the table she measured the reservoir of drying blood taking a sample. Rammed into a well-worn butchers block she again photographed and measured from the end of the hilt to the block. It would help determine the force with which the blade had been forced into the wood.

'Our murder weapon,' she announced as she stood back. Going closer again she spotted something and pointed so that Atherton could identify what she was examining.

'There...' she pointed 'where the handle meets the choil there is a small trace of blood left behind. The killer has tried to wash the blade clean but blood is sticky and sometimes difficult to remove.'

Checking around the sink drainer and taps she found several more traces. Like Atherton she went in close taking her keen nose as close to Arthur Benson as she dare. She saw Atherton nod.

'Do you know what it is?' she asked.

'Pentobarbital.'

'She agreed puffing up her chest then deflating her lungs. 'Which suggests quite possibly that this unfortunate victim was alive when his parts were removed.'

'If you establish a time of death Marjorie I'd be interested to know when only it'll give us something to base our investigation on.'

Hearing the footfalls of a man behind he turned to greet Michael Hargreaves the County Coroner. Hargreaves acknowledged both.

'You will forgive me if I don't shake your hands but the damn gloves that they produce nowadays always make me feel like a shop window manikin.' He stepped into the kitchen.

'That poor woman in the police vehicle out front, did she find him sergeant?'

'Yes Sir.'

Hargreaves followed the route that Atherton and Marjorie had taken minutes before. Lifting up the deceased's left hand he let it drop testing the degree of rigor mortis. 'It must have been quite a shock for her to come across a scene such as this...' he took himself to where the genitals hung limply from the mouth pointing at the penis where it had been clamped tight by the teeth. 'The murder forced the upper jaw onto the lower mandible hence the dental abrasions embedded into the penis.'

'Would the victim have been alive when that happened?' asked Atherton, the need to know essential.

'I think the mutilation took place as he watched.' He moved to the victims head again. 'See here...' he pointed 'the eyes are looking down. It is my opinion that this poor soul was forced to watch the removal as the horror in his eyes would suggest. He would have suffered not just physically but mentally as well. I'm surprised that his heart didn't give out as he bore witness to his mutilation.'

Atherton was satisfied 'A revenge attack.'

Marjorie broke away from what she had been examining.

'Nobody in their right mind goes around exacting this sort of reprisal... it's positively insane. You hear of the rare case abroad concerning a jealous wife who seeks revenge on an unfaithful husband but most cases like this occur mainly where a red-mist individual has a temper to match their volatile nature.' Hargreaves agreed.

Taking himself into the next room Atherton left them to get on with the job of establishing a time. He saw Pete Byrne talking to Emma Crandon wondering what part if any she might have played in this murder. It was possible as she had access to a key. Around the same age she and her employer could have been lovers. From the kitchen he was called back in.

'We believe that death occurred sometime around one this morning when most of the residents would have been in their beds.'

Hargreaves further stated that he would perform a post-mortem later under clinical conditions but in the meantime Marjorie would continue to gather evidence for the investigation. They did however have some findings that would help.

Hargreaves again lifted up the deceased's hand. 'See here sergeant, there are ingrained callouses especially just below the fingers and palm which suggests that the victim had been used to hard graft, a labourer maybe.' He let go of the hand. 'Have you found anything to indicate his profession or place of employment?'

'Not yet Sir... and the blood around the fingers... can that be explained,' Atherton asked 'did he realise the extent of his injury after he regained the use of his senses?'

Hargreaves examined the hand once more then looked down at the exposure in the groin.

'I would say that his touching was an involuntary reaction, knowing that something was wrong, something was missing.'

Hargreaves dropped the hand. 'Think of a soldier that loses a leg on a landmine the shock instantly blankets the horror but sometime later the victim will search the body for the missing limb, a natural instinct to ensure that everything is in order. We come into the world whole so we should expect to leave intact. This poor man however witnessed the attack but his mind refused to accept the revulsion that had been inflicted upon his person. He had to know. It would be no different for any other person, man or woman. His eyes recorded the cataclysmic seizure that he witnessed.'

'And he couldn't call out?' Atherton asked.

Hargreaves noticed a very small puncture wound on the side of the neck.

'Intravenously he was drugged.' He looked at Atherton then Marjorie 'although I think you know that. Paralysis of the vocal cords would have prevented him calling for help and our killer knew this long before he arrived. He examined the wound in the lower abdomen. 'The same as he knows how to cut.'

Pentobarbital.' Atherton said. 'It's what I believed the killer used.'

Hargreaves agreed. 'That would certainly work and suit the circumstances.'

He went in close to the mouth. 'There is a metallic presence that you would expect from the body after death although there is a secondary element.' Eyeing the front door he righted himself. 'How long has the door been open?'

'Since the cleaner arrived, approximately an hour maybe.'

Hargreaves rubbed the underside of his chin with the back of the gloved hand.

'Time enough for other odours to penetrate the interior. The air outside, scents from flowers in the properties either side,' there were no mention of anything in Arthur Benson's garden 'traffic fumes from the police vehicles arriving, a smoker in the crowd, anything that would interfere with perhaps an analysis. I won't say what until I've run a toxicology test.'

Not wishing to leave either of them disheartened Michael Hargreaves nodded 'Pentobarbital however would work and given the right amount would render the victim sufficiently conscious so that they were aware of what was happening but unable to defend themselves. A terrifying predicament.'

Hargreaves looked at his watch mentally recalling his schedule for the day.

'I can perform the autopsy at two this afternoon. Would that allow enough time for your interim enquiries sergeant?'

'Ample time, thank you Sir!'

He left them alone again heading off to check the rest of the house going into the adjacent room which had been used for dining purposes, which struck him as odd as the occupant already had a table in the kitchen. To the centre was an old wooden table and four chairs one that didn't match. Under the window was an armchair where the back cover had a heavy grease stain where Arthur Benson had laid his head back and watched the birds nesting outside. What surprised Atherton the most was the lack of creature comfort. Devoid of framed photographs, the odd painting or ornament the place was lacking in material memories and goods. The furniture looked old and shabby, discoloured and second hand, hand-me-downs that had been given out of sympathy. Going through each of the rooms he found pretty much the same.

On the landing above and over the kitchen below he stood momentarily in silence gathering his thoughts. Closing his eyes he let the house talk to him and give up its secrets. All about him he could feel the energy of many souls pushing and pulling, asking and demanding so much of his attention but Daniel Atherton could not appease them all. Reopening his eyes he concentrated his focus on the airing cupboard.

With the door pulled open he had to immediately stand back fighting off the discharge of dust and smell of urine from the linen on the shelves above the copper cylinder. Pushing to one side he checked under and between folded bed sheets, items of underwear and towels, nothing new and some past their sell by date. Some items of clothing although laundered had black stains possibly from oil or grease. The jacket around the cylinder red in colour was torn and where it was badly damaged had limp sections of thin foam hanging down. All the time he felt the pressure on the back of his neck and shoulders pushing into him but Atherton had seen enough. Closing the door he went into the bathroom but other than a worn flannel, toothbrush, razor and tube of toothpaste there was little else to see.

In the front bedroom the furniture again was no better than the floor below. Pushed against the chimney breast was a double bed although from the way that it had been made and left nobody had slept in it for a very long time. Under the window was an old fashioned crafted vanity dresser with an angled mirror. He could not see a hand brush or comb and also absent were bottles of aftershave, perfumes or jars of cream. Atherton sensed that Arthur Benson had been expecting a female guest to stay at some time only it looked as though she had never arrived.

Pushing aside the door to the rear bedroom it was marginally better although in one corner the wallpaper had come loose and was water damaged due to a misplaced roof tile. The double bed was larger although it had definitely been used. The sheets lay in a state of disarray as the occupant had left in a hurry. Housed behind the door were a pair of old laminated timber wardrobes and set against other walls around the room and either side of the window were a single chest of drawers, a blanket box, two small bedside cabinets and a chair over which the deceased had smoothed out his trousers and shirt. Lying crumpled on the floor beside the chair were a worn pair of socks and carpet slippers. Central to the bed and on the wall opposite was a large wooden cross which had been secured into the plasterwork and brick by two screws.

Checking the drawers, blanket box and wardrobes Atherton found a bible and a small square tin. Examining the bible he found the initials *AB* pencilled into the top right corner. They were the markings of a small child. The tin contained a number of old photographs mostly taken at a park and others coastal landscapes, although he wasn't sure where.

'Find anything yet that will help?' asked Marjorie as she entered the rear bedroom. Atherton pointed at the bible and open tin.

'There's not a lot to go on. What about you?'

'Same as downstairs. The victim didn't have a lot to shout about. I would say his furniture came from auction houses as most of it is mismatched and has seen better days elsewhere in somebody else's home.' Picking up the tin with her gloved hand Marjorie added. 'Have you noticed that there are no paintings or family photographs?'

Atherton handed over the images that he had. Marjorie flicked through the photographs as he replied.

'It's almost as if he didn't want to be haunted by the past!'

'I find that eerily creepy. I know that I would be lost without my photographs.'

She handed them back as there was nothing significant about children playing and a few holiday snaps.

'Has Michael Hargreaves gone?'

'Yes, he had to leave as he was already running behind schedule. The van will be here soon to remove the deceased. He said to say that he would see us later.'

'Pete Byrne won't go.' Atherton admitted, receiving a wry smile from Marjorie.

'No, I guessed not. He seems to shy away from the mortuary and post-mortems.'

'He's just not comfortable around them and I don't push it!' Neither did Marjorie.

'I came up to say that we could be here for another two to three hours and although this isn't a big place and it's hardly furnished sometimes it is the empty shells that cause me the most problems.'

Daniel Atherton heard her descent on the staircase as a cold shiver entered the room passing through his soul. He wasn't shaken or perturbed by the experience because it had happened many times before and as before there were no signs to indicate who.

Out of respect he replaced the bible putting it back in the bedside drawer before shutting the lid of the lid slipping the photographs into the pocket of his suit jacket. Taking one last look around the bedroom he pulled the door shut and descended to the floor below.

Outside in the front garden he found Pete Byrne talking to Emma Crandon and standing next to her was Amanda Jones and Simon Preston. He smiled at Amanda Jones.

'You good?' he asked.

'I am now, although I admit sarge it was a shock!'

'Why don't you both go next door and see if they know anything. With a bit of luck they'll have the kettle on only you've been here since the call came in and you look like you could do with a good strong cup of hot tea.'

When Atherton saw the rings on Emma Crandon's fingers he realised that Arthur Benson had none although it didn't say much as a many men didn't wear jewellery.

'And how do you feel now Mrs Crandon?' he asked.

'I'm alright and it ain't that I've not seen a dead body before only not naked and with its bits missing. I was married once only my Eric passed away ten years ago with a heart attack although he was fully clothed at the time. Now the lazy lump of lard who occupies my Eric's chair thinks he owns me but he is under delusions of grandeur.'

Atherton nodded an accord with what she had said. 'Me neither. I've never come across anything quite like that I assure you!'

Emma Crandon saw Amanda Jones disappear into the house next door.

'I'm not sure know how she'll cope it right shook her up!'

Pete Byrne was on hand to help. 'Amanda Jones... she'll be alright. A few more bad incidents under her belt and she'll be rocking along like an old hand.'

Emma Crandon wasn't convinced. The young woman was tough on the outside but soft as putty beneath.

Atherton pressed her some more 'Is there anything else about this morning that you could help with something that you might have forgotten to tell my colleagues?'

'About Arthur?'

'Anything Mrs Crandon. Any memory helps with our investigation and of course I would like to hear what you think happened?'

Emma Crandon repeated what she had told Pete Byrne. She cleaned at the house twice a week, had been given a spare key by her employer and she had never encountered any trouble with Arthur Benson. The deceased had never made any physical advances towards her, never used offensive language in her presence and never been suggestive. He asked her about the wooden cross on the wall in the bedroom but she could only say that she had been asked to keep it free of dust and polished.

After a few moments of silence to let it sink in she added 'Arthur always paid me in cash. It weren't enough to declare to the tax office but enough to get me by. We never had us any paperwork just a gentleman's arrangement like you do!'

Atherton thanked her and said that they would be in touch. Walking with Byrne back over to where they had parked the car he said that they would need to check her alibi. He believed her story but even the most deceitful of murderers had been known to slip through the net.

'Emma Crandon has been around the block a few times,' remarked Byrne 'and I bet she could tell you about the affairs of most households up and down this street plus her own.'

Atherton nodded although necessarily agreeing 'She's holding up well for somebody who only this morning found that inside.' He thumbed at the front door which had been closed by the CSI team.

'You know I have a funny feeling in my bones Pete, something about this house that we've missed.'

'Like what,' Byrne asked 'the place is a dive inside from top to bottom and there's hardly anything worth looking through that will give us any clues to help sort this murder.'

Atherton watched as Emma Crandon was stalked by several members of the waiting press.

'What I mean Pete is that there's an energy inside wanting to be heard. I felt it was stronger when I was upstairs especially in the rear bedroom where Arthur Benson slept.'

'A voice from the grave?' Byrne asked. Since teaming up with Daniel Atherton Pete Byrne had become accustomed to his sergeants unconventional ways and voices.

'So did Hargreaves have anything to add?' he asked.

'Only that the post mortem is scheduled for this afternoon.'

Pete Byrne immediately lost interest. 'And our resident vampire, how is she getting on?'

Atherton lowered his head so that Byrne missed his smile.

'You know Pete, Marjorie is one hell of a forensic examiner and I'd have her on my team before a lot of others that I have come across in the past. If only you two could cut each other some slack you would find working alongside one another a whole lot easier.'

Byrne raised his hands defensively 'Okay, I'm willing to give it a go for the sake of the job but I just wish that for once she would jump into the grey areas of an investigation. Marjorie tends to bend with the safety of everything black and white.'

Atherton was quick to come to Marjorie's defence.

'There really isn't any other way Pete not with forensic science. The evidence is either there or not, only Marjorie digs a lot deeper than most. Keeping to the guidelines is how she secures a prosecution for us. A good defence barrister could destroy our evidence if she didn't comply and do it by the book.'

Atherton saw a lone figure possibly Marjorie cross the window of the bedroom above.

'Marjorie delves into places that I don't think to look. Give her a little more love Pete and she'll come up trumps for us, trust me!'

Byrne removed his sterile gloves screwing them up and putting them in his pocket.

'Have you tried the *'hooky spooky'* stuff yet?' he asked.

Atherton grinned. Confiding in his colleague soon after joining the department, Byrne had found the revelation fascinating. The hooky spooky as he so eloquently put it was in fact a psychic gift that Daniel Atherton had acquired from his maternal grandmother where he could sense the energy of the dead, not see or communicate with them but hear their voices.

As Pete Byrne had remarked earlier *voices from the grave* only some spirits would not rest until the matter of their demise was resolved. Atherton's gift was nothing magical, remotely hocus pocus and definitely not considered paranormal, instead it involved listening and feeling. It was why he sensed that the house still had some secrets left to reveal.

'There are unanswered questions that we've not uncovered yet Pete.'

With a determined look masking his expression Pete Byrne turned back around.

'Then why don't we go back inside until they present themselves!'

Pete Byrne sniffed hard.

'Alright then I'll ask, only maybe it's time she found out how much I love her!'

Chapter Two

Byrne promised Marjorie that they would not interfere or get in the teams way insisting the reason that they could not return to the station without some answers. Reluctantly the head of the forensic department appreciated the detective's position and agreed.

'We have an accord detective as long as you agree to call me if you find anything.' They said they would. On the landing above they discussed tactics.

Atherton sucked in the atmosphere, suggesting. 'Put ourselves in Arthur Benson's shoes. There's with a knock at the door, somebody has rung the bell or he senses somebody coming, let's be his spirit before one a.m.'

Pete Byrne took up the challenge.

'Okay, he's in bed probably asleep, when he has a caller a visitor that he knows because there are no signs of a forced entry. Roused from his slumber he goes downstairs in just his underwear, where the rest of his clothes are slung over or beside the chair in the back bedroom. He lets the killer in unseen by any of the neighbours. There is no door slamming, no argument or abusive disagreement, everything is quiet.'

Atherton paced along the short landing thinking as he listened.

He carried the conjecture forward 'at which point our killer stabs the syringe in the victim's neck and seconds later probably paralysed with fear or uncertainty Arthur Benson collapses under the effect of the pentobarbital. Dressed only in his underpants Arthur is helped through to the kitchen at the rear of the property where he he is assisted up onto the kitchen table probably having lost the power of speech as his tongue numbed together with the sensation of being strangled.

'So he wasn't able to ask any questions why?' added Byrne.

'Possibly not. Assuming he was powerless to speak or react I think he knew his killer and why he had come visiting so late into the night.'

29

'But if you found yourself in that position prior to the visit, you'd leave a clue about, a note saying who was expected!'

'You would have thought so unless Arthur felt the revenge was justified.'

'That's like committing suicide!'

Atherton looked to where Pete Byrne was looking through the airing cupboard. He didn't tell him that he had already searched the cupboard in case there was anything that he had missed. Coming across the oil stained clothing Byrne was still suspicious of Arthur Benson's social activities.

'I'm still convinced that there's a sexual motive involved. Not just between two consenting adults but...' he paused, reconstructed his thought before continuing 'okay let's say it was someone Arthur knew, picked up a month beforehand in the pub. A friendship developed and they are intimate but for argument's sake let's say the killer is a younger man and soon the attraction wanes but Arthur is besotted and unwilling to call a halt to the affair. Sensing that he might be blackmailed into staying in the relationship the younger man does the only thing possible. In a fit of silent rage he tortures Arthur to get across the message then realises that his actions have gone a bit too far. Arthur lies bleeding out on the kitchen table with his tackle in his mouth and sometime between one and seven dies.'

Atherton stopped pacing.

'A crime of passion!'

Pete Byrne didn't like anything associated with queers. 'Hardly, but it gives us another angle.'

'And a reasonable motive. It's good Pete.'

'Did you see his underpants in the kitchen?' Byrne asked quizzingly.

Atherton shook his head. 'No, I had wondered about that earlier... not unless the killer used them to wipe his hands after removing the body parts. There was a tea towel on the worktop but it looked to be untouched.' Byrne made a mental note to check the waste bins out front.

Going from the landing into the rear bedroom they continued their search finding a medical leaflet concealed at the back of one of the wardrobes advising on chronic obstructive pulmonary disease.

'I doubt Arthur could have put up any kind of a struggle.'

Byrne scoffed 'either way Benson was *fucked!*'

Atherton agreed 'and that is possibly something else that our killer knew about Arthur. Still drowsy from being woken he was then injected with a powerful anaesthetic. Arthur would have been easy prey.'

Keeping his thoughts to himself Pete Byrne had little sympathy for the victim.

'Alright, so now we have an insight into Arthur's medical condition which proves he was in no fit state to put up any sort of defence needing help to get up on the table. I'm bloody sure that if somebody came near me intending to remove my manhood I would have fought like a mule.'

Going through the scenario in his mind Atherton quickly put together the facts. No struggle meant no bruising or defensive cuts. A missing pair of underpants. A bible in the bedside drawer, a few photographs and a bloodied knife in the butchers block. A medical leaflet and a wooden cross on the bedroom wall. They resembled the pieces from a children's game only the slaying of a defenceless victim was no game.

'Me also...' Atherton replied his thoughts wandering elsewhere. 'We need to ask Emma Crandon if she's thrown anything out recently, anything of significant value and not necessarily monetary but of sentimental worth. Perhaps something that the killer might have come looking for?'

'She might not tell if she's our suspect!'

Atherton shook his head disagreeing. 'No, I'm still convinced that she's not involved not unless she was after Arthur's bank balance. Emma Crandon was purely instrumental in finding the body.'

Byrne raised his hands shoulder height. 'Then we don't have a lot to go on.'

Atherton suddenly felt a shiver pass through his body.

'It's suddenly got a lot colder in here,' remarked Pete Byrne.

'Like Arthur's spirit refuses to leave.'

'Yeah, something like that, although I'd say Arthur's hanging around because he knows that he's guilty of some past misdemeanour.'

'Guilt.' It was another motive to add to the list of possibilities.

They went back out and into the front bedroom.

Taking the photographs from his pocket he handed them to Byrne.

'Strange that he had pictures of kids playing in the park?'

Byrne studied the images in the pictures. 'Maybe he had a thing for young kids too. Child Protection are aware of a paedophile ring operating somewhere along the coastline. It's not inconceivable that Arthur wasn't connected.'

Atherton put his fist under his nose automatically rubbing the underside, the suggestion was another for the list.

'We might need to have a look at their files and see if this address is on the radar.' Atherton went to the front window paused and looked at the crowd outside. 'We might need to ask around.'

Sucking through his teeth Byrne was already reluctant.

'Good luck with that. This area is well known for not helping the police with their enquiries. I would say that fifty percent of my arrests have come from within a two mile radius of Parkway Drive.

Atherton however was unperturbed by non-cooperation or anti-police views.

'Then we need to get some of our people into local boozers and buy some pints!'

'Any other theories?' asked Byrne hoping that he would be selected for the task.

'That this was a domestic motivated incident. Maybe not random but planned. The energy force in this place is heavy with burden.'

'I'd prefer and go along with that theory rather than being spat at and kicked around by a gang of local thugs.'

'Our problem with that theory is that there's little evidence here to suggest anything domestic.'

There was even less in the front bedroom than there had been in the rear room. Watching Pete Byrne move about Atherton wanted to know why the feud had existed between Byrne and Marjorie Matthews. Keeping his voice he asked.

Byrne checked that she wasn't around before he replied.

'Rumour has it that she is shacked up with some other forensic know-it-all from the west side of the county. We've tried to find out who but with no success. Marjorie blames me for starting the rumours only I had nothing to do with them and then make matters worse somebody in the station knick-named her Amaunet.' Gnashing his teeth together he imitated a vampire.

Atherton was less amused.

'Whoever the moron that gave her the name knows nothing of mythology only Amaunet was an Egyptian goddess and vampires are the origin of fictional novels penned in the wastelands of Transylvania. Maybe it's time we put the rumours to bed.'

With a flick of his finger Byrne had another idea. 'Arthur could have been the victim of a satanic ritual slaying!'

It was a wild notion but not unheard of although from what Atherton had read about such cases they were normally undertaken in a place where a pentagram had been drawn placing the victim inside.

'I've never dabbled in anything like that myself,' admitted Byrne.

'We did as students but only for fun and when we'd had a bit to drink. In the cold light of day however I had regretted taking part. Black magic can be powerful stuff and should be dabbled with lightly.

Byrne mockingly sucked through his teeth. 'Although such practices still take place. Do you recall that the Met had a case down south where the headless body of a teenage boy was found floating down the Thames. The investigation deemed then that the motive had been a ritual slaying!'

Atherton nodded remembering. 'Yes, I read about that case when I was at university. Okay, we'll add black magic to the legend board but let's keep it from Jasmin Yates only I don't want her leaking anything as sinister to her counterparts in the press. It would blow this case all out of proportion.'

Byrne closed an empty wardrobe door. 'I think I'll cut across the street and ask the neighbour at number sixty five some questions.'

'Who's that?' Atherton asked.

'A woman by the name of Millicent Watkins. She was lurking about when I was talking to Emma Crandon only I got the distinct impression that the pair of them don't get along. She could provide some useful background information on our cleaner and Arthur Benson.'

Turning around Atherton saw the curtain in the house opposite drop and number sixty five had a commanding view of the properties across the road. Sensing that somebody had come up behind them they both turned to see Marjorie standing in the doorway.

'How long have you been standing there?' asked Byrne.

'Long enough,' she replied looking back at him directly. She joined them at the window. 'I take it that you was referring to the woman across the street, the one with the large bust and dyed hair.'

'Yes.' Replied Atherton.

'Interestingly she's been watching this house ever since we arrived. In my opinion I would say that there's not a lot that she doesn't see, whatever the time of the day or night!'

'That was my impression.' Pete Byrne smiled at Marjorie before stepping away from the window.

'We found this under a pile of magazines near the larder.' Marjorie handed over a thin biscuit tin. 'A cobweb covered the lid indicating that it not been disturbed for some weeks, maybe months. Our killer obviously didn't know that it existed.'

Inside the tin contained a number of old payslips stamped with the logo of Chopping & Sons, a local cotton mill. A letter of employment where Arthur Benson had been a skilled maintenance engineer keeping the machinery oiled and in good working order. Sifting through the last payslip was dated the twenty second of December two thousand and two. In a long buff coloured envelope they removed papers recording his redundancy package.

'That backs up Emma Crandon's explanation.' Byrne smoothed out the folds of the redundancy document. 'She told me that Arthur never discussed his package but that the introduction of new technology had confused his trade, replacing the old machines with a new stream lined production run by computers. She mentioned that when she had come cleaning Benson would hack a lot.'

There was another envelope and letter from a respiratory clinic consultant. Atherton read out aloud the important passage.

'Arthur Benson is fighting a courageous but futile battle with chronic emphysema. Although I have no physical or documentary evidence to suggest otherwise in my opinion I blame forty years spent in a dust laden environment for the onset of the condition. Arthur told me at out last meeting that the workshop was adjacent the flax store.' A copy of the letter had been sent to Arthur's doctor.

He passed the report to Marjorie then Byrne.

'In a way the inevitable was already foretold for Arthur Benson. Michael Hargreaves's will confirm how far advanced the emphysema had taken a hold at the post-mortem this afternoon.'

'I know Chopping & Sons,' Pete Byrne intervened 'do you remember Marjorie, we had a burglary there early last December?' He looked at Daniel Atherton 'just before you got promoted.'

'And was anything stolen?' Atherton asked.

'That was the strange thing about the incident, when I went along after uniform had taken the initial report there appeared to be nothing missing, just some damage to some filing cabinets where they had been forced open.'

'And the petty cash?'

Marjorie jumped in 'I remember that. No, the petty cash was in the safe in the next office but the safe was untouched. We dusted for prints eliminating the members of staff who had access to the two offices but came up with no suspects. The crime was recorded and local youths blamed for the break-in.'

At the bottom of the tin they found several old service invoices, council tax bills and statements for gas and electricity. Lastly although oddly there was a small collection of official programmes for Liverpool Football Club.

'At least we now know what he did on a Saturday afternoon. We'll have to check to see if he went with anybody.'

Pete Byrne immediately saw a way out of attending the afternoon post-mortem.

'I'm sure that the women at Chopping & Sons will remember me, why don't I cut along there instead of going to the autopsy. My time would be better served gathering information than seeing Arthur cut again!'

Atherton saw Marjorie lower her head and grin, he agreed it was a waste of time all three of them going. Standing beside Marjorie he watched her tense as a shiver travelled through her body making the hairs on the back of her neck rise.

'That's the second time that, that's happened since I arrived,' she revealed 'this place has a restless spirit walking through the fabric.'

'We experienced similar not long ago, we think the dead are trying to tell us something!'

Pete Byrne was surprised when Marjorie readily accepted the conjecture. Maybe she did see the grey as well as the black and white.

'You believe that?' he asked.

'Yes, had you been downstairs about ten minutes back you would have witnessed the deceased move as an involuntary muscle decided to come out of spasm. Even to a seasoned investigator like myself, I still jumped!' Marjorie left them looking through the contents of the tin realising that she had been away long enough from her team.

Picking up a match programme something fell from between the pages. Byrne reached down and picked up a Polaroid image of a church with a headstone in the foreground.

'I recognise this...' he exclaimed 'the church is St Cuthbert's at Alton Cross. Anne, the girls and I attended a christening there a couple of years back when her brother's son was baptised.'

On the back was a pencil mark, barely recognisable but it was there. Atherton twisted the image in the light to make the markings stronger but the carbon was faded and smudged. He passed it across to Atherton who failed also to read the inscription.

'Maybe photographic can help enhance back and front. If Arthur Benson felt it was necessary to keep the image then it must have some significance.' They put everything back in the tin and shut the lid. 'Come on,' said Atherton 'let's go visit Millicent Watkins.'

Passing by Gabrielle George on the staircase they found her bent over a section of worn carpet gingerly extracting hairs from the loose fibres of the weave. She edged to one side to let them pass safely protecting her bit of tread. Atherton smiled and apologised for the interruption in awe of her tenacity. Without forensics detection would be sometimes impossible.

Outside of the house like a pack of waiting hyenas members of the local press had jostled one another for prime spot in order to be the first to ask questions as cameramen flashed anything that moved. Eager to hear what the detectives had to say local residents were right behind. Atherton looked around the many faces hoping to see Jasmin Yates from the press liaison office but she was nowhere to be seen.

'I suppose that I had better say something.'

Flanked by several uniformed officers Pete Byrne stood aside and watched as his colleague addressed the crowd.

'As you are no doubt aware a tragic set of circumstances at number seventy two involving the occupant a Mr Arthur Benson has resulted in the police being present and setting about an investigation. At this stage we are unable to determine the cause of death but hope to have more details later following a post-mortem. In the meantime we would ask that if anybody has any information regarding Mr Benson or what took place here during the night, that they contact Southport Police.'

Somebody amongst the crowd shouted out 'Old Arthur never did have any balls' which immediately caused an uproar of laughter and smiles from those that didn't know of the victim.

Walking back over to where Pete Byrne was stood waiting Daniel Atherton shook his head in dismay. 'Word travels fast in these parts!'

With a supportive hand on the shoulder Byrne looked at faces in the crowd, some he recognised and they were aware of him.

'You did well although the crowd still want blood. Around this neck of the woods death is nothing new and revenge attacks are common place especially amongst the rival gangs fighting a turf war. Around here they sort their own problems and don't involve the police. The law of the jungle still exists in some places north east of the river. Anyway what you did say will keep Tavistock happy.'

Atherton muttered something back but with the impetus of the laughter what he had muttered was lost in the air.

Standing by the corner shop a lone figure wearing a long dark coat with the hood down low covering the eyes watched as the two detectives crossed the road then went down the path to the front door of the house opposite. He waited until they were across the threshold before he turned away.

Pulling shut the van door the stranger turned the key in the ignition then listened as the piston rods fired up and down in the cylinder head. When the engine was idling nicely he released the brake and engaged first gear.

His work was done at Parkway Drive and he could tick another from the list, however the list was long and there were others to visit.

Chapter Three

Millicent Watkins had wanted to be inside her front garden when the detective had spoken to the press and the crowd wanting to hear what he had to say but she had lived in the area long enough to know how quickly the mood could swing against the police and turn ugly. When some of the onlookers started to drift away she rushed back to the safety of her hallway where she left the door slightly ajar checking herself in the mirror to make sure that her bosom was evenly set inside her lace brassiere.

Before Atherton could depress the button on the doorbell Millicent had pulled the door open eagerly checking the street for prying eyes. She loved being recognised in the street by the neighbours albeit it was deemed dangerous talking to the police. Standing near to where the reporters were gathered Millicent saw Emma Crandon watching. Gesturing that they could go through to the room at the front she announced as the parlour she quickly shut the front door.

'Arthur never had that many visitors,' she said in response to Pete Byrne's question 'he always struck me as a bit of a loner.'

'He must have had some Millicent!' Byrne pushed her a little harder.

Millicent gave it some thought 'Well, there was an elderly couple sometimes only not that often mind but when they did visit there would be a right to-do about the occasion and on the front steps as well. It was a good few minutes before Arthur relented and would let them in.'

'So you knew him as Arthur?' Atherton asked sceptical of her familiarity.

Folding her arms purposely beneath her chest, Millicent inhaled with Byrne sitting by her side. She had an obvious liking for the older detective believing that he was handsome whereas the younger policeman was okay but needed some grit between his teeth to taste the reality of life's hard lesson. The long and short of it was that Atherton wasn't her type, too educated and devious around edges.

Millicent sucked in again ruminating over her response. 'Before she came on the scene, Crandon that is... I had already done a couple of mornings over at Arthur's house, you know doing a bit of dusting here and there earning me keep washing up the dirty crocks, laundering his smalls and making the bed only for some reason it didn't last!'

'And why was that?' Atherton asked.

'Well for one thing I couldn't stand old Arthur's wheeze, it sounded like a dirty old man creeping up on you. Then there was the times when I caught him fiddling with himself every time I bent over to rake out the fireplace.' With a single movement of her crossed arms her bust heaved one way then the other like a pair of boats bobbing about on calm waters.

Millicent shuffled a little closer next to Pete Byrne.

'Naturally I ain't suggesting that I was being suggestive or anything, but god gave me these assets and there ain't a damn thing that I can do with them. I reckon before I called it a day my knockers near drove poor old Arthur mad. Sometimes his front bedroom curtains would be pulled for a week and it's no wonder he had that wooden cross nailed to the bedroom wall. I reckon he was up there all week repenting his sins!'

'Meaning, he could see you if you went to the bathroom upstairs?' On the way in Atherton had seen the opaque glass over the porch roof.

'Course he was dirty old bugger. I bet that didn't help his wheeze none!'

Pete Byrne coughed getting Millicent to look his way.

'You say that when the elderly couple came round to visit that inevitably it ended up in a heated debate on the front steps. Have you any ideas about what?'

Millicent pointed up to the fanlight in the window.

'Not even with that open could I hear what they were saying. As I said it was always a few minutes before he stood aside and let them in though.'

'And how long did they stay?' asked Atherton.

'Not that long, long enough for a cup of tea.'

'Do you know who they were and where they came from?'

Millicent shook her head 'I never asked and Arthur was never one to give away much. Secretive bugger at the best of times he was.'

Atherton thought about the articles that had been found in the biscuit tin. Millicent was right about Arthur's circumspection.

'When you did the dusting at Arthur Benson's was there something special that needed attention, something like a document box something that Arthur wanted especially kept clean?'

Millicent frowned 'like what?'

Atherton didn't reply allowing time and the silence to help jog her memory.

'No, not really. I polished the furniture only because he asked and it made the place smell nice although he'd watch my tits wobble inside my top. I would then change his bed linen and make sure that the cross on the wall was straight.' She shrugged her shoulders closing down the vision that had fogged her mind. 'That was about it, it took most of the morning to do that lot!'

'The cross in the bedroom, was Arthur a religious man or did you ever see him go to church?'

'He told me that he prayed every night although I never asked what about. I mean you don't ask do you and those sort of things are private.' She shook her head from side to side. 'No, I never saw him go to church.' She then looked directly at Pete Byrne 'Christ with the thoughts he possessed I doubt god would have let him in.'

'What about boys and girls,' asked Byrne 'did you ever see Arthur Benson bring any home or maybe catch sight of one or two leaving?'

She nudged his arm playfully 'are you asking me if he was one of them paedophile's?'

Atherton was quick to intervene and put her straight.

'No Millicent, we're just shutting down a line of enquiry and asking if you saw any visitors go to the house who were children, like a niece or nephew?'

Running the tip of her tongue along the underside of her top lip she inadvertently removed a layer of recently applied lipstick. Millicent could feel the heat from where her leg touched Pete Byrne's. It had been a long time since she had such a good looking man cross her threshold and the older detective was all man. She could feel her juices staring to flow. With a sigh she imagined him handcuffed to the bed upstairs. Regrettably she had to look back at Atherton.

'No, I gathered from Arthur that he was an only child.'

'Are you married?' Byrne asked realising his mistake the moment that the question left his lips. Millicent however was on it like a flash.

'Why you proposing detective?' the prospect fluttering both her heart and eyelashes.

Using the same ploy Atherton had employed Byrne did not answer.

'I was once... only not nowadays I'm not.'

'Are you divorced then?'

Sorting her posture once again she sighed heavily.

'Twenty years back the old bastard got up one morning, told me that he was going down to the corner shop for some fags and a racing paper only he never came back.' She scowled 'you can image the gossip and the rumours were rife up and down the road. I heard from a reliable source that he had got himself a fancy woman, some young tart and that he had been cavorting with her for almost a year before he up sticks and done the vanishing act.'

Millicent let the memory out through her nostrils disavowing herself from her husband's betrayal.

'Daft bugger lives over Manchester way now, still it serves him right. The tart,' she scoffed 'she had a son by another man so he got saddled with the brat as well.'

Feeling the tightness in her chest where it still pained her Millicent put a hand up to support her forehead. 'The thing that hurt most was that we had been trying for our own kid for ages and I'd even thought about that

43

IVF stuff.' Suddenly clamping both hands on her breasts she finished off her tale of woe. 'I suppose that when it came down to it a pair of knockers on the NHS just didn't do it for him anymore!'

Millicent dropped her hands down to her knees before clamping her left hand onto Pete Byrne's upper thigh feeling the solid muscle beneath his suit trousers.

'If your old woman ever throws you out detective, you know that I've a warm comfy bed for the night upstairs!'

'How do you know that I'm married?' Byrne asked interested to have her release his leg.

Millicent laughed out loud 'because you're like a flaming cat on a hot tin roof sitting next to me. Christ I ain't that bad looking am I...?'

Byrne studied hard. Ignoring the crow's feet etched in deep around the sides of her eyes, the bottle dyed hair and NHS extras Millicent wasn't half bad for her age, twenty years on from now he might still be tempted.

'No, not at all,' he replied being kind. She released her grip on his leg before slapping it just the once.

'That's what a girl likes to hear.'

Sitting opposite Daniel Atherton was amused to see his colleague squirm.

'If he does get kicked out Millicent, I will personally see to it that he comes here!'

Suddenly without any warning Millicent straightened herself on the settee. 'What I've said this morning, I hope you don't both think that I'm one of those nosey old broads, one of the curtain twitching brigade with nothing to do all day only I can assure you that I've plenty to keep me occupied.'

Byrne looked across at Atherton who replied. 'Without members of the public like you Millicent we would be lost on investigations like this!'

She relaxed, much calmer less defensive.

'Did Arthur Benson have any hobbies, any that you noticed when you were cleaning?'

'Besides watching my tits wobble. No, only his football,' she replied. 'I know that he supported Liverpool as there was a red scarf hung over the coat peg in the hall.'

'Any other hobbies you can recall?'

'Photography I think although he was never one for taking holidays but he did once visit the Lake District, he told me so.'

Her recount explained the landscape photographs in Atherton's pocket.

'And what about you Millicent do you get out much?' Byrne asked.

She frowned. Had he noticed the slight pull on her right knee where arthritis had started to set in?

'I did only not as much as I would like too, bingo once a week and down to the corner shop... why?'

'We were just wondering if you had noticed anybody strange hanging around the area lately.'

Millicent shrugged her shoulders.

'We're always getting those door knockers calling, selling double glazing, new boilers and wanting to repair the roof, otherwise the only ones that I see hanging about are the bloody teenagers who sit on their bikes controlling the junction. They're a confounded nuisance and intimidating. Can you do something about them?' she asked.

Byrne gently patted the back of her hand. 'We let the local mobile patrols know. They can stop and have a word with them next time they're in the area.'

'Daft thing is...' she continued 'they were all young kids at the local nursery when I knew their mothers. Nowadays most of the elderly around here are too frightened to venture that far for fear of being mugged, burgled or assaulted. Most people keep themselves to themselves, it's safer.'

It had not been the case for Arthur Benson.

Atherton looked at his watching wanting to wrap it up. 'You've been a big help Millicent and we're almost done. Just out of interest what time did you go to bed last night?'

'Around half ten although I couldn't sleep and Percy my cat wanted to go out around eleven so I opened the back door and booted him out. Trouble is though I worry about him when he's out what with all those other feral cats in the area. Some are really vicious always wanting to fight so around half past midnight I got back up and let him in. We settled down about a quarter to one after I had made us both some nice warm milk.'

'And you didn't see anybody hanging about?'

'Nobody, not without my contact lens.'

Atherton left his contact card with Millicent rather than have Pete Byrne leave his. Setting the wrought iron gate back onto the catch they both noticed that the CSI vans were still parked outside the house opposite.

'We might need to revisit Millicent again soon whilst the memory of last night is still fresh but for now there are other things that we need to be doing.'

He settled himself in the drivers as Pete Byrne secured his seatbelt. 'Are you okay?' he asked.

'I'm fine... although she's a randy old cow. I'm surprised that Arthur Benson didn't have a stroke watching her stoke the fire.'

Atherton grinned drumming his fingers on the steering wheel gathering his thoughts together.

'You know women like Millicent Watkins expect another visit from the police. She has a lot more to give but she'll do it in her time and keep the attention level simmering. Did you notice that she is slightly deaf in one ear?'

Byrne housed the end of his seatbelt in the metal catch. 'Yeah the right ear.'

Byrne reported to the receptionist at the cotton mill as Daniel Atherton battled with the pre-lunch traffic heading back to the station. He was climbing the stairwell to CID when he came across Gregory Tavistock taking an unplanned rest on the landing between floors, the one-time force rugby captain was rubbing and nursing a dodgy knee. More recently the pain had been coming in excruciating waves so he had refocused his energy on the less arduous sport of golf.

'Ah Daniel I am so glad that our paths have crossed only I've just come from your department. How are things at Parkway Drive?'

'Unusual Sir, the victim was viciously mutilated before he died.'

'So I heard.' Tavistock sucked in hard as the pain started to subside. Atherton waited patiently for the imminent advice that was forthcoming.

'Domestic attacks do have a nasty habit of turning violent and Neil Johnson in the control room appraised me of the incident as soon as I arrived for work this morning. Bad business and Parkway Drive is on our intelligence radar. We had a mobile unit bottled there the other night, did you know?'

'Yes Sir, I did.

'Anything positive to go on yet?' Tavistock asked.

'Pete Byrne's chasing down a possible lead and I'm off to the autopsy soon. I had just popped back to get the team working on other enquiries.'

Tavistock straightened his back now that his knee had stopped hurting.

'Byrne's been around the block enough times to know the score, he'll come up trumps for you I guarantee as will the others in the team.'

Encouragingly he gave Atherton's shoulder a couple of strong raps. Since the appointment to DS the detection league tables had steadily risen, caseloads had been distributed evenly around the office and arrest rates had also peaked. Taking everything into consideration Gregory Tavistock's division was the best in the county. It bode well for his personal ambitions.

'Good man Daniel,' he said turning on the landing 'we knew that we had picked the right man for the job at the beginning of the year.'

Tavistock stepped down onto the first tread of the stairs descending towards the canteen, without looking back he called up after the man above and asked that Atherton keep him appraised.

He watched until the older man was out of sight thinking that Tavistock resembled a rugby ball, slightly rounded with blunt edges where the stitching had frayed due to overuse. Golf or so somebody advised was a gentle remedy to help keep you fit and healthily and yet Tavistock looked to be suffering all the more. He surmised that most of the exercise was spent in the club house bar.

Atherton briefed the other members of the department of the circumstances surrounding Arthur Benson's death admitting that they had little to go on but at least two out three listening had a keen look in their eye. Scribbling down notes as he spoke Lucy Fancham, George Gunn and Tim Robbins began compiling a list of enquiries that needed to be made. Lucy opted for checking the voters register, digging out the names of neighbours and residents in Park Drive, before delving into other records such as employment and previous convictions.

George being the drinking man of the team opted to do the pubs and clubs in the area, leaving any local amateur photographic societies and Liverpool Football Club down to Tim Robbins. Leaving them to their tasks Atherton went back to the car with only half an hour to spare before Hargreaves was to begin the post-mortem.

'It sounds domestic,' said Gunn flicking through a list of known pubs and snooker clubs. 'I'll lay ten to one that it's the ex-wife with a score to settle, probably still waiting for an alimony settlement.'

'If you keep drinking the way you do George, Jenna will divorce you soon!'

Gunn grinned as he looked across at Lucy Fancham. He blew her a kiss. 'Is that you hoping princess, waiting for the day that I am free so that we can shack up together?'

'In your dreams George, get back to your pub list!'

George Gunn was still smiling when Tim Robbins looked up from his laptop.

'In the end most women come around to my charms, watch this space.'

Tim Robbins nodded back but the information he sought was slowly materialising on screen. He agreed with Lucy, George was slowly drinking himself into an early grave and especially after his second wife had walked out on him because of his many after works sessions at the local Conservative Club bar. Daniel Atherton knew about Gunn's problem but for the present he was happy just keeping an eye on George's behaviour.

Several minutes of silence were disrupted when Tim Robbins wanted to know why George had made the reference to ex-wife.'

Gunn spread his hands wide 'look at the area Tim, we all know what Park Drive is like. There are more domestics and social disturbance in that one road than in the whole of Southport. I'm just saying that I'd lay money on it being a domestic!'

Lucy Fancham took a crisp five pound note from her pocket and laid it on George Gunn's desk. 'Alright a fiver say's you're wrong.' Tim Robbins did the same. 'My opinion for what it's worth is that the killer originates beyond the family tree.'

George added his own stake then concealed the notes in an envelope rummaging through his desk drawer for a drawing pin.

'When Atherton and Byrne come back we'll see if they want in as well. I'll guarantee Pete will although I'm still not sure about Atherton?'

'He's alright,' replied Lucy 'and he gets results, that's what counts.'

'Yeah I know, it's just that he's young and still a little wet behind the ears.'

Lucy turned back to her screen although refusing to let the older detective have the last word. 'If I were you George I would keep my opinions to myself. Daniel Atherton is highly thought of by Tavistock and those in headquarters especially Harry Lane. So far he's proved his worth and raised the standard in the department.'

Silently George Gunn accepted that Lucy could be right realising that his own chances of promotion had long since passed him by and now the only prospect for the immediate future was retirement in three years' time. George had big plans for when that day arrived vowing that they wouldn't see his arse for dust as jetted away to some sun kissed Spanish island never to be heard of again, wife or no wife.

He rubbed the underside of his nose 'whatever, but you wait, I'll be prove right I can feel these things in my water!'

Tim and Lucy laughed as he pinned the envelope to the department notice board.

'The only feeling you have in your bladder George is from last night's session!'

They settled down again to some serious research going through respective sources. Lucy hit on a family living nearby Arthur Benson that had a string of convictions for assault, burglary and car theft where the sons were well known to police. She added them to her list knowing that there would be others like them to follow. Later when the list was complete she would check with the intelligence office and council although it would not surprise her if pseudonyms had been used and different addressed recorded. Using her initiative she added local surgeries and hospitals to her ever growing list. She highlighted the line *closed circuit security cameras* wanting to check with petrol filling stations and night clubs to see who was out and about between the hours of midnight and dawn.

Heading west Daniel Atherton called Pete Byrne and checked on progress wanting also to know that Chopping & Sons were giving him their fullest co-operation. Taking the call outside of the HR department Byrne took the call.

'They remember me so no problem getting in. The manager is on holiday but his assistant is helping. She's optimistic of finding Arthur Benson's file although it looks like most from the burglary, the older records have been stored down in the storerooms below the main hub of the mill. It's where Arthur Benson had his workshop.'

'Have a nose about if you can Pete, only you never know an old photo or piece of football memorabilia might leap out at us. See if any of the other engineers working there now can shed any light on Arthur's social habits. We need anything we can lay our hands on. I met Tavistock on the stairs and he's already writing it off as a domestic!'

'Tavistock's a...' Byrne didn't complete the sentence. 'Okay I'll see what I dig up. Where are you now?'

'On my way to join Hargreaves. Give a call when you're done there and I'll pick you up.'

With the call complete Pete Byrne slipped the mobile into his suit pocket and went back where the assistant was waiting to show him inside the storeroom. The filing cabinets had been changed since the burglary, more substantially manufactured and with locks. The assistant read his thoughts.

'Mr Chopping junior thought it would be safer to keep the records undergrounds although I doubt that there's much that can be gained from the few scant details that we keep on file on past employees.' When she located Arthur Benson's file she passed it over to Byrne.

'You're right, there's not a lot inside the folder!'

All the same he was left to his own devices to forage through the files and search for anything else that might help. The assistant went back to her desk where she had her own work piling up.

Engaging the brake and switching off the engine Atherton sat alone for a few moments absorbing the peace and quiet. It helped him think. As a young boy he had spent many happy times with his aunt, his mother's sister, spending weeks at her bungalow with his older sister just lazing about her long enchanting garden which came to an abrupt end at a slow running stream at the bottom of the garden. Quiet moments would help put things into perspective.

Removing the photograph again from his jacket pocket he studied the image more closely. Something about the expressions of the children's faces were engaging with his thoughts. He sipped water from a plastic bottle remembering when he and Sarah would play on the swing before looking up at the stars as they started to appear on a summer sunset. He wondered how old the children were now and if any would shed a tear for the dead Arthur Benson.

Leaving the Saab parked around the corner from the coroner's building he walked along the paved path going around the side of the building. Like most Victorian designed edifices they were majestic in blood red brick, sprouting a few gothic gargoyles from beneath the eaves, notably to ward off evil spirits and yet interestingly inviting. 'Taylors Knife' as the coroner's building had been aptly named was a constant reminder of the man who had the building constructed.

A naval doctor of the late seventeenth century Louis Albert Taylor had been around when large fast clipper ships had crossed the Atlantic carrying precious cargoes perilously undertaking the long voyage across treacherous seas. The ship's owners in both wisdom and reverence had employed Taylor as the ship's surgeon thus preventing the captain from losing valuable time in different port's to deal with on-board injuries or sickness.

Growing older and developing a dislike for the continuous rough seas Taylor resigned from his naval post to take up a land position in Southport as a general practitioner however the authorities wanted value for their coin and so he was installed as the county coroner. After a lengthy verbal exchange lasting several weeks with the county officials he was given sufficient financial funds to build the grand edifice. He had the bricklayer etch *Taylors Knife* into the wall beside the entrance as a reminder of all who passed through the door, not that many ever came out.

Pushing aside the imposing oak door he was greeted with an engaging smile by a smartly attired receptionist. 'Please go on down detective, Dr Hargreaves said that you would be attending soon.'

Descending the stairs to the floor below Atherton entered the white tiled chamber where neither design nor décor had changed in the past two hundred years except for the modern introduction of fluorescent lighting, central heating, advanced instrumentation, steel tables and cabinets. Aware that the soles of his shoes squeaked on the old tiled floor he took his place opposite Michael Hargreaves at the occupied examination table.

'Ah good… thank you for coming sergeant, is Marjorie Matthews not joining us?' he asked.

'My guess is that she's still at the address. You know Marjorie thorough to the last!'

Hargreaves adjusted his fingers in the thin latex gloves 'she's a very fine forensic investigator and I would be proud to have her on my team.'

Extending the height of the ceiling mounted microphone Hargreaves activated the record switch. Lying naked and almost occupying the length and width of the long stainless steel ribbed table Arthur Benson had his head supported at the nape by a wooden block where armed with a consistent flow of water the mortuary assistant was ready to wash away any unwanted body fluids.

Methodically working his way up and down the cadaver, checking both sides and lifting up tufts of hair, pulling forward the ears and manipulating the jaw Michael Hargreaves satisfied himself that the deceased had no other injuries, other than the obvious. Nodding at Atherton he peered over the rim of his spectacles indicating that he was ready to begin.

'The deceased is Arthur Benson aged sixty five, born on the twenty seventh of February nineteen forty five. At a time between the hours of eight and nine this morning being Thursday the ninth of September two thousand and ten I did attend number seventy two Parkway Drive the last known residence of the deceased.

'In the ground floor kitchen to the rear of the property I saw a naked Caucasian male who was lying lengthways on a wooden table positioned central to the room. The deceased was on his back facing the ceiling and both lower and upper limbs were dangling unsupported both sides and the end of the table. The most significant injury present was the removal of

both testes and penis which I found forced into the cadaver's mouth. Other than this on visual examination there appeared to be no other physical injuries present, suggesting that a struggle had not taken place.

'It is not known how the deceased got up onto the table albeit of his own volition or whether he was assisted. At the time of my examination Arthur Benson weighs a hundred and five kilogrammes including all body parts. He is a hundred and seventy three point five three centimetres tall. The record should also show that due to extensive blood loss through injury the amount left in the body can only be calculated to be no more than a litre perhaps two.'

Hargreaves then recorded an account of the head, stating hair colour and condition, colour of the eyes, number of teeth, accidental and surgical scars, old injuries and work related conditions of the skin. He added that Arthur Benson had been a skilled engineer employed at the Chopping & Sons cotton mill where he maintained the plant within the property until the deceased had been pensioned off. There was no mention of his lungs until the coroner went inside the chest cavity.

Applying deft movements Hargreaves took hold of the scalpel, placed the sharp blade against the skin quickly cutting a 'Y' incision between each clavicle, coming together at the sternum bone and then down in a straight line to the round knotted depression of the naval. The assistant helped by clamping back the loose folds so that the organs inside could be clearly seen without any obstruction.

Pointing with his right hand so that Atherton could lean forward Hargreaves held what was left of a lung with his free hand.

'As unfortunate as the circumstances were of today sergeant, in my opinion the deceased would not have lasted much longer. The emphysema as you can see had gripped our victim in a stranglehold from which no amount of surgery would have prevented the inevitable.'

Cutting and dissecting valves, tubes and sinew Hargreaves removed, examined and weighed everything. Within a short matter of time the stainless steel table resembled a butcher's block awash with the dead man's heart, kidney, lungs, liver and intestines. He took blood samples, labelled and made each ready for the toxicology machine.

Daniel Atherton watched as Hargreaves danced his post-mortem tango, twisting one way then another as he meticulously performed his duties. The coroner had once said that he precariously danced with the devil as the demon from below had claimed many of his victims. Forensics he would add was an exact science and the minutest scrap of missed evidence could be the undoing of a criminal prosecution. Taking scrapings from under the fingernails he moved to the inside of the mouth, the nasal cavity and lastly the ears.

When the assistant brought the plastic bag to the table containing what was left of Arthur Benson's manhood the contents resembled the giblets taken from a Christmas turkey. Opening the bag Michael Hargreaves matched them to the body noting the expression change on Daniel Atherton's face.

'I need to satisfy myself sergeant that they belong to the deceased only I would rather foolish in court if they belonged to somebody else, not that that is likely in this particular case. However in my profession I cannot take anything at just face value or for granted.'

Taking up the knife that had come from the kitchen at Parkway Drive, Michael Hargreaves placed it against the skin. Switching back on the microphone he continued.

'A knife found in the kitchen of the deceased's property is part of a culinary set. It was used as the instrument to cut into the groin and remove the testes and penis. The incision is clean and well executed except for where the killer had to change his or her position and continue the circular motion. To remove this part of the anatomy should in my opinion have only taken ten to twenty seconds. There is a small amount of evidence of blood on the steel handle and choil which when tested will I suspect belong to the deceased.

'There is a small puncture wound which is identical to the insertion of a syringe needle going into the jugular vein. Toxicology will determine the drug used although I suspect that some form of anaesthetic had been applied rendering the victim conscious but without the use of his limbs, muscles and power of speech.

'Death was caused by fear and from bleeding out which eventually stopped the heart from beating and rendering the brain as a dead cell.'

Hargreaves switched off again concluding the examination. He promptly extended both his arms stretching the sinews in his back. 'This profession can be very unkind on the spine sergeant. Tell me, did you find anything of interest at the house?'

Atherton told him about the oddments in the biscuit tin and of the photographs, he showed Hargreaves the one of the children in the park. Hargreaves studied the image.

'This was without doubt premeditated, a planned execution and the killer knew that there would be knives in the house which he could use. Although the idea might seem abhorrent to most the removal of the sex organs would not have taken long to perfect. A butcher, an abattoir worker, even a vet would know how to perform such an operation and the list could go on and on.'

Working alone in the background his assistant was replacing body parts including the ones that had been found in Arthur Benson's mouth. A simple running stitch along the length of the chest would soon bring together the folds again and other than the funeral parlour nobody else was likely to notice the impatience of his handiwork.

'And the pentobarbital Sir, could that have been what made Arthur Benson compliant?'

Scrubbing the examination from his hands despite wearing gloves Hargreaves looked through the viewing glass at the analysis machine working away in the next room.

'When I'm done we'll go through and see what the machine tells us although by whatever means the killer subdued his victim it was an act of extreme brutality.'

'The actions of a psychopath?' added Atherton.

Hargreaves towelled his hands dry rubbing in some dermatological cream.

'Not necessarily as the line between a psychopath and a sociopath is definitely fine, take todays case for an example. The killer has problematic, significant issues as no right minded individual would go to such lengths to inflict such an appalling injury.'

He threw the used towel into a laundry basket. 'However for a refined list of idiosyncrasies I would suggest that you consult with a psychologist, a professional who deals with the mind.'

Atherton however had his own views. His understanding of the subject was that a psychopath killed at random without remorse acting entirely on impulse, getting a buzz from the high level of self-gratification upon which his methods had caused the maximum suffering by the victim whereas a sociopath suffered a distinct personality disorder manifesting into antisocial attitudes and behaviour. Some professionals would argue there was a distinct mix of both conditions in any disturbed killer.

He followed Hargreaves into the next room where the analysis machine was disgorging a paper record. Pentobarbital was present in the body.

'You've a dangerous killer on the loose sergeant.'

Michael Hargreaves turned off the toxicology analyser. 'Pathology was always easier than Psychiatry when I was studying for my exams. I can cut into the brain anytime down here in the basement although I am unable to see into the mind of a living breathing soul when they pass me by in the street.' He wished Atherton luck with his enquiries and said that his secretary would send all the toxicology results across electronically.

Leaning against the driver's door Atherton's thoughts were interrupted by a flock of geese heading north for the winter. They made the journey look remarkably easy. What Michael Hargreaves had said was right and somewhere out there was a very dangerous killer. Atherton reached for his mobile knowing that every second counted.

'How'd it go?' Byrne asked when he saw who was calling.

'Much as we expected. Arthur Benson was a smoker before he contracted emphysema and between the nicotine and dust at the cotton mill his lungs were as shot up as the ducks at a fairground shooting gallery. Anything new at Chopping & Sons?'

'Not a lot really. Back in two thousand and seven, the mill survived the recession losing some employees along the way through redundancy. Although for Arthur it seems as though redundancy was an unexpected bonus. From his file I managed to get his bank details, the exact figure of his redundancy settlement and the pension plan that human resources put into place.

'Arthur was punctual and never missed a day through illness not until his condition kicked in big time. Soon after that he joined the NHS wagon visiting numerous clinics until transferred to the chest clinic. Seemingly respected by young and old alike he never picked fights or had any altercations. Arthur Benson was a very private person, rarely going for a pint after work although he did have an annual membership at the works snooker club.'

'And contact details, family?' asked Atherton.

'Stanley Benson, the father is named as next-of-kin. He lives at a hundred and ten Rochester Road, Southport although there was no recorded telephone number on file. Oddly enough though in the unexpected circumstances of Arthur's death there were no recorded details of any beneficiary for the pension.'

Twenty minutes later Atherton drew up alongside Pete Byrne. His colleague eased himself into the passenger seat looking tired and hungry.

'What say we head over to Rochester Road deliver the agony message and then I buy you a pint in the conservative club on the way back home?'

Byrne lay his head back against the headrest and shut his eyes wanting the day to end. It was almost five in the afternoon and the traffic was already swelling.

Standing outside of the Rochester Road address Atherton instinctively felt that something was amiss. All the curtains in the detached house had been pulled shut cloaking the property in a dark veil. Everything was quiet, too quiet.

Using the doorbell they received no reply.

'You check with next door Pete and I'll wait here in case anybody does show!'

Raising the metal flap of the letterbox the inside was darker still shrouded like the underside of a bats wing. Catching a whiff of something metallic Atherton checked to see where Pete Byrne was before taking a step back and kicking hard at the door. As the lock snapped open the glass in the viewing panel shattered. Reaching in he flicked on the hallway light before heading straight for the kitchen knowing what to expect, moments later he was joined by Pete Byrne.

'Fucking hell...' announced the older detective *'can this day get any worse?'*

Reaching for his mobile he called it in.

Chapter Five

Byrne passed the details of the address to the control room requesting back up seeing the offer of his ale slipping away with every passing moment. He couldn't work out whether his throat was unusually parched or the metallic tinge in the air was to blame.

With both chins resting on the tops of their chests the man and the woman sat slumped at the kitchen table illuminated only by the glare of a single low wattage bulb. Their hands had been pulled around back and tied into the fretwork of the chairs with twine. If that wasn't frightening enough both victims had serious head wounds where the sides of their skulls had been caved in by a series of heavy blows.

Atherton noticed that amongst the hanging mass of neurons which had seeped from the fissure in the skull nests of buff coloured pupae of the blowfly had already started to grow in size. Resembling the tendrils of a dying squid the uneven strands of brain had come to rest uneasily on the shoulders of each cadaver.

'Marjorie and the circus are on route.' Pete Byrne announced.

Circling the table Atherton mentally recorded every detail in his mind, the looks in their eyes the horror etched upon their face as the killer struck one then the other.

'Thanks Pete. Do you need to call home?'

Byrne looked at the dials on his watch 'I'll let Anne get the girls settled before I make the call otherwise they will keep me chatting for ages.'

Atherton respected his colleague's decision, envious that Byrne at least had somebody at home with whom he could converse and offload the day selling his soul to a thinking, breathing person. Daniel Atherton lived alone in a comfortable bachelor flat in a developed part of the town but tastefully designed and decorated the interior lacked a woman's touch, her feminine scent and bodily contact. Somewhere in the distance the two-tones were growing in intensity.

Lying on top of the drainer was a bloodied steak mallet, they both knew why it was there but neither man made any comment.

'If this is case about a family secret then this is some bloody secret!'

Byrne slowly worked his way around the kitchen touching nothing but seeing everything. Like Park Drive he felt that the place was unusually cold.

'They've been dead for over forty eight hours, I'd say.'

Atherton nodded. 'The blowfly.'

'No...' he held up a newspaper which had been on the side of the kitchen. It had blood splatter across the front page. It had been printed for Tuesday's edition.

'I think it's safe to say that they met with the same killer as Arthur and the dead man here is Stanley Benson. This might be the wife but we will need somebody to identify both.'

Byrne nodded 'or maybe some poor bugger who happened to just come round to visit or alternatively an elderly woman collecting for charity.'

They searched the lower floor before climbing the stairs to the bedrooms above making sure that there was nobody still in the house or anybody else dead. Stranger things had been known to happen in the past.

What was immediately different from Arthur Benson's house was the quality of the furnishings, the décor and comfort. Most of the walls had hanging paintings, photographs and ornaments, mementoes of happier times.

Arriving around the same time as the marked units Marjorie was as keen to see an end to her day as much as Byrne and Atherton. She dropped her equipment bag in the hallway assessing the man and the woman sat at the table, besides the two dead people the only other thing out of place in the kitchen was the steak hammer on the drainer.

From the floor above she heard movement knowing that the detectives were upstairs she called out to let them know that she was downstairs. After a few minutes they joined her.

'I understand that the dead man could be Arthur's father Stanley Benson?'

Lightly tapping a photograph on the kitchen wall Atherton pointed to the two people sitting on the jetty. They looked happy in the sunshine as a boatload of sightseers pulled away to travel down the lake.

'Going on profile alone I would say the man on the jetty is Stanley Benson and that's his wife.' He looked at the dead woman's left hand, she was wearing a wedding ring.

'It would have been good to have known who took the photograph.'

Atherton looked again at the image. 'Possibly Arthur Benson did, remember Millicent told us that he took himself off to the Lake District one summer with his camera. It's possible that he went with his parents.'

Once again Marjorie was armed with a handful of plastic markers and her camera as she prepared the scene for examination. Using a slide rule she measured the pupae of the calliphoridae pod.

'Initial guess is that they've been dead for over thirty six hours. These pods are getting ready to change colour.' She rubbed the underside of her nose detecting an odour in the immediate vicinity.

'And that could be periodontitis. Many old people suffer the condition through poor dental hygiene.' She looked across to where Pete Byrne was stood. 'Would you mind cracking open the window a little please only a slight injection of fresh air would be most welcome.'

Byrne was happy to oblige. To the rear was a fair sized landscaped garden. The sudden influx of air helped abate the offensive odour.

She took a sample of blood from either end of the table then closely examined each wound.

'This wasn't really necessary, these victims were elderly people they could not have put up much of a resistance!'

Marjorie had attended and been witness to many crime scenes down the years but young children and vulnerable people would always affect her emotions the most and the more extreme the modus operandi used it was evidently clear that violence was on the increase and many of the perpetrator's caught unashamedly admitted to enjoying the moment of when they would inflict as much pain and terror as was possible.

Pete Byrne was surprisingly in agreement.

'The killer didn't give them much of fighting chance, tying their hands behind the chair backs.'

Lying on the worktop was a ball of parcel twine. Much stronger than string although coarse and in time would have cut into the skin.

'He likes the control factor.' Atherton added. Also on the table were three cups and saucers with the remnants of cold tea. 'This proves our theory that they knew their visitor.'

Marjorie placed three numbered markers beside each item of crockery.

'They could prove valuable and perhaps we'll be able to lift the killers DNA from the rim of the tea cup. I doubt we'd get anything from the handle as it's too thin.'

Marjorie noticed that Pete Byrne looked somewhat distracted as though his thoughts were elsewhere rather the kitchen.

'Are you okay?' she asked. It pleased Atherton that they were more civil with one another.

Byrne looked back up and nodded. 'Yeah, sorry… I was just thinking. Do you remember the serial killer we had running the county. He would sexually assault his victims before he killed them.'

'The *wheel man killer* replied Marjorie her memory as sharp as the time she had collected evidence at the various scenes.

Byrne nodded. 'Yeah, that's right. 'He would wait for them to exit the pub or a restaurant late at night before following a short distance before he pounced. Each victim was found in or around the side of a disused railway sidings.'

Byrne looked over at Atherton. 'Most were found lying next to train wheels. All had been raped and marks about the body suggested that some form of torture had been used as an instrument of fear. He was named the *wheel man killer* as most were found chained or tied to old rolling stock. The terror he inflicted upon the young women had been to satisfy his sexual self-gratification. Looking at the couple here tied to the chairs brought back memories of the case.'

'And was he caught?' Atherton asked.

'No, we got close several times but somehow and I was never sure how, he escaped before we arrived. Despite the amalgamation of a special squad made up of detectives from three neighbouring forces the bastard always managed to slip the net. I've always expected him to strike again someday!'

Marjorie used a mirror from her bag to look into the man's eyes as he stared down at the tea cup. The terror was there for each of them to see.

'If you were to ask detectives, I would say that the man had to watch the woman be tortured before he was attacked. Her injuries are to a degree less severe than hers!'

'Our killers searching for something?' Atherton implied. He watched a maggot disappear back inside the cranium.

'In what way?' Marjorie enquired.

'First Arthur and then Stanley and his wife, presumably Arthur's mother. Most killer's disturbed in the house attack their victim leaving nothing to chance. The assault is brutal but over in a matter of seconds whereas all three have had to witness their demise. A prolonged attack to interrogate them perhaps before they die!'

Atherton specifically looked at Byrne.

'This *wheel man killer* were any of his victims related?'

'A pair of cousins who had attended a hen party together were abducted together, raped and murdered together. They were found within yards of one another. We did think at the time that there could be two perpetrators working together but body hair found at the scene suggested that the killer was one and the same man.'

'And nothing showed in system?'

Marjorie shook her head. 'Nothing, no match no previous convictions. I'm with the detective on this one in that it still worries me that the killer is going to strike again one day.'

Atherton was trying to tie together any loose ends and not jump at the obvious.

'It could be that our killer here was known to the family, a friend say only not with any blood ties. Someone that had a disagreement that needed sorting.'

Byrne spurned the suggestion 'Well he's made sure that there won't be any other disagreements!'

Marjorie started to remove more equipment from her bags hinting that she need the space to manoeuvre as the rest of her team came in through the front door. Before they left to resume their search she asked if anything conclusive was found at Arthur Benson's post-mortem.

'Only that as we thought, pentobarbital was present in the body. Hargreaves secretary is sending a copy of the toxicology report electronically.'

On the landing above both took a few moments to engage their thoughts. A second look about assembled fresh opinions and ideas.

'Old Arthur could have been cut out of the will for some reason,' Byrne suggested 'it would account for the verbal altercation when his parents came visiting.'

'It's a good theory Pete. As you say it would account for bad feeling. Could be that our killer had also been left out of any legacy.'

'Well this place smells of money and suggests that Stanley wasn't badly off. This is a good area much like where you live.'

Atherton agreed. 'I know but my parents helped with the down payment on my place. I could not afford it without their help. Whatever any dispute the Benson's didn't do the same for their son. Arthur Benson's house was virtually spartan compared to this.'

'That would create bad blood. I know that I'd feel pretty hurt if mine or Anne's parents did that to me.'

'The motives are there Pete, we just need to unravel them.'

'We could do with finding an address book for a list of relatives.'

Atherton shook his head checking the time with his watch. 'I'm surprised Tavistock hasn't called yet, this latest find could seriously affect his league tables.'

Byrne was pleased to hear the remark proving that despite his promotion Daniel Atherton had some scruples left to doubt the policing methods of the top floor management of the station.

'At least it'll give him something to talk about at the next rotary club dinner!'

Atherton smiled. 'I'd like to also say thanks Pete for giving Marjorie and team some slack.'

Byrne grinned back. 'They do a good job, I recognise that it's just that we got off on the wrong foot a while back and every time that I've tried to broach the subject Marjorie brought down the shutters.'

'Well thanks anyway only it's good now that we're all on the same side as we have enough to do without any infighting.'

Byrne nodded accepting the pat on the back.

'I we're profiling our killer, then we're looking at somebody younger than our victims?'

'Seems to be heading that way.' Replied Atherton. 'I'd also stick my neck out and say that are or were at some time local. They know their way around. They possibly know what time the likes of Millicent goes to bed and when best to strike. They are strong to catch Arthur especially off-guard then haul him up and onto the kitchen table. We're looking for a fit youngish man.'

Dividing their efforts Daniel Atherton was almost finished in the back bedroom when Gabrielle George asked him to come back downstairs. In the front living room she showed him a football programme lying on the coffee table beside the settee. It was creased where it had been folded, dated Saturday the ninth of May nineteen ninety two. The front cover picture was of the two teams competing in the FA Cup Final, Liverpool and Sunderland. The venue Wembley.

'I thought that you would want to see this only I found it between the cushions of the settee' she carefully took hold of the programme to ensure that there was nothing hidden inside 'it's like the ones we found at Parkway Drive, only it's here.'

Atherton agreed, it was. So far he had found nothing else to suggest that Stanley Benson was a keen supporter of either team or soccer. He asked Gabrielle to bag it and test it back at the lab for prints.

He was about to climb the stairs again when Michael Hargreaves walked in attired in evening dress. Atherton shook the extended hand. 'Good evening Sir!'

Hargreaves raised his eyebrows 'It was certainly turning out to be good sergeant until I got this call.'

Hargreaves suddenly felt a shiver run through his body as he rubbed his hands together. 'Is it cold in here or just me?'

For the month of September the interior was remarkably chilled.

'With two dead souls looking for a way out I'd be inclined to agree with you Sir, it is distinctly chilly!'

Hargreaves nodded. For some time he advocated that when the dead lay dead the energy about the scene changed, influenced by the elements outside, the body temperature of the deceased, how warm or cold it was in a building or unscientifically whatever was around. Seen as a medical practitioner and forensic scientist Hargreaves was open to all reason, living or dead.

'And the dead are Arthur Benson's parents?' he asked

'Stanley Benson definitely although as yet we've not found anything to confirm the female victim. Odds on that she is Stanley's wife.'

Hargreaves caught Marjorie with a pair of stainless steel tweezers clamped between her teeth and a reel of fingerprint tape wrapped around her hand. She nodded appreciating his coming.

Hargreaves caressed the underside of his chin deliberating over the scene.

'On reflection this is almost certainly the work of a psychotic psychopath. The disconnection with reality and fantasy is reprehensibly self-evident.' He removed his dinner jacket and rolled up his sleeves. Tom Skerritt assisted by handing over a disposable examination all in one. Leaving the three of them alone in the kitchen Atherton re-joined Byrne on the floor above.

'Michael Hargreaves?' Byrne asked.

Atherton nodded then told him about the supporters programme. 'Arthur could have put it there having visited before the old couple were killed.'

'Or our killer did.' Byrne was sceptical that Arthur had been anywhere near the property for some time. He didn't drive and couldn't walk with his poor health, unless he took a taxi. It was another line of enquiry that would have to be investigated.

'You mean a calling card?'

'Yeah,' agreed Byrne 'serial killers do that only they say it gives them a buzz.

I know this isn't relevant to this case but our *wheel man killer* would keep the investigators on their toes by leaving clues behind at the scenes. Like small tokens he'd leave the business card of a pub or a restaurant that the victims had been visiting. In a way he was helping but taking the piss out of us at the same time. It was like he was undermining our ability to find him. I think our current killer is doing the same. Two crime scenes in less than twenty four hours. We've got to piece together both and reach a satisfactory conclusion.'

Byrne paused letting his thoughts catch up with what he was about to suggest. 'At one point in the *wheel man killer* investigation I admit, that I started taking a long hard look at the faces of the team investigating the rapes and murders thinking that we could be hunting a police officer.'

'That has been known to happen.' Atherton admitted. 'Did a pattern develop?' He asked.

'Not intentionally. We gathered together every business we could lay our hands on from every, pub, nightclub and restaurant, highlighting each location on a map of the area. A sort of pattern materialised but when we focused on one particular hotspot the killer move elsewhere. It's why I considered somebody in the squad being involved or at least tipping off the killer, a brother, uncle or nephew perhaps. He was like a modern day Jack the Ripper. After so many killings it stopped almost overnight and the perpetrator vanished, simply disappeared.'

'So you think that he could be leaving us a false trail, getting us to think that it could be linked to an outsider, somebody that went to football with Arthur when he was in better health?'

Byrne nodded. 'Killer's like to flout the law, show that they are quicker off the mark than us. They like to play games to see how close we can get before they change direction. If we had a crystal ball we could sometimes get one step ahead, just once.'

Atherton too was thinking. 'Connected or not it might be worth looking at some of the old case files from your investigation just in case our killer is older, wiser and had a change of heart. He could have a condition that prevents him from being sexually active but has decided to show himself again only this time around he's inflicting pain in a different way.'

Pushing shut a suitcase from on top of the wardrobe Pete Byrne was incensed.

'I blame the movie channels. We don't let the girls watch any of the late night films as a majority of them are poorly scripted depicting a high level of graphic violence, influenced by sexual arousal, ending with a hundred and one ways to kill the neighbour next door. *Fuck* we see enough bad things in our job to give us all nightmares without my family becoming the victim of some loony screwball and his idea of a good night out!'

Atherton wanted to laugh but Pete Byrne was soberly right in what concerned him. Television did influence the dangerous and unstable members of society. With the search almost complete he asked Pete to organise the officers outside and have them begin house to house enquiries. Taking a moment to look out of the window as expected a large crowd had gathered, restlessly waiting for information.

Searching through the contents of a bedside cabinet he found a bible similar to the one found at Arthur Benson's only there was no inscription. More interesting though he located an address book only checking the pages he tossed it frustratingly to one side having it land on the bed covers.

'That's unlike you,' remarked Marjorie as she entered the bedroom.

'Somebody has deliberately torn out the sections marked A-M. My guess would be because the Benson clan don't go beyond the second half of the alphabet.'

Marjorie picked up the book and examined where the pages had been removed. 'I'll still fingerprint it just in case.'

'I came upstairs because I saw Pete Byrne go outside and I wanted a quiet word with you. At university part of our study work involved psychology and sociology. One of the chapters was about criminal profiling suspects. If you're interested Daniel I could help begin a profile analysis running through what we have and see what it throws up?'

'I'd be grateful for any help Marjorie and thank you. However if you find any odd patterns developing will you let me know before anyone else.'

Marjorie nodded although her eyes were deep set penetrating his thoughts. 'Did Pete tell you that they suspected the *wheel man killer* to be a police officer?'

'He did, how do you know that?'

'I was on the CSI team investigating the crime scenes. Pete Byrne was a young detective at the time although extremely conscientious. Often he would work longer hours than some of the others on the task force. I watched him over the months put together a profile matrix. Charting everything he added a final category was entitled *'possibles'* and below the column heading there was a question mark alongside where he had pencilled in three words *'one of us'*. I wasn't sure quite what he was implying at first but I soon cottoned on. He's a good detective and nobody's fool.'

'No, he's not. Pete gives the impression that he doesn't car less but he's just the opposite and of all my team Byrne is as sharp as a nail and invariably wrong.'

Marjorie sighed. 'There'll always be a bad apple in any big organisation.'

She picked up a small framed photograph from the dressing table. It was inscribed around the edge with the phrase *'angels are born although we don't always realise until it is too late'* she showed it to Atherton.

'That's an odd inscription.' The photograph was of Stanley and Evelyn Benson at the beach.

'I'll remain objective in the matrix and see where it leads us!'

Atherton sensed that there was something else that Marjorie had come up to discuss, he asked.

'I know you're going to think me as a feminine sentimentalist but have you considered a crime of passion?'

She had Atherton's ear and he asked her to go on.

'This could very well turn out to be a domestic situation that's blown all out of proportion but what if our killer is a female, somebody aggrieved by a situation in the past.'

'Like what?'

'Before Arthur contracted emphysema he might had been involved with a woman say from work, the cotton mill but Stanley Benson might have thought the relationship doomed and said as much. A woman scorned can be a deadly threat. Perhaps cast aside by Arthur she might have sought revenge. It would explain his injury and the old couples.'

It was worth considering and one that Atherton had not thought about.

'Love, the pain and bane of many young couples. Romeo and Juliet a good example.' It would account for how the family deaths were connected. Why and how they had died. Atherton nodded. 'Add that to your matrix too Marjorie. If only we had the first half of this address book it would have seriously helped.'

'Talking of pain, have you felt the energy in this house, it's very nicely decorated and furnished although there's a sinister presence here, that has long lived here?'

Daniel Atherton was slightly taken aback by Marjorie's admission. He would not have thought it possible, not from somebody so pragmatic.

'Like a heavy depression. Yes, I experienced the same when I first entered the property. It was weird as though there were two forces present, one good one bad. One wanted me to be here and the other not, only I've been able to determine which belongs to who?'

Marjorie nodded understanding. 'I thought it would be worse downstairs although coming up the stairs is just as consuming. I get the impression that one wants to communicate with us. I felt it at the address in Park Drive, only I didn't say anything because I wasn't sure.'

'And now?' he asked.

'It's why I mentioned the crime of passion. I have this oppressive weight pressing down on me as though the answer lies deep underground. 'As though the dead are trying communicate!'

Daniel Atherton exhaled loudly. 'Wow Marjorie... that is some revelation and I would never have thought it of you. Maybe we should keep this between us as well for the sake of both our careers. Off the record however I agree wholeheartedly with you but for the moment we'll see how this investigation pans out before we throw caution to the wind!'

With a smile she agreed. 'Oh and the last reason that I came up was to tell you that the neighbour next door neighbour has kindly made coffee and tea.'

Atherton thanked her for everything stating that he would be down in a minute. Standing on the landing he watched Marjorie's shadow pass along the hall wall heading towards the front door leaving Tim and Gabrielle behind to secure the scene. There were a good many things that nobody back at the station or indeed the division knew about Marjorie Matthews but now Daniel Atherton knew a bit more than most. It pleased him that she had felt sufficiently confident to confide in him and spiritually he sensed that an understanding had developed between them. In time it could prove useful.

When the house fell silent he closed his eyes inviting the energy on the landing to come forth as he knew that it had been waiting. Almost immediately his head was full of different voices some recognisable others not as clear. He heard them arguing, bickering with one another, passionately wanting to be heard but there were so many. Suddenly he saw the colour red, not pinkish but blood red and not his own but another's.

Channelling his thoughts on one point he asked if the blood belonged to the elderly couple downstairs but an unfamiliar voice replied telling him that he would find it elsewhere. Daniel instantly opened his eyes and leant over the bannister rail. He was in time to see the shadow of a cloaked figure head towards the outside door. Descending the stair treads two at a time he reached the front door in seconds to find the gravel drive and front garden empty.

When Pete Byrne walked through the side gate carrying two mugs of coffee he asked if he had just seen a clocked figure leave.

'No, should I have?' he replied.

Atherton shook his head 'No, it was probably just my imagination.'

'There was tea but I thought coffee would keep us going only its seven now.' He noticed the pensive look in Atherton's eyes. 'Are you okay?'

'Yeah I'm fine only don't ask how or why but we need to be on the lookout for someone wearing a dark hooded coat.'

They took the coffees around back and sat in the garden where it was quiet except for a thrush singing.

'Before I went to organise the troops and have them start resident enquiries I checked the knot that had been used to restrain the old couple. It wasn't any normal knot but a friction hitch, the type that would

74

be used by an engineer to lift heavy machinery, a mechanic replacing a car engine, or a maintenance man changing the loom at a cotton mill.'

'That's interesting,' replied Atherton as he watched the thrush open and shut his beak. 'That suggests Arthur could have killed his parents then went home where he too had an unexpected visitor. This case is full of endless dead ends.'

From his pocket Atherton produced a duplicate photograph of the children playing in the park playground.

'I thought you'd left that back at the station?'

Atherton produced the original from his other pocket. 'This was hidden behind a framed image we found in the master bedroom. A strange place to hide something significant, wouldn't you say.'

Pete Byrne produced a photograph of Stanley and Evelyn Benson on their wedding day that he had found in the downstairs sunroom.

'The next door neighbour identified Evelyn Benson from the photograph. We can take that as a formal ID.' He looked at the image that Atherton was holding. 'It's like the clues are in the photographs only none of them are talking to us.'

They heard the side gate go and seconds later Jasmin Yates appeared. She was her normal cheerless self, the sides of her mouth curved down like that of a depressed clown.

'What do you want me to tell the members of the press?' she asked ignoring Pete Byrne.

'Tell them that we have several lines of enquiry to pursue although until we get something to eat we won't be able to string two sentences together!'

Yates again ignored the older detective.

'And you Daniel, what is your official take on this unfortunate incident. I have to put some meat on the bone otherwise the press will just invent something, anything that will sell papers!'

'Alright Jasmin,' said Atherton. 'Tell the press that the elderly couple inside died in suspicious circumstances however at the moment we are unable to give the exact cause of their death. We do not want them printing anything that will have our perpetrator think that we are on top of things here or the incident this morning at Park Drive. I want to keep this killer guessing our next move not the other way around.'

The three of them walked back down the side path to where the press were out front waiting beyond the hedge. Pete Byrne was surprised when Atherton caught her by the arm and gently spun her around.

'This circus has just got going Jasmin and in under thirty six hours we have three corpses at two different locations. Tell the press that we believe it to be a tragic domestic situation. Whoever the killer, he or she is very dangerous and likely to continue killing. That last bit is not for the press release just yet!'

For once Jasmin Yates cowered down and understood the severity of the situation. For once Daniel Atherton had exercised the authority of his rand and status. They watched as she approached the waiting pack of hyenas.

'That told her...' said Pete Byrne suspiciously 'only I'm still not sure about her, her eyes are too close together.'

Atherton took Pete Byrne's coffee mug heading for the gate between the two properties.

'I don't suppose her role is ever that easy Pete. Jasmin Yates gets the bare bones from us but I can't have her making up stories. We need to give away as little as possible, that way we eventually gain the upper hand.'

Byrne nodded as he held the gate open. 'The officer in charge of the *wheel man killer* investigation gave too much away to the press. I always thought then that he had said too much. Had the press not goaded the killer I doubt some of the victims would been snatched, raped and murdered!'

Coming back out of the neighbour's house they saw the mortuary van arrive to collect the bodies.

Pete Byrne watched as the press photographers took pictures of the van. 'You'd think they'd never seen one of those before!'

'Pictures sell newspaper's Pete.'

'Still Tavistock will be happy with the domestic angle. It keeps the old aggravated assault line from peaking on his wall chart.'

'You're not keen on him are you?'

'Tavistock nor David Cherrington, our illustrious Chief Constable. Both men are statisticians for the police commission. Once this gets out that this isn't domestic then Cherrington will haul Tavistock's arse up to the big office in the ivory white tower and you can just imagine the conversation can't you *'Gregory these murders in your division, they're extremely bad news and could seriously influence your application for Assistant Chief Constable. Get that bastard Byrne working harder or transfer him to traffic. I want both sorted like yesterday.'*

Atherton was grinning and laughing at the same time 'I take it that neither have invited you to the annual golfing dinner!'

Pete Byrne shook his head cursing under his breath.

'No, me, Cherrington and Tavistock go back a long way. We have history hence why I don't sit in your seat. Wolves hunt sheep at night and naïve shepherds get made to be the scapegoat. When the shit hits the fan they know how to duck lower than anybody else. I know because I have seen it happen to some good officers, better men than me.'

Atherton watched Marjorie head back to the house to relieve Gabrielle and Tom. Her day wasn't quite over just yet and neither were theirs.

He conveyed Pete Byrne back home politely declining the invite to join Anne and the girls for supper heading instead back to the station one last time. On his office desk he found a brief note weighed down from Gregory Tavistock asking for an update regarding the circumstances at Rochester Road before he went off duty.

Looking at the clock on the wall Atherton decided it was way too late to disturb the commander at home. He threw the note in the bin and turned out the desk lamp.

Chapter Six

The hooded figure crouched low amongst the twists of dense hawthorn, wild brambles and blanket of heavy ivy, hidden from view as the dark night clouds passed overhead. With only his eyes visible the uninvited stranger watched the men pass the silver hip flask back and forth their haughty laughter echoing through the night air. Hung low over the crook of their left arm were a pair of shotguns at present broken but it would only take a second to lock them again and be ready to fire.

Breaking free of his concealment he passed silently to the trees nearby no more than twenty maybe twenty five feet from where the men were stood talking.

With one final tilt of his head the older man finished off the contents of the flask before replacing the cap. Always so sure of himself Sir Roger Edington-Forbes was an abhorrent disrespectful landowner, a successful farmer and brutal husband. His philosophy, which he only believed was to grab everything regardless of the cost, financial or human. An existence that had many of the locals and neighbouring farmers turn their back on the man, negotiating any transactions with his eldest son Richard.

Overhead the clouds danced across the night sky every so often blocking out the moon casting the estate below in long episodes of shadow. The wood as the men understood was the ideal lair for the fox to hide and move about using the rugged landscape to its advantage. For a good two weeks the creature had been stealing chickens from the hen coop and worrying the young sheep.

Feeling the chill set deep in his bones Sir Roger was adamant that tonight would be rightfully theirs for the taking. 'This damp does my arthritis no good.' He complained.

'There's an extra scarf in the glove compartment if that would help,' exclaimed his son as he kept eye on the shadows.

But the brandy had already worked its way down and his bladder was screaming to be released. 'In a moment Richard, first I need to use the trees!'

Hearing his father walk towards the thicket Richard Edington settled himself on the tailboard of the land rover and gazed up at the house lights way up on top of the hill wishing that he was sat before the fire with his wife and daughter rather than with his father. It had been at his father's insistence that they had undertaken the night vigil hoping to flush out the fox rather than leave the matter to the more able gamekeeper. Richard thought of Reg Cullen nicely entrenched at the pub with a beer at his side throwing darts for the team. He had every Thursday night off an arrangement that had been longstanding.

Muttering a profanity he envisaged a long night ahead. He checked the time with the illuminous dial of his watch, there were only a few minutes to go before nine o'clock.

Passing around the swollen water of the flume channel where the recent rainfall had flooded the lower field the estate owner trod carefully knowing that with all the water about the earth would be treacherously boggy. So far they had been out an hour already and the only stirring amongst the trees had been the pigeons, a few rabbits and an owl.

Still watching Richard saw a shadowy outline move across the window of his apartment on the west wing. It was probably his daughter and her nanny wondering where he was as she looked out into the dark unable to see anything beyond the house lights. What had started as a calm evening had the threat of worse weather to come.

Edington Hall was a grand edifice, moated for three quarters of the surrounding grounds it had been Sir Roger's folly to have it installed believing that as king of his castle he would be better protected. Richard lowered and shook his head in disbelief. What sort of deluded man was his father? He heard his footfalls crunch the fallen branches underfoot as he found a suitable tree with which to relieve himself.

Grunting to himself Roger unzipped his fly then sighed as the hot fluid washed the bark of the tree. He closed his eyes realising that he was passing water more frequently of late and soon he would have to consult the doctor as to why. When he opened them again everything was seemingly darker than before. All about he could hear small creatures scurrying to and fro going about their nightly ritual foraging for food and the need to stay alive. From somewhere behind he heard the echo of a twig crack. Moments later a large sharp hunting knife came to rest against the fold of skin beneath his chin.

In a whisper the intruder issued a warning. 'If you move or utter a single sound I will slice you where you stand pissing and leave you for the creatures to gnaw upon, do you understand?'

Sir Roger gulped gently nodding as the knife was pulled away so that he could reply.

Using his free hand the hooded figure took the shotgun snapping it shut and ready to discharge its shot. The end of the barrel dug hard into the small of the older man's back.

'Now walk you contemptible piece of shit back to the vehicle, do it slowly and with no sudden movements!'

Finding his way back around the flume channel Sir roger looked for anything that would give him the opportunity to overcome the man but there was nothing and anything that had been there earlier was now buried beneath the mud. Watching nearby between the gaps in the bush the fox followed the route taken by two men as they went closer to the land rover.

Sir roger looked up at his grand hall seeing the lights but they were from his son's apartment not his own which was on the far side of the house. He wondered if his young wife and daughter-in-law were back from their shopping trip in London. Much younger than he by fifteen years she was still good to look at although the shift of power in the bedroom had begun to turn in her favour. It had been some time since they had slept together and his frustration was beginning to show in hi mood swings.

In places the ground was extreme slippery, thick with mud and rotting vegetation and hard to find a foothold but he managed to concentrate and keep his footing. Still sat on the tailboard Richard heard him approach only didn't bother to look as it would be a matter of seconds before he returned. His father had been in a foul mood all day and had insisted that they went out that night and deal with the fox. It would serve Richard best not to agitate his mood any deeper.

It was no wonder that his step-mother was of late becoming more distant and he sensed a divorce looming on the horizon. Love meant only one thing to his father and that was getting his women to submit to his unusual depraved demands. Richard Edington felt sorry for Francesca Forbes. The same as he felt sorry for the maids that his father had deflowered down the years, his black heart destroying their lives. With time to contemplate his father's grip on people's lives, Richard understood why his two younger brother's had long since escaped Edington Hall.

When his father went stumbling past the tailboard landing face down on the brownish bracken Richard jumped from the tailboard to assist but before he could get to his father the end of a shotgun was placed against the side of his neck. Looking right he could just see the outline of a man in a long hooded coat although he could not see the face. He also realised that his own firearm and gun belt were out of reach lying on the tailboard. Still watching in the bush the fox sniffed the air deciding that it was time to go hunt its supper.

With a swift kick to the back of the knee Richard Edington went down landing near to his father.

'What in blazes are you doing man and who the devil are you, I demand that you show yourself?'

Kicking the sole of the older man's right the pain shot up Sir Roger's leg attacking his arthritic hip. He let out a yelp to the amusement of the intruder.

'Shut up you loathsome bastard and keep still. The night is growing cold and damp, my trigger finger might slip and take off a limb or two!' he pointed the barrel of the shotgun down at both legs.

'At last I have you just where I want you. It's been a long wait but I knew that if I bided my time this moment would be granted to me.'

Swinging the barrels right he pointed the end of the shotgun at the younger man.

'Are you Richard Edington?'

He nodded and said that he was, leaving it at that not wanting to antagonise the stranger holding the shotgun. Whereas his father had a different opinion of the situation.

'Do you know who I am and who you are dealing with?'

The air was suddenly cut in half with the shrill of laughter, a convulsive cachinnation of mockery.

'*Fuck* who you are you bastard, do you know who I am is more important?'

Richard intervened quickly before his father's black mood sent them to hell. He shook his head.

'No. Perhaps if you told us we could somehow work out this misunderstanding.'

The hooded intruder stopped laughing. He switched the shotgun barrel back to the father.

'You should be more polite, like your son.' Keeping the barrel pointing at Sir Roger's legs he looked back at Richard Edington. 'On reflection, it is not prudent to let you know who I am just yet but soon enough you'll know.'

Lying on the ground supported by his elbows Sir Roger noticed the fox run up the hill towards the hen coop.

'Down there you don't look half as powerful as you make out that you are. I've been watching your progress from afar only I wanted to see how mighty you could become before I intervened and took it all away. I watched your wife get on the train this morning and head off to London with her sister-in-law. Neither are part of this so it was best that they were out of the way.'

'And my daughter?' asked Richard concerned for her safety.

'She like her mother is safe.'

Like an audience watching in the wings of the theatre the moon reappeared flooding the field in a sheet of white light.

'In times gone by the authorities would have dragged you screaming from your house, butchered your hide and left you for the crows to feed upon for the things that you have done. Down the years you have stolen innocent lives and sent their soul to the devil. Long ago justice meant something but now money talks and judges can be easily bribed. I stand here before you tonight as both judge and jury and I find you guilty of the heinous crimes that you have committed against young women in your employ.'

Sir Roger opened his mouth to speak but the end of the barrel fell onto his shin and the hooded intruder shook his head.

'Don't interrupt my deliberation or you'll lose the leg.' He sent another shock wave up the leg bringing about another scream instantly lost in the night.

'You destroy young lives as though they were no better than carrion, showing no mercy for their pleas. Instead you laugh and cast them aside when you're done with them. Tonight I sit in judgement of you and your past, of you both!'

Sir Roger Edington-Forbes was not used to being spoken to like this, not by a reminiscing fool. He had dealt with worse down the years, tenants on his land, other farmers and market traders. He started to rise uttering *'fuck this'* but the intruder reversed the shotgun jamming the butt of the stock hard into the old man's shoulder sending him sprawling back down.

'I won't warn you again!'

'Don't be a fool father, do as the man asks!'

Nursing the ache in his shoulder Sir Roger was less passive.

'That has always been your undoing Richard, you have to stand up to lesser men and put them in their place. There always has been masters and there always will be. Those that serve have their place in society and should not rise above it.' His eyes were set hard as they had always been

84

set when he had chastised any of his three sons. 'Have you learnt nothing that I have taught you?'

Richard Edington looked down at his chest awaiting the inevitable, it was useless trying to reason with his father and if a divorce was looming he would willing sign a deposition in favour of his step-mother.

'I suppose that you've come for money, that's normally what most men want from the rich and powerful?'

The shotgun had been sung back around again.

'Money...' laughed the intruder 'I've no use for money, where I'm heading money would not bring me happiness. I only seek what's rightly mine... justice!'

But Sir Roger believed that any man could be bribed. Relentlessly he tried again.

'There is twenty five thousand at least in the safe in the house, if you let us go I'll will have my son get it for you. No questions asked and you can just disappear back into the wood from where you came.'

Alongside him Richard Edington shook his head in shame. 'Is that the going rate that you levy upon a person's life father, do I mean that little to you.'

Sir Roger however was undaunted by his son or the stranger.

'Life is cheap Richard. You grab what you can and ignore those that cannot feed themselves. It has always been like that!'

He looked up at the hooded figure and pointed with his good arm.

'One day the authorities will catch up with you. Madmen like you never succeed.' Sir Roger suddenly stared hard at the eyes, the features beneath the hood. *'You look familiar, don't I know you from somewhere. Give me a moment and I will remember!'*

Richard Edington tensed shutting his eyes. All about the breeze was chilling his bones as the moon overhead continued to watch. With the shotgun only inches from Sir Roger's right foot the hooded man didn't wait for the recognition. He pulled the trigger discharging one barrel of shot. Instantly the foot vanished leaving a bloody stump just below the ankle bone. The scream that followed pierced the night as a shrill of a wild banshee as wood pigeon flew from the branches nearby and smaller creatures sought a place to hide.

Calmly the stranger spoke 'you see it doesn't pay to annoy me.'

He broke open the shotgun and flicked out the used cartridge making sure that it still had a charged round, he cracked it shut once again.

'I'm not mad, not half as I was before today. You're all the same just because you have wealth, land and title. You believe that gives you the right to belittle, abuse and degrade the lower classes. Have you any idea what it is like to be alone and frightened at night cowering in a room not knowing when you are going to be fed again, when it is safe to come back out and when the voices in your head or the ache in your chest will stop. Do you know what it's like to feel totally unloved?' He looked at the man agonisingly holding the end of his leg. 'Have you ever experienced hell on earth?'

Richard Edington opened his eyes. 'No, I don't,' he replied 'maybe if you explained why you are here, we can help you.'

'Atonement!' came the reply

'Atonement, for what precisely?' Richard Edington looked puzzled.

Throwing off the hood the eyes were almost black in the shadows.

'Atonement for the repeated violation of somebody that I loved more than I loved myself. However, the evil that existed in your family, in your father and possibly you, destroyed everything that she was. A gentle soul she lived out a living hell until her death.'

Richard Edington was no fool, a much better man than his father he realised the predicament of their lying defenceless in the ground.

'Before I die,' he wanted it to be known that he was not afraid. 'I have the right to know to whom you refer and who you are. For years I have done my best not to be like my father. At least grant me the courtesy to tell me who?'

Walking back over to the gun belt lying on the tailgate the stranger reloaded the empty barrel.

'Telling you would make it no easier upon your soul. You say that you are not like your father and yet you abused a young woman when you could have retaliated and shown your father that what he was doing was wrong. What you both did to her broke the last of her spirit. She was no more than a walking corpse. You both took from her, her body and her mind. You destroyed one of god's angels.'

Locking the shotgun barrel into the stock he made the firearm ready.

'Do you know what a walking corpse is?' he asked.

Slowly the tears began to run down Richard Edington's cheek.

The intruder explained. 'When there is nothing left inside and the soul has become an empty void that person believes that they are dead. They cannot hold onto anything solid enough to support them, upon which to feed, to live. As a walking shell they deem themselves worthless so being dead is better than being alive. Endless cruelty will make them a walking corpse. Eventually the mind snaps as their body becomes infested with illness. Death is a welcome end.'

Fighting back the nausea in his throat and the pain in his leg Sir Roger was beyond caring for his life or that of his eldest son.

'This is a mere figment of your imagination. If however you knew such a person then she was better off dead!'

From his side Richard Edington uttered only one word knowing to whom the stranger was referring *'sorry!'*

Mustering the last of his energy Roger Edington-Forbes slapped the side of his son's face.

'Be quiet you fool. We are Edington's and we do not bow down to any insolent cur holding a gun.' He scoffed at the hooded figure *'if she were here now I would do exactly the same, fuck her until she begged for mercy!'*

Levelling the shotgun he took the head clean off from the shoulders of the older man before pointing it at Richard Edington. The headless corpse flew back several yards before coming to rest.

'Did your father coerce you into raping that young woman?'

Pulling his hands from over his eyes Richard Edington stared back at the intruder. His eyes were soft yet knowing. The end was soon to come.

At Edington Hall down in the basement a kitchen maid busy at the sink heard the gunshot followed by a bloodcurdling scream. She looked over to where the cook of the house Agnes Maitland was stirring a large ladle around the edge of a stewing pot.

'Don't you be fretting none Mary, I've told you before that the vixen always cry out in the night for their young. Living in the countryside you get used to the different sounds.'

Mary Thomas nodded, accepting the cook's explanation. It had not been that long since she had been employed at the grand hall and things were as Agnes said different. Looking up at the wall clock she set about her duties once again as the mistress and Richard's wife were due back any minute.

'And besides,' Agnes added 'you know that the masters are out hunting the vixen who has been stealing our hens.'

Mary felt the shiver run down her spine at the mention of the dirty old man who had trapped her in the kitchen store when Agnes had been in town shopping. Providence had descended over the occasion and for some reason Sir roger had suddenly gripped the front of his trousers and rushed away. The experience however had left her very wary. Beyond the kitchen window besides the howling of the wind all was quiet again.

'It was inevitable that one day somebody would come for my father. In a way it was a fitting end to his life. I know about the young maid that you mention. She was only a few years older than myself, pretty and had a nice smile. On my sixteenth birthday my father dragged me from my bed manhandling me to her room in the attic where he forced me to be with her.'

Richard Edington breathed in deep taking a full intake of the night air. 'You must realise that I had no choice. Had I disobeyed my father would have horsewhipped me until my back was raw.'

'How many times was you with her?'

'Only the Once. I was so ashamed of myself but my father only laughed as he took me back to my room. He told me that I would no longer have to prove myself as a man.' At last he felt the weight of that night ebb from his soul. 'I understand why you came here tonight, please forgive me for I am truly sorry!'

'Did you know that she had a son, a bastard?'

Richard Edington shook his head. 'No, I didn't.'

'Tell me does the stable-hand who was employed the same week as the young maid still work on the estate?'

'William Benjamin. Not long discharged from the army. Yes, I remember him although he was killed in a riding accident about two years after the maid left the house.'

When the moon disappeared behind a large black cloud the shotgun barrel discharged the last round blowing a gaping hole into Richard Edington's chest. Like his father he was blown backwards coming to rest almost alongside. Most of his organs had disintegrated in the blast including his heart.

Picking up the shotgun that had been left on the tailboard of the land rover the killer walked over to where Richard Edington lay dead. Placing his hand over the man's eyes he gently closed the eyelids.

'I am sorry too. So often without our approval we carry the burden of those that we once loved, those who went before us. Dark mysteries, family secrets can send us mad, as mad as a dead corpse walking.'

Spitting contemptuously at the headless body the killer replaced his hood. He turned and headed towards the trees. On the bank of the flume channel he heeled both shotguns beneath the mud pushing down hard until they were no visible, then looking back just the once he left. At last it was done although there was no time to rejoice nor rest as others needed to run and hide.

Back in the basement kitchen Mary Thomas heard more shots only this time there was no scream. She shrugged her shoulders then cut four equal sized slices of bread. It was almost time for her to head up to the attic bedroom. Soon the master would return to the house. She knew that she would have to barricade the door as he was always more demanding when he had been out shooting and drinking.

Chapter Seven

Friday Morning

Daniel Atherton stood alongside Marjorie as they watched Michael Hargreaves delve into the chest cavity before extracting the heart that had once beat for Evelyn Benson. In a silent moment of condolence Marjorie prayed for the departing soul of the dead woman. In her many years as a forensic examiner she had witnessed more female deaths than male.

At her side Atherton sensed her reverence.

'I was just paying my last respects,' she whispered.

He nodded raising his eyebrows. Hargreaves was weighing the liver when Atherton felt his mobile buzz in his jacket pocket. He apologised for the interruption excusing himself from the room returning in a couple of minutes looking decidedly anxious. Noting the change in the detective's expression Michael Hargreaves stopped what he was doing.

'Again, I must apologise Sir that call was to inform me that we have a double fatal shooting incident out at Edington Hall near Waxford Hammock. My informant tells me that a father and son have been brutally murdered.'

Without hesitation Hargreaves released them both stating that as soon as he was done with Evelyn Benson he would make his way out to Edington Hall.

Outside of the coroners building Marjorie parted company needing to get back to the station to mobilise her team and collect the necessary equipment required for an open scene. Atherton headed directly for Edington Hall.

Having driven along the winding drive interspersed with shrubs and trees he found Pete Byrne waiting anxiously at the top of a grassy knoll. He looked tired and somewhat haggard as he ran his fingers through the mop of brown hair.

'You look like you could sleep for a week!' remarked Atherton.

Byrne stifled a yawn. 'I'm okay although there are times when I seriously think I should have been a bus driver at least where I knew the hours would be regular.'

Not far behind were a pair of white CSI vehicles.

'Have you been to the scene?'

'Not yet, I had only just arrived myself. Control told me that the gamekeeper found the bodies and that he's waiting down near the woods below.'

Treading the grass underfoot they all decided to the leave vehicles up top and walk down the steep incline of the hill as the ground. Way down below they saw a man waiting patiently beside a dark coloured land rover.

'That must be the gamekeeper, Reginald Cullen.'

'And it was he who found the men?' Marjorie asked.

'About an hour ago. Story goes that both men were out hunting a fox last night only when they failed to return this morning the gamekeeper was sent to search for them.'

'By who?' Atherton asked.

'Lady Francesca Edington-Forbes, the mistress of the hall.'

'And both died from gunshot wounds?' Marjorie was already gathering facts for her record.

'That's right,' replied Byrne 'one with a head and foot, the other with a massive chest wound.'

'Any idea why Cullen wasn't on the shoot as well?'

'Thursday's by all account is his regular night off.' Alibis would have to be verified. Byrne warned them to watch where they placed their feet as the field was flooded in places and where it looked dry was in fact nothing better than a quagmire.

'There was a lot of rain during the early hours of this morning!' They all looked to where Gabrielle George was trailing behind. 'I know because I couldn't sleep so I got up around one thirty. Made myself a cup of tea and a short while after that it started to rain.'

Aware of the company she was in she appeared a little hesitant to continue. Prompted by Tom Skerritt she did. 'Only when I went to the window to look at the rain falling outside I thought I saw a man standing on the corner opposite. He was looking directly up at my flat and me. I did think about calling control but when I looked again he had gone. It unnerved me a bit so I didn't get to bed until around four this morning!'

'Me neither,' admitted Byrne.

'Next time Gabrielle call it in,' Marjorie advised 'it's better to be safe than sorry!'

Gabrielle saw Atherton looking, he winked at her supporting what Marjorie had advised. She liked Danielle Atherton, he was always so kind and helpful especially if she didn't quite understand something at a scene. She liked Pete Byrne too although he had always reminded her of her father.

Near to the scene they were met by two uniformed officers who were unravelling and threading a roll of crime scene tape in some sort of wide circle. Propped against the rear side panel of the land rover was Reg Cullen. He righted himself as they came closer.

'Can we start by getting the tent up as soon as possible,' Marjorie asked 'as the clouds looming overhead don't look overly promising!' She introduced herself to the gamekeeper shaking his hand. 'And, if you could just tell me what you've touched so far we can begin by placing markers?'

'Nothing...' he replied 'not even the gun belt.' Marjorie placed her first marker on the tailboard.

'Excellent,' Marjorie replied 'we'll take your fingerprints later!'

Reg Cullen moved across to where Byrne and Atherton were looking around taking it all in.

'I bet she's fun to work with!'

Byrne smiled 'you want to be with her when she's having an off-day.'

Atherton looked on but said nothing. He studied Reg Cullen looking for signs of hesitant guilt. There were none.

Byrne rubbed his hand together it was surprisingly cold for a September morning.

Cullen sniffed as though testing the air. 'We could be in for a harsh winter the sun is much lower than usual.'

Daniel Atherton held out his hand to which Reg Cullen responded. 'I'm DS Atherton and this is DC Byrne. 'Are you okay?' he asked.

Reg Cullen's grip was firm, stronger than they imagined it would be.

'Aye, I've seen worse!'

Byrne frowned 'And when would that have been Reg?'

'A while back now in the seventies when I'd done my tours of Northern Ireland!'

Both detectives had read about and seen the newsreels on the troubles in Northern Ireland and been made aware of the sensitivity that surrounded the mainland with the bombings in Hyde Park, Birmingham, Brighton and Mill Hill. Reg Cullen would have experienced similar.

'And what unit was you in?'

'The Royal Lancashire's. I can show you my colours if you need to verify my claim.'

Atherton looked over at what was left of the two men lying on the ground. 'No, that's alright Mr Cullen we can undertake any checks later. Do you know if anybody else has been down here prior to you finding the bodies?'

Reg shook his head. 'As far as I'm aware it's just been me. We do however get a few dog walkers in the wood sometimes. The master would encourage their visits believing that the dogs would help reduce the grey squirrel population. They're a damn pest the grey much worse than the red. As I came over the ridge I realised that something was wrong. You get a sixth sense for these things when you've been around death for some time.'

'Do you know about what time they began the hunt last night?'

'Around eight I think although I couldn't say for sure because it was my night off.'

'What time did you leave the estate?'

'Earlier, about half six.'

'So how did you know it was around eight?'

'I asked cook before I went looking for them this morning!'

Atherton kept observation whilst Pete Byrne asked the questions. Cullen's story seemed plausible, genuine. Over by the trees a small muntjac raised its head inquisitively wondering what all the fuss was about. He caught sight of a lone figure standing at a window on the nearest corner of the west wing. It was too far away to distinguish whether it was a man or a woman.

'Is it always like this down here when it rains?' Byrne asked.

'More or less,' replied Reg Cullen 'worse when the winters been and gone though, although that's when it floods real bad. The master had this flume channel put in eight years back to help with some of the excess drainage it helped a bit although not as much as I had hoped. We don't let any of the cattle graze this part of the estate as it's too soft after the rain. The daft bugger's tend to slip over and can't get back up. Last year we lost a cow to drowning.

'I don't suppose the temperature helped last night?' added Atherton.

Reg nodded. 'There was a slight breeze when I left to go play darts and keener when I left the pub only it was worse around three this morning.' Just as Gabrielle had said it had been.

Emerging from between the trees a man with his dog was stopped by a uniformed constable before he came too close. On the advice of the officer he put the lead around the dog's neck.

Reg pointed over their way 'That's Harry Flowers, it was probably his dog that I heard barking earlier. Harry walks Marmalade out for about two hours each morning, reckons it saves him going back out in the afternoon.'

Atherton watched the dog sniff the ground near to where he was on the lead. The canine was a brown, tan and white medium haired Brittany Pointer, a good looking animal. 'Does Harry always take the same route every day?' asked Atherton.

'More or less although you'd best ask him. Marmalade's still very young and boy off the lead can he run, especially if he spots a squirrel.'

Leaving Byrne to ask more questions of the gamekeeper Atherton went over to see how Marjorie and her team were getting on. The examination tent was erect and now covered both bodies hitched up to include the rear panel work of the land rover. He lifted the flap and went in. Inside was like the Tardis deceivingly bigger than what you' would expect. Surrounding each body were a dotted line of yellow plastic markers.

'Stand still please Daniel,' Marjorie asked as Tom Skerritt took a quick series of digital frames getting in each of the markers in correlation to body parts or parts missing.

'This could prove difficult lifting prints!' It was both a statement and a question from Atherton.

Marjorie always the optimist looked at the tailboard, where the gun belt was still in the same position that it had been left by the killer.

'Be positive and you will be rewarded in heaven. The overnight rain and wind might have done some damage but there's always something, always!'

Gabrielle George was methodically working her way around the side of the vehicle where she was busy marking out bits of brain, bones and hair that had once belonged to Sir Roger Edington-Forbes. He watched her wondering how a young woman could be fascinated with such a gruesome and harrowing crime scene. Watching him watch Gabrielle, Marjorie read his thoughts.

'She's really good Daniel, always quick to listen and learn. Gabrielle applies an open mind to each crime scene and in a few years she will be a first rate forensic examiner.'

He agreed then pulled Marjorie to one side. 'I was a bit concerned about what she had to say regarding the stranger watching her flat that worried me.'

'That worried me too. I was going to suggest an alarm in the flat only the tech lab will do anything for Gabrielle and I am sure that they would fit up an alarm for her. Although I would be hesitant to installing any cameras as I don't her parading around the flat naked and being posted all over the station website!'

'Can I leave you to make the arrangements?' She said she would.

'Tavistock won't be pleased with our latest crime scene!' Atherton detected a slight amusement in her tone.

Daniel Atherton agreed. It would not please wither Tavistock or Cherrington alike.

'Some of them have forgotten what it's like down at ground level. To some crime is measured in commission statistics, mission statements and performance management. Real policing is left to the likes of you and me.'

'I wonder why they left it until this morning to come looking for them.' She asked nodding.

'It's a good question although according to the game keeper they weren't due back until the early hours.' He looked around at the various markers. 'Have you come cross any firearms yet?'

'No, I find that odd. All we've got is a gun belt and some cartridges.'

Atherton thought about the man with the dog.

'They could have been disturbed or they themselves come across a poacher. For the sake of argument which turned into an exchange of fire, ending with both men dead. It might be that the killer took them home.'

Marjorie was less enthusiastic about the notion. 'It's possible, although something tells me that they're somewhere nearby.'

There was a sudden knock on the side of the land rover. Marjorie stuck her out through the door of the tent to where a uniformed officer was stood holding a styrofoam beaker. Inside was an empty shotgun cartridge.

'We found this near that storm channel. I picked it up with a pen so it's not been contaminated or handled Marjorie.'

She dropped the beaker and cartridge into a clear evidence bag. 'Well done Mike this could prove valuable. If you could just show me where you found it I'll give the bag an evidence tag.'

Atherton added his thanks before going back over to where Pete Byrne had let Reg Cullen go back up to the stable block as he as needed to check-in the normal Friday morning deliveries.

'What do you think?' he asked watching the gamekeeper go over the ridge of the hill.

'Normally I'm an old sceptic but I tend to believe old Reg. When questioned he said Roger Edington married Francesca Forbes for her money to keep afloat the assets of the estate. Her father is a wealthy banker working for an Italian Corporate Bank in London.

'Two years ago he was knighted for his services to the industry a much reviled accolade amongst the other landowners and farming community in the area. Reg reckons money exchanged hands to add him to the list.

'From he knows and had seen with his own eyes Sir Roger was a much despised man. He has three sons, two who are abroad and the one lying inside the tent alongside his headless father. Richard Edington is married, lived in the west wing of the house and is survived by his wife and young daughter, she's nine. As far as Reg Cullen knows she's not been told about the tragedy involving her father.'

Atherton let a low whistle and profanity leave his lips 'That's going to be tough. What did the son do for a living?'

'Fifteen years back he took himself off to agricultural college where he came away with a diploma in farm management. From there he has acquired more knowledge of how to handle the estate better than his father.

'Reg went on to say that Sir Roger was a tyrant who would relentlessly beat his boys when they were young and probably did the same to their mother if truth be known. Many employed at Edington Hall and beyond the boundary fence hated the man.'

'And Reg Cullen, what did he think of his master?'

'There apparently existed a mutual respect. Being from the army and serving in Northern Ireland old man Edington was wary of Reg.'

Atherton saw the list as long. 'We could have any number of suspects from wives, sons and ex-employees, stable hands to any number of farm workers or local landowners.'

'A nightmare scenario,' insinuated Byrne as he rubbed his brow. Atherton considered that his colleague definitely looked tired.

'How was Anne when you got home?' he asked.

'Pissed as usual although that's nothing new. The girls had gone to bed and when I looked in on them they were both asleep. Anne had wanted to join them but she feels obliged to be there when I walk through the door providing it's not over late.

'She's a really good wife and mother, but I get the impression occasionally that I could be stretching the supportive part of our vows a little over the line. The microwave reheated my supper although when she was upstairs in the bathroom I gave it to the dog.'

Pete Byrne let forth a long sigh. 'The only good part of yesterday was the hot shower I took before I crashed down on the bed. It don't get any easier.'

'With a bit of luck we will get away at a decent time today. Why don't you treat Anne and the girls to a nice meal out and add the bill to my tab, call it an early Christmas present.'

'Thanks, I will.'

High above on the ridge of the grassy knoll a new looking 4x4 slowed to a halt. Moments later a uniformed man got out of the passenger seat.

'Don't look now,' warned Byrne 'but Tavistock has just arrived.'

Daniel Atherton turned around in time to see the divisional commanders heading their way.

'Why don't you go talk to the dog walker Pete and leave me to deal with Tavistock.' Pete Byrne was away faster than a whippet needing no second prompt.

This time there was no pleasant handshake or smile. 'This is embarrassing I knew Sir Roger Edington-Forbes personally, we played golf together and dined out at the annual round table charity ball. The man was a hard working decent, generous and titled landowner, who does this sort of thing sergeant?'

Atherton was totally uninterested in Tavistock's problems in that he would have to find himself another golfing partner.

'That's what we are here trying establish Sir!'

Taking a few moments to access the scene, the tent, land rover, the woods and the man with his dog Tavistock adjusted his trousers around his waist.

'And ideas, have we any?'

'Our initial thoughts are that Sir Roger and Richard, his eldest were confronted by a night-time poacher resulting in a stand-off situation and double shooting.'

It was simple, on paper would look even better. Tavistock nodded his agreement.

'And the poacher,' asked Tavistock proving that he was hopelessly out of touch with reality 'what of him?'

'Our enquiries will search far enough to visit, hospitals, surgeries, local farms and estates. At some point he'll turn up.'

It sounded positive and straightforward, Tavistock liked uncomplicated crime scenes.

'So there is no connection here to the Benson murders?'

'Not that we have found any evidence yet to make a connection Sir.'

To have said there was would have left the matter open for further discussion. Atherton had remembered Pete Byrne telling him that Tavistock had been a detective.

Pointing over to where CSI had their tent he asked. 'Are they under the tent?'

'Yes, they are.' Atherton took a step in front of Tavistock to block his way. 'However Sir, perhaps for the sake of remembering your friend as he was and letting Marjorie and her team get on with amassing evidence it would best that you don't take a look inside. It's not for the fainthearted.'

Tavistock looked at the tent and then at Daniel Atherton he admired his pluck and honesty.

'On this occasion I will bow down to your judgement.' Lowering his head once in respect he also shook it from side to side. 'Damn shame really that his life should end this way. Roger was a gentle giant, a big-hearted family man and not one to hurt a fly intentionally!'

He looked up at the house where he had left his police driver and vehicle. 'Maybe my visit would be best served consoling Lady Francesca Edington-Forbes.'

Feeling the weight lift from his shoulders Atherton smiled weakly 'Thank you Sir, I am sure that the lady of the house would greatly appreciate your taking the time to visit.'

Tavistock nodded as he watched Pete Byrne talking to the man with a dog.

'And the unfortunate incidents of yesterday, how are they proceeding.' He asked 'only I spoke with Jasmin Yates before I came here and she firmly believes that both incidents are because of a grudge, a family feud. Is that right?'

'Family problems is about the size of it Sir.' He watched the lines on Tavistock's forehead ebb away.

'That's what I said it would be and I know George Gunn agrees with me. I had Cherrington on the phone to me last night asking all sorts of bloody stupid questions only incidents like that of yesterday have far reaching consequences, reflecting in bad moral and serious doubt of our ability to clear up crime in our area.'

Tavistock acknowledged Byrne and the two uniformed officers over by the trees with a solitary nod of his head before turning around heading back up the rough grass. He was about ten feet away when he suddenly turned again.

'By the way Daniel did you not get the message that I left you last night about giving me an update?'

'No Sir, I was late getting back to the department and the cleaners had already been in, in all probability it ended up in the bin. I'll have a word with them when I see the supervisor.'

Tavistock sniffed turned and continued up the field. Pete Byrne waited until he was a safe distance away before he came over.

'What did the voice of wisdom want?' he asked.

'Unbelievably to sing the praises of the departed Roger Edington-Forbes.'

Atherton's thoughts however were elsewhere focusing on something that Tavistock had said about the ability to resolve crime in the area.

'Humour me Pete, when did you first come across Tavistock?'

'When we were on the *wheel man killer* investigation together. He was a detective but three months in he got promotion to sergeant. I'd just become a detective but we didn't get along as I was always wary of Tavistock. There was something about him that I didn't. His eyes are too close together and that's always made me cautious even as a child. The DCI in charge of the investigation split the squad into four teams each taking a quadrant of the city. Luckily I was with a sergeant and we took the southern section. Tavistock lead a team that took the west side between the railway yard and the Mersey.

'So in eight years Tavistock made a meteoric rise to commander of a division, that's interesting.'

With the help of the two constables they checked the trees but no shotguns were found, the explanation of the mysterious poacher seemingly having some credence. They checked with the dog owner but he too had not come anything remotely like a pair of shotguns.

'Did anybody get in touch with the local press and request copies of the photographs taken outside Parkway Drive and the Benson's house?' Atherton asked.

'Yeah Lucy,' Byrne replied 'I thought she would handle the asking better than George and Tim.' He paused to catch his breath. 'We could be seen as stepping on Jasmin Yates toes again!'

'I'll live with it,' replied Atherton smiling.

They were in time to see Gregory Tavistock open the passenger door and slip inside before he was driven back to the station by Alf Barrett.

'He didn't stick around long.' Byrne remarked sarcastically.

They went to the front door where they were shown into the study by a member of the household staff. Francesca Edington-Forbes was nothing that they imagined her to be, casually dressed she was more naturally attractive than most women her age. Atherton noticed that there were no tension lines or tear stains on her face. On the table between the chairs was a tray of fresh coffee, tea and home-made biscuits.

'Mary, the kitchen maid saw you walk back. You can just see the top part of the field from the library where I was choosing a book. Having despatched your commander back to the station I wanted to relax with a good book. She made no mention of her dead husband or her stepson. Byrne hoped that Tavistock had not received the same courtesy.

Daniel Atherton made the introductions taking her hand in his. Her skin was warm and unblemished by the harsh living of running an estate.

'We would like to express our sorrow for your loss.'

Francesca Edington-Forbes acknowledged with a series of short nods as she poured the coffee into the cups asking that they help themselves to the biscuits.

'Perhaps I should begin by explaining that I am Roger's second wife. Felicity his first died many years back in childbirth. I am almost twenty years younger than my late husband. I did not need to marry for money as I have my own and as far as I know there is no will. Roger was insistent that he would live well into his dotage.'

She took a seat opposite theirs. 'Like a good many other things he got that wrong as well. You will however not find me shedding any tears of sadness for my dead husband. Many on the estate and for a good twenty mile radius will rejoice when they hear the news. Roger was a much hated man. My heart instead goes out to Ginette who introduced me to Roger, Richard Edington's wife.'

'How did you meet?'

'We had just completed a modelling assignment in Blackpool when Ginette suggested that we went for a drive in the country. We came across Richard looking through an antique shop in Stockport. Maybe had I not been in the shop next door I might have got to him first, however Ginette's long legs and fluttering eyelashes won the day.

'Invited to tea at Edington Hall by Richard I ran into Roger. At first he was charming and thoughtful, everything a girl looks for in a man. He knew how to wine and dine a lady as well flying us both to Paris a month later he proposed to me at the top of the Arc' de Triomphe. It is fair to say that the marriage was a disaster and in time I would have been looking to divorce him. Importantly thought gentlemen as much as I kept my husband from my bed, I did not kill him!'

Daniel Atherton put down his cup gently upon the saucer.

'You appear not to be disappointed that your husband is dead!'

Francesca sipped her coffee from the edge of the cup, her refined years of a good education showing through.

'No sergeant I am most definitely not. The marriage was a complete charade. He was a servant to the devil with an evil past and a lust that had no boundaries.'

Munching silently on a biscuit Pete Byrne looked up. Had she just put her late husband in the frame for the *wheel man killer* case?

'Roger had a vile temper and his mood swings were completely unpredictable. After our honey the sexual demands became more bizarre and I refused he would use threats saying that he would besmirch my father's name. Later when I grew more resilient he would hit me but I hit back, I am Italian after all. In time I came to realise that all Roger wanted was a young female to share his bed late at night.'

All the victims from the *wheel man killer* case had been young women.

'Things only became more complex when Ginette married Richard. I felt trapped staying in the house for her sake and safety. Had I left and returned to Italy he would have vented his anger on Ginette. I had no alternative but to stay.

'Only last week with Richard's help, the three of us planned to leave Edington Hall taking their daughter with us. We intended starting a new life in Switzerland far from here. Richard had secured a job out in Geneva and with my money we could live out our lives happily.

'Somehow we think Roger got wind of our plans which is why I think he insisted on Richard accompanying him on the fox hunt last night. I only found out about it when we were on the train back from London. Ginette was almost beside herself with worry.

105

'This morning before I heard the tragic news of Richard's death I noticed that my passport was missing from the safe in my room.'

She pointed to an antique looking cabinet standing in the corner of the study.

'This is Roger's room and I would say categorically that my passport is inside his safe. The problem I have is that I do not have access to his combination.'

Pete Byrne knew of a few locals that could help out.

There was a sudden knock at the door and a pretty young maid entered apologetically realising her mistake.

'Oh, I am very sorry madam I thought that I had best check in case you wanted any more coffee?' Her eyes dropped low although not quite low enough that she could not see the handsome young detective sitting closest to where she stood.

Francesca was unperturbed by the interruption, she smiled obviously liking the maid.

'That's quite alright Mary and I assure you that there is no harm done. Will you please give us a few more moments alone and then I will let you know when the tray can be taken.'

Mary Thomas returned the smile stepping back and closing the door on her exit, not before she took one more look at Daniel Atherton. It was not missed by her mistress nut Francesca was pleased to see the maid happy. At last she hoped that the curse of Edington Hall had disappeared along with the passing of her late husband.

Watching Mary leave Atherton latched onto the moment.

'Could you tell us please, what did the staff think of your late husband?'

Francesca inhaled slowly and fully expanding her lungs.

'An obnoxious, loathsome employer. Roger was constantly belittling or berating their incompetence although really they were simply just petrified of his bark. Of course I have nothing with which to prove what I tell you but feel free to ask around. I am confident that they will tell you the same.'

She momentarily lowered her eyes unable to look at their faces.

'I feel ashamed to say that in my refusing his evil demands of my body I only succeeded in sending him towards the staff quarters. I do not need elaborate what went on throughout the night!'

'Can you vouch for your movements yesterday until you went to bed?' asked Byrne.

She relaxed back in the chair taking her coffee cup with her.

'It would be my pleasure detective. Ginette and I spent the day in London shopping. We caught the train home to Stockport then from there we travelled back to the house by taxi. The ticket collector will vouch on what train we arrived and cook can verify that we got back just after nine pm. We spent an hour in Ginette's apartment eating supper where we let Clare from the stable go back to her room in the staff block Clare had been looking after Yvette whilst we were in London.

'Because they were out shooting I wanted to stay with Ginette and Yvette, safety in numbers if you like only Ginette and I had no idea what my late husband had planned for Richard having found out about Switzerland. When they both failed to return this morning I called for Reg Cullen and asked that he scour the estate.'

'Is there anybody in particular that you can think of that who would want your husband dead, an old adversary perhaps?'

She scoffed 'believe me Mr Atherton the list would be too long and the pen would run dry of ink. Roger hired and fired staff at random, some lasting less than a week. His fuse once lit was hard to extinguish.' She stopped to think. 'If Gregory Tavistock was right about the killer being a lone gunman then again I am not at all surprised. I am however extremely saddened about Richard's fate. Ginette is extremely distraught and so is Yvette, that little girl adored her father. Richard had two other brothers both younger, did you know?'

107

Atherton thought it interesting that she didn't mention anything about the granddaughter being adoring of her grandfather.

'Yes, Reg Cullen told us we will be talking to them later.'

Francesca shook her head 'I doubt that they killed their father although you'll have to check with passport control. One lives in Ireland and the other France. They were the lucky ones who escaped their father's tyranny.'

'Could you tell us about Reginald Cullen?'

She replaced her coffee cup on the saucer.

'Reg Cullen is probably the longest serving member of the estate staff. He was one of the few that Roger did like. I suppose because Cullen had served in the army and seen action, Roger liked that sort of masculine machoism. Reg Cullen also speaks his mind and if there's something to be said he's not afraid to say it. This morning I asked cook what time Reg had left for the pub and she told me around six thirty. Nearly every Thursday he has a light supper about half five leaving in time to arrive at the Duck and Drake which is the nearest public house to the estate. Reg is a regular member of the darts team.'

Pete Byrne wrote the pub name in his notebook, they would have to verify Reg Cullen's movements with the landlord.

'Was it bad,' Francesca asked looking directly at Daniel Atherton 'the shooting I mean?'

'Reg Cullen identified your husband and step-son. They were found down near the woods so you don't have to go through the stress of attending any formal identification. If you would take my advice I would not press the undertaker for a private viewing.'

'The rumour amongst the stable yard staff is that my husband had his head blown off, is that the case sergeant?'

They both nodded but Atherton replied 'the rumour is true.'

Francesca Edington-Forbes offered more coffee but they declined.

'The lord acts in mysterious ways to punish the sins of man. Roger met with an end befitting his miserable existence. He made many suffer and in the end I hope that he suffered too. Retribution can be swift or prolonged.'

She sipped from her refilled cup once again looking directly at Atherton.

'And Richard, what of poor Richard?' she asked.

'His death was quick, over in a second and I doubt that he suffered.'

'Thank you. It is of little consolation but I hope that he did not suffer. He was only there under Roger's insistence. He would not have been involved otherwise.'

'We'll make arrangements to have any personal effects returned to you as soon as possible.'

Francesca dismissed the notion with slight wave of her hand.

'I don't want any of my late husband's property. Stuart and Robert Edington will decide what is to become of the house and the estate. They are both level headed young men and thankfully nothing like their father. There not a lot of love between the brothers as Richard was always his father's favourite son.'

'And what about you, what will you do after the funeral?' asked Pete Byrne.

Francesca smiled 'me detective, I'll probably stay while to support Ginette and Yvette. Maybe then we'll continue with our original plan, I'm not sure yet. Why, is it important?'

'No. I was just curious. I'm a family man myself and I was wondering what my family would do if anything happened to me.'

She smiled again, told them that she had things to arrange and that if they needed to look through her late husband's room she would have one of the house staff assist. Within minutes of her departure Mary Thomas returned with a replenished tray of refreshments and baked pastries made that morning by cook.

Byrne rubbed his hands together 'food that hasn't seen the inside of a microwave, now there's a novelty.'

Taking the used tray and crocks Mary smiled at Atherton then left. Making an excuse that he needed the bathroom he ran after her and caught up with her in the lobby leading into the downstairs kitchen.

'You can come in if you want,' she invited him into the kitchen pushing the swing door aside with her shoulder 'there's only me here until lunchtime.'

It a large kitchen and in days gone by would have been better used with more cooks, scullery maids and servants but big houses had also suffered and owners had tightened their belts.

Atherton was grateful of the warmth as the rest of the house appeared cold including the study.

'Where's Agnes?' he asked.

'In town. She always goes Friday morning to oversee the meat order. She likes to choose the best cuts. Come over here and plonk you beside the Aga it's lovely and warm and the heat from the oven will help keep the chill from your bones.'

Up close Mary was naturally pretty, a fresh complexion with the hint of freckles bridging her nose and hazel coloured eyes.

'Do you always invite strangers into your kitchen?' he asked mischievously grinning.

'Only the handsome ones.'

He held out the palm of his hand 'I'm Daniel Atherton.'

'Mary Thomas. Is the older policeman your boss?' she asked.

Atherton laughed 'No, Pete is a detective and I'm a detective sergeant.'

'Why did you run after me, is it because of what's happened to the masters?'

He placed his hands on the thick warming plate, instantly feeling the benefits as the heat passed up through his arms.

'We're investigating a double murder Mary so we need to speak to everyone in the house and the stabling yard. Like any investigation from what we learn we can build a picture of what really took place last night. You're not under suspicion although anything that you can tell me will help, anything at all?'

Mary lowered her eyes 'He used to scare me sergeant... at times he would frighten me real bad!'

'Daniel, please call me Daniel.' He asked.

'At night when I would go to my room after working in the kitchen master would come knocking on the attic door although I pretended to be asleep. To prevent him from getting in I would have to place the back of the chair against the door handle. He would rant and rave something awful making all sorts of threats but come the next morning it were as though nothing had taken place the night before. I'm sure that the mistress was looking out for me. As much as possible I would keep out of his way.'

'Was you here before Lady Francesca married Sir Roger?'

She shook her head. 'No, I've not been here that long but Agnes said things changed after he got married again. At first it was calm but after a few months there were arguments and long periods where neither talked to one another. When I came here I soon noticed that the master was always watching me move around the house, when I brought up the breakfast, lunch or serve the evening meal. At night I would pull my bedroom curtains even on a summers evening as I felt him watching from the garden outside.'

'Has he ever hurt you?'

Again she shook her head. 'No. I was always wary of him so I'd get to my room first. He had eyes that would undress you. They were creepy. I would feel a shiver run down my spine just thinking about him. I wasn't the same however with the stable girls, some left because he pestered them.'

Atherton wished Tavistock had been present when Mary was describing the dead landowner.

Mary went across to the swing door to make sure that nobody was about before coming back to stand alongside Atherton.

'I honestly don't know why the mistress married him. I mean you've only to look at her to see that she is beautiful. Agnes told me that she used to be a model before she came to Edington Hall.' Mary sighed. 'Is it true that the master had his head blown clean off from his shoulders?'

'More or less. He won't be pestering or undressing any other women with his eyes!'

'Am I bad for saying that he deserved to die like that, only I've heard some stories from the stable lads about the master and they weren't very nice.'

'No, you're not bad Mary.' He smiled to show that he cared about her. 'Can you tell me about Richard Edington and his brothers, Stuart and Robert, how did they treat you?'

Mary relaxed. 'Richard was always kind and smiling. As for the brothers well I've never seen them. In the short time that I've been at Edington Hall they've never once come visiting. Agnes told me that they are like their brother, kind and intelligent. Besides the mistress, Lady Francesca I feel really sorry for poor Mistress Ginette and little Yvette. Richard was always so loving when they were together. He was a good husband and father.'

'And where was you last night Mary?' he put up his hands to gesture that he had to ask.

'It's okay, I thought you'd ask me sooner or later. I was in the kitchen until just after nine.' She paused to get the order chronologically correct. 'Let's see, Reg Cullen come in around five thirty for his supper, game pie with salad and a roll. He left about an hour later only he plays darts every Thursday with his mates at the Duck and Drake. The master and Richard went out shooting around half seven and Lady Francesca and Mrs Edington arrived home just after nine. I know because I saw the taxi swing around on the drive outside. Agnes and myself were busy in the kitchen until about half past nine as we had to give them their supper which they took with them to the west wing where Master Richard has his large apartment. After clearing away the supper things I went up to my attic bedroom around a quarter to ten. Normally it's not that late but because of the shopping expedition and their coming back from London on the train Agnes and I were both required to work a little late.'

'Did you hear any gunshots?'

'That's strange that you should ask that because just after the mistresses had returned I heard what sounded like a single gunshot followed by a scream. When I mentioned it to Agnes she told me that it was almost likely to be the vixen calling for her cubs. I wasn't so sure though only to me it sounded human.'

'And later,' he asked 'there were more?'

Mary nodded 'A little while after the first I heard others maybe two perhaps three although I'm not exactly sure. I didn't take much notice after what Agnes had said as I wanted to get my chores completed in the kitchen and return to my room before the master came home.'

'How long after the scream do you think the other gunshots were fired?'

'Five maybe ten minutes. I should have looked at the clock.' Mary placed her hand on his forearm. 'I know it's awful what's happened but at least I am no longer afraid.'

'Then some good has come out of a tragedy.' Replied Atherton. Mary let her hand slip from his arm.

'Thank you!'

'Another few questions and then we're done. 'Do you have any idea what time Reg Cullen got back from the pub?'

She shook her head. 'No, the attic room overlooks the kitchen and the field down to the wood. Reg has his rooms over in the staff cottage sharing with the stable boys. The females have their own quarters adjacent to the boys. In the past Reg has arrived home around midnight.'

'Are there any dogs on the estate?'

'No. The master wouldn't keep any. Agnes said that Sir Roger likes dogs but he couldn't put up with their constant baying at night when the foxes were about the estate.'

Atherton was more than comfortable standing against the aga and alongside Mary, he didn't want to move but he had one last question.

'Have you any idea who would have hated Sir Roger so much that he or she would have wanted him killed?'

Mary Thomas looked at Daniel Atherton her hazel eyes burning through to his soul.

'Not many liked the master. Most here despised him, were wary of him. Others in the village or on the other estates hated him. There would be many that would wish him dead.'

'Including you?'

She seemed surprised that he had asked.

'If I was honest yes. In time I think he would have found a way to get me alone and attack me, so I'm not sorry that he's gone…' she lowered her voice 'and neither is the mistress if truth be known.'

'Last question. Have you ever fired nay kind of gun?'

She shook her head 'No, never guns scare me.'

'Thanks Mary, you've been really helpful and what you've told me has helped build a clear picture.' He gave her a contact card with his direct dial details.

'If you think of anything else, you can call anytime!'

'Would that also mean if we could go out and have a drink together?'

'When this investigation is over, that would be good.'

Mary smiled feeling her body go tight with excitement. He gently squeezed her arm and thanked her again and for dispelling the cold from his bones. He was about to leave when he thought of one other line of enquiry.

'Just out of interest Mary, who keeps the staff records at the hall?'

'Reg Cullen I think. Master Richard managed the house and the estate. Reg was in charge of the stables and farm. When I joined Edington Hall, it was Reg who recorded my details.'

Atherton promised to be in touch. Walking back along the basement corridor he stopped at a storeroom where the door was slightly ajar, peering in he saw at least three dozen game birds hanging from butchers hooks. If Roger Edington-Forbes went shooting for game he did so on a regular basis. A killer waiting and watching the estate would know this.

In the kitchen Mary listened until she could hear his footsteps no longer. She liked the handsome detective, liked him a lot. There was a way in which he smiled and looked that made her tingle. Suddenly taking the front of her apron in her hands she placed it over her face and started to cry.

Never again would she have to listen for the tell-tale squeak on the wood stairs leading up to her bedroom or have the brass handle of the door rattled in the middle of the night. At last Mary Thomas could sleep and rest easy at Edington Hall.

She was still crying when a pair of strong but sensitive hands went around her back and pulled her in close. Without looking she knew that Daniel Atherton had come back. She sobbed with her head on his chest letting go the fear of living under the constant threat of being assaulted. After while the memory had been erased from her mind. He held her for a long time until she could weep no more.

'It's over now Mary and the nightmare has passed!'

Chapter Eight

Friday lunchtime

Reg Cullen was busy with an inventory in the tack room when Byrne and Atherton walked in. He had been expecting their visit only not quite so soon after having been quizzed at length by Byrne down at the field.

Having asked around several others had verified Reg's night at the Duck and Drake pub. Atherton didn't think that he was responsible for the murders as Mary had heard shots shortly after nine in the evening, what he was more interested was the records of previous and present staff. Reg suggested that they went back to his office where it was warmer than the yard. From a large metal filing cabinet he produced a well-documented ledger.

'You can keep that for the meantime if you think it will help,' he said laying the ledger on the desktop randomly selecting where the pages had fallen open. 'There's names and addresses, dates of birth, place born, national insurance numbers, next of kin details and last known employment in case we ever needed a reference.'

Flicking through the various pages the detectives were surprised to see that there were so many.

'And these were all employed here at Edington Hall?' Byrne asked.

'The full-time staff and some part-timers, plus seasonal workers.'

'Working where precisely?'

Reg held up his hands 'anywhere sergeant, anywhere where work was needed. Assisting in the stables, picking fruit in the orchard, sorting vegetables from the walled garden and harvesting the crops. We also have two herdsman Jed Bullen and Sam Filch but they've both been with the farm for years. The milking sheds are tucked away from the main house down near the outer farm.'

You've more outbuildings?' Byrne was surprised how big the estate and farm actually was.

'Plenty, some big others smaller. Cowsheds, a large holding pen for the sheep, cow byres and then there's the hen coop. Edington Hall is virtually self-sufficient. Come market time we would be extremely busy and without all the extra help we would never manage.

'When Master Richard took over running the estate, things however changed dramatically and for the better. He increased the yield in the fields, increased the herd, doubled the sheep and began a proper rotation of crops. What we didn't have enough of was willing hands and so we would employ seasonal help, cheap labour but they were well fed and watered. You'll find a few foreign names amongst the list but every big estate has casual labour.'

'And the seasonal workers, do you know where they went after leaving here?'

Cullen shook his head exhaling through his nostrils.

'No that's almost impossible to keep track of their movement only they come and go as they please. They'd disappear as quickly as they appeared for work. *Agricultural Spooks* we would call them. A pity because some of them are really hard workers and better than some of the local help we get turn up on our doorstep.'

Atherton saw that taking the ledger would prove ineffective wasting more of their time. The killer could be amongst a dozen or even a hundred recorded in the ledger.

'Thanks for the offer but you keep it here Mr Cullen. Should we find evidence that matches a name in the ledger then we might have to come back and take another look.'

'I still think you'll be looking for a poacher!'

'Why so sure?' asked Byrne.

'I've caught the buggers hiding down in that part of the estate before chasing our game birds. We've normally given them a flea in their ear and warned them not come back. If we caught them a second time we called the police. The woods on that part of the estate are thickest and it is easy to hide unseen. The master and young Richard knew the estate like the back of their hand and would not have so easily been taken by surprise. I'd stake a month's wages on it!'

'At the pub last night, did you stay for after's?'

Reg nodded. 'We always do after a match. Leonard does everything above board, pulling shut the curtains and supplying the pints free of charge. Normally there's only four of us that stay behind. Me, Sid Rawlings, Henry Tonks, Ray Leighton and Gerald Gray. We all went to school together and we've been part of the same darts team since I came out of the army.'

'So what time did you get home?'

'About one. Like I normally do I check around the hall and the stable block before I retire to my rooms.'

'Did you know that Sir Roger and his son Richard were still out?'

'No. I never check the garage or the cars. They all had their own vehicles plus the land rover which was mainly for estate work and when the master held his special seasonal shoots. There's a multi-use garage with eight bays around back of the house. The first that I knew about them being missing was when Lady Francesca called me to ask that I go look for them.'

*****

Leaning on the bar of the Duck and Drake Pete Byrne watched the landlord pull the pint then let the contents settle before bringing over the glass. Standing to his right Atherton had ordered a sparkling mineral water for himself. Screwing down the lid on the bottle Pete Byrne looked on with an expression of despair masking his eyes.

'We'll never make a man of you,' he remarked.

Atherton laughed as he handed over enough money to include a complementary drink for Leonard Pryce. The landlord. 'Maybe I don't want to end up like George!'

Byrne readily agreed knowing that for as long as he had known George the man had been knocking back pints and shorts nearly every day.

'It's his loss,' added Leonard 'only some of these are the finest north of the midlands.'

He thanked them for the drink and promptly poured himself a half pint of *old barge brew.*

'Does Reg Cullen like a pint?' Atherton asked.

Leonard Pryce supped the froth from his glass then laid it down before him.

'I thought you pair had a look about that said old bill.' He ran the drying up cloth around the inside of a wine glass that had been drying on the side.

'Old Reg likes his pint the same as a good many others that come in here to sample some of our brews and especially on a Thursday night when we have our darts league games. He can hold his own but I guarantee that when Reg leaves here he is stone cold sober.'

'And Reg was in here last night?'

'All evening until around half past midnight. After the regulars have gone off home a few of us share a jar together, we're old school chums. The tradition was set a long time ago whether the team won or lost we'd still celebrate the occasion. Not much tradition around nowadays though.'

Leonard Pryce made sure that the cyclists huddled in the corner wasn't listening in. He lent over the bar top coming closer.

'That was a bad business up at the big house.'

'News travels fast!' said Pete Byrne looking at Atherton.

'Aye that it does in these parts,' replied Leonard 'I had to call Reg first thing this morning to tell him that he had left his spare set of darts behind the bar. Team members can be very particular about their darts. He told me about the Edington men. As I said, a bad business.'

'What did you make of the Sir Roger, Leonard?'

He righted himself standing up straight.

'I didn't care for him much and he didn't come in here much which pleased the regulars on account of them not liking his company. Whenever he did grace this place with his presence the atmosphere… well it changed. Some of the other landowners and farmers would get up and leave, some not finishing their drink and men around her don't walk away from good ale. That should answer your question.'

'So he was despised?' It was Atherton asking.

'That would be putting it lightly. Most thought his knighthood a travesty and for helping other farmers would be an insult. More like he would be the ruin of some and death of others. Edington was not a popular figure about these parts. Whereas his wife was a different kettle of fish, always polite and charming. She would order a drink and buy others theirs. She and the lady Ginette, a right nice pair. They were always welcome here.'

'And Richard Edington?'

Leonard hung the glass upside down on the bar shelf.

'Nothing like his father thank goodness. An upright intelligent, respectful young man. He was well liked by his peers and regulars. According to what Reg had told me in the past, young Richard virtually ran the estate and the old man wined and dined on the profits. Did you know that before Richard got his diploma's Edington Hall was heading for receivership and word was that is why he married somebody so much younger than himself.'

Daniel Atherton nodded knowing that there could be a different reason and not just for financial gain but one involving depraved cravings.

'And the other sons Stuart and Robert, what of them?'

Pryce picked up his pint glass.

'No trouble, like their older brother equally as charming. One I believe lives in Ireland the other France.'

'Doing what exactly?'

Leonard shrugged his shoulders 'Stuart is in Antiques in Dublin and Robert as far as I know dabbles in wine near the Dordogne, nice place so I understand. I wouldn't mind Robert popping in when he comes back for

120

the funeral only we could set up a deal with the vineyard. Over the weekend this restaurant is packed and punters appreciate a good wine with their dinner.'

'What else do you know about the father, other than he wasn't very well liked?'

Leonard Pryce leant over the bar top again gesturing that they also come closer.

'Rumour went around that after his first wife died old Roger was one for the girls and I don't mean women, I do mean girls. A few of the lasses from the local villages only lasted a few days up at Edington Hall before they left.

'One night after visiting a pub over Upper Marsh way Edington was set about by a group of unidentified men. He ended up in hospital quite badly beaten. Rumour went round that he had been set upon in revenge for having assaulted a young stable girl from the village. The odd thing was that Roger Edington never made any complaint to the police.'

Byrne made a mental note to check the hospital casualty records.

'When he did drink, say here or elsewhere, what was his tipple?'

'Brandy or whiskey mainly, he never showed any interest in our home brewed ales.'

Atherton left his contact card with Leonard Pryce although he never expected to get a call, publicans were a breed apart from other commercial outlets and so were the people who ran them. Sitting in the car outside Atherton put the key in the ignition but didn't start the engine.

'What do you think Pete?'

'At this moment in time we could have a never-ending list of possible suspects. I'm game to go along with the theory that the mystery poacher had an entanglement with the landowner and his son whereby they were fatally shot. There are a lot of poor families still in these parts, especially in the outlying cottages.'

'I'd agree except for one factor, why shoot off old man Edington's foot before his head and then add Richard Edington to the incident?'

'Wrong place and a witness!'

Atherton nodded, as often it was the case.

'There could have been an exchange of gunfire which meant that out mystery killer might also have been hurt. We need to check hospital emergency rooms, surgeries or medical clinics in case our man walked in last night with such an injury. The other thing that doesn't add up is that both the Edington guns are missing. Reg is adamant that they went out with a pair of shotguns.'

'Back there in the pub, what was the angle with the old man's sex life?' asked Byrne.

'Both Reg and Mary, the housemaid have said that old man Edington was at the maids and the stable girls day or night. Mary Thomas told me that she had to barricade herself in her attic bedroom most nights to prevent him getting at her. Sir Roger was a rapist and not the bloody saint that Tavistock makes him out to be!'

'Tavistock knew him?'

'Yes, he told me that they attended golf and charity functions together.'

Pete Byrne's suspicions were pricking his conscience, he couldn't help but think that there was another link somewhere else. 'Which is why Edington didn't report the assault that put him in hospital.'

'That's about right.'

'In which case our mystery poacher could well be female.'

Atherton sighed 'Instead of narrowing down the list of suspects, we have just made it a hundred percent bigger!'

Byrne had a much bigger picture in his mind 'I could try fishing around Upper Marsh only our young stable girl will be a fully mature woman now. You never know she might want to have some closure knowing Edington is dead and put the matter to bed. I'm not looking to open up old wounds or hunt the vigilante pack that went after Sir Roger, just help close down one avenue of our enquiry.'

Atherton was all for his approach. 'Okay, only don't let Tavistock know what you're doing. He's keen on the poacher being responsible and this being an accident. How you shoot two men in cold blood blowing off one's head and leave a gaping great hole in another beats me. He must have been one hell of a detective!'

Pete Byrne scoffed 'He was a *fucking* hindrance that much I know!'

'We also need to go speak to Millicent Watkins again and discuss what she does see sitting at the window.'

Chapter Nine

Friday afternoon

They checked hospitals and surgeries in the area although found no recorded shooting injuries overnight. Next they went to gunsmiths, auction houses and pawn brokers searching to see if any shotguns had been registered for sale but again drew a blank.

As Byrne kept searching Atherton went back to the station to catch up on paperwork and what they did know seeing if the incidents were connected. An hour later Byrne also returned without anything new to give.

'It's as though our killer vanished with the night!'

Atherton had been adding to the legend sorting a sequence of events, names and places. To the left of the board he had added a vertical line.

'What's going in there?' Byrne asked.

'Thoughts, I'm open to any suggestions however ridiculous they may seem. How did you get on at Upper Marsh?'

Byrne shrugged his shoulders. 'Going around circles. They don't like the police and deal with problems their own way. The only information I got from an elderly woman was that girl who was attacked had married and moved away possibly gone south, Devon way.'

Atherton added Upper Marsh to the legend adding a question mark next to the village name. He stood back and looked at what they had so far.

'It's not much and doesn't inspire much but there's something there Pete, something we're missing.'

'We were there last week,' said Marjorie as she entered the department.

'On anything of interest?' Atherton asked.

'Only to take some evidential photographs of an assault which turned out to be two cousins fighting over a girl that they had both met at a dance.

The custody sergeant released them with no charge stating that it was a waste of police resources. Upper Marsh is an odd place and I got the feeling that there was a lot of interbreeding going on.' She looked at Pete Byrne and grinned 'The eyes give them away, being set to close to one another!'

Byrne laughed 'The funny looking buggers that I talked too were like that.' He thought about Tavistock.

Marjorie added photographs from the crime scene at Edington Hall to the legend.

'That's another oddity and although we did all we could, I had this feeling that I'd missed something important.'

'We were of the same opinion.'

'Have you never heard of Locards Exchange?' she asked. They both shook their heads. She sat next to Pete Byrne to explain.

'Edmund Locard was a French doctor who specialised in forensic science, born eighteen seventy seven he died in nineteen sixty six. Regarded by many of his peers as the father of forensic principle Locard believed that every contact with a surface left a trace.

'When a perpetrator enters a crime scene they touch surfaces leaving evidence, not necessarily fingerprints but other trace evidence such as footprints, human hair and fibres from clothing, anything vegetable, mineral or textile.'

Marjorie stood and went over to the legend tapping the photograph taken at Edington Hall.

'Blood and semen is indisputable. The same as when a surface becomes contaminated evidence can be obtained. On occasion we have found evidence almost invisible to the naked eye buried in the scratch of a piece of furniture and it should never be ignored but every piece of evidence collected tells a story.

'Think of evidence as a mute witness looking down on the scene, watching the perpetrator at work. Remember evidence does not go away unless other factors are present mainly weather and contamination. Failure only exists if we do not appreciate the value, study it or understand it.'

Daniel Atherton stood up as well and went to the board. 'Of course *fragmentary evidence*, I remember the instructors telling us about that on my promotion course, not just what you see but what you cannot see.' He picked his mobile up from the desk and looked at Pete Byrne. 'We need to revisit Parkway Drive.'

'I would come with you,' Marjorie said 'but my caseload is stacking up fast and I have the crown prosecution service requesting statements for a case beginning next Tuesday.'

Atherton smiled grateful for her intervention 'Don't worry, you've helped already.' He asked if she had found anything significant at Edington Hall.

Gabrielle is checking with manufacturers to identify a set of boot prints that we found in the mud beside the flume channel.'

Atherton nodded 'They didn't belong to either of the victims?'

'No. Almost certainly someone else, maybe our killer!'

Atherton was thinking. Reg Cullen had said that once he found the bodies he hadn't moved. It was highly unlikely that the prints belonged to him.

'And still no firearms?'

'Not a trace. Tom's going over the empty cartridge to see if there's anything worth noting.'

On the journey to Park Drive Byrne took a call from the office of the Registrar of Births and Deaths who had been looking through their ledgers. They found two witness signatories recorded on the marriage certificate for when Stanley married Evelyn. The first a Bertrand Benson, Stanley's father and second David Strong, Evelyn's father. The clerk stated that both men had passed away in the late eighties.

'What are you expecting to find at Arthur's house?' asked Byrne.

'I'm not entirely sure. It was what Marjorie said about evidence being hidden or buried. I want to have another look at the airing cupboard.'

Pete Byrne continued to look out of the car window. He missed most of the faces of the pedestrians going by his own thoughts elsewhere returning to an era gone by when he had been involved in another investigation, one in which Tavistock had been a detective like him.

As soon as she saw the car draw alongside the kerb Millicent Watkins left her seat and rushed to the front door. With a wry grin Atherton winked at Byrne. 'I can do the house, you talk some more with your number one fan!'

Watching her pull open the garden gate and swing their way Pete Byrne was in the least disinterested. *'Oh for fuck's sake, I'd swear that she's had additional implants since we were here last!'*

Atherton made sure that he was the first out of the car.

'Hello Millicent, Detective Byrne was just coming across to see you!'

'Are you coming as well?' He noticed her shoulders sag as she asked.

Smiling he responded 'me... oh no, I have something that I've got to check at the house opposite.' Instantly her shoulders righted themselves. She heaved her massive bosom up under her cardigan and grinned across at Pete Byrne.

'I'd just put the kettle on, we have ourselves a cuppa before we settle down on the settee!'

Pete Byrne looked across at his sergeant said nothing but was already throttling him. Linking her arm through Byrne's she guided him across to the open door. 'Take your time sergeant, the kettle will still be warm when you're done!' Millicent didn't look back as she closed the front door with the heel of her shoe. Atherton shook his head in amusement as he headed up the stone steps to the front door.

Standing alone in the hallway the house seemed exceptionally quiet unwelcome. The only light was gloomy small shafts of natural daylight from under the curtains that had been pulled together to prevent prying eyes.

Knowing that Arthur Benson had walked across the bare boards and tatty carpet Atherton began his search in the kitchen. It seemed eerily different without his body stretched across the table. Opening and shutting cupboards the house had been invaded by particles of dust, damp and the smell of death. In the front room the fireplace which had long seen any warmth smelt of charred soot. Finding nothing of interest he began climbing the stairs.

On the landing above the atmosphere was different. The air was infused with an aura as though somebody or something had sprayed a mist of humiliation, sorrow and misery into the upper floor of the house. In his thoughts he imagined Arthur Benson crying into the pillow of his bed although he did not know why.

Suddenly the energy changed pricking his skin. Atherton closed his eyes and waited. Moments passed before a shaft of sunlight parted the gloom penetrating the bathroom window and casting a long ray of bright light along the landing floor before settling itself upon the airing cupboard door. Like a sleeping dragon having been rudely awoken Atherton pulled open the door. Going past outside a heavily laden shook the floorboards.

All about the voices were engaging, some calling others raising their voices to be heard. Ignoring their demands he emptied the shelves as he had done before leaving only a loose wire which brought power to the hot water cylinder. Remember said Marjorie *'hidden and buried'.* Pulling aside the front of the cylinder jacket he inserted his hands either side of the copper storage unit feeling his way around back and up and down. When he touched something plastic he pinched the corner and withdrew the item from where it had been concealed. Holding the bag up to the light inside was a set of female underwear. Replacing the linen back on the shelves he closed the door. Almost at once the voices vanished.

Taking the bag into the bathroom where the light was best he examined the contents more closely leaving them in the bag. Atherton was suspicious of why the bag had been so well hidden, without doubt not wanting to be found. Maybe, he thought Pete Byrne had been right and Arthur Benson did have a secret past. He was on his way back downstairs when he saw a shadow at the front door.

Pete Byrne was ready to give Atherton both barrels of his frustration when he saw what he was holding as the sergeant held open the door.

'Where did you find those?'

'Well and truly hidden around back of the hot water cylinder. Only Arthur Benson would have known that they were there!'

Byrne looked over to where the curtain twitched. He stepped inside the hall and pushed shut the door. 'I told you that there was something not altogether right about Arthur Benson.'

He examined the bag, nodding 'they wore stuff like this back in the late fifties, sixties and seventies.'

The seam keeping the bag airtight was slightly yellowed suggesting that it had been behind the cylinder for a good length of time.

'Well one thing, it proves Arthur had women here!'

'We'll give it to Marjorie and her team. Maybe DNA will tell us more. She said that every piece of evidence could tell a story.'

Looking through to where the sunlight was shining through the kitchen door Pete Byrne had a thought. 'You don't think that we've got any bodies under the paving slabs do you?'

Shaking his head Atherton wasn't sure. 'At present let's think positive. If anything else shows up we might have to consider the possibility. How did you get on with Millicent and your cosy chat?'

Byrne muttered an initial reply but he was still looking out back. 'Even when I told her that I was happily married and showed her a picture of Anne and the girls it didn't make the slightest difference. Millicent has a determined streak in her.' He turned to face Atherton. 'She did however tell me that rumour had it Arthur had a love child!'

Daniel Atherton looked surprised 'That adds a different complexion to the equation.' Maybe the underwear wasn't so much of a surprise. 'Any information as to whom and when?'

Byrne sucked through his lips ending in a squelching sound. 'That's the bit Millicent can't recall.'

Atherton gently fisted the end of his chin in frustration 'We'll just have to keep pumping away at Millicent until she remembers more. Something must trigger a memory, a name, place or face. Maybe somebody else around here remembers such a rumour.'

'Well the next time you can accompany me to have a cosy little chat, Millicent Watkins is dangerous!'

Parked a little way back up the road the occupant of a dark blue van watched in the rear view mirror as the two men secured the property then went back to the car. One had something in his hand but from so far away it was difficult to see exactly what.

'If Arthur Benson had a love child, then they could be the only surviving relative alive. The trouble we have now is knowing who that person could be?'

'The killer possibly?' added Byrne.

'Maybe,' Atherton replied 'although it would have to be a very strong motive to kill your father!'

As the Saab pulled away from the kerbside the curtain at sixty five Park Drive settled back into place. Millicent Hawkins smiled to herself knowing that they would be back.

Chapter Ten

New week - Monday morning

Surprisingly it had been an exceptionally quiet weekend. Daniel Atherton had been in work Saturday morning hoping to catch up with some overdue reports looking for an excuse to visit Edington Hall although without one his visit might have been seen as imposing.

By seven thirty Monday morning he was in work again. Closing the door quietly behind him he crossed the floor of the forensic department and placed the plastic bag of underwear alongside where Marjorie had been working. The others busy at their workstations looked up and acknowledged his presence but they were actively engaged and did not have the time to talk. Slipping on a pair of gloves Marjorie came back over to her examination bench.

'Been weekend shopping Daniel?' she inquired. Her eyes were bright and enthusiastic as she examined the bag and its contents. She also had managed to rest on Sunday.

'Unfortunately not me. I found this Friday afternoon at Arthur Benson's house, it was concealed behind the hot water cylinder. I left it locked in my desk over the weekend where it could not be tampered with.'

Tearing a metre square strip of brown paper from the roll she laid it out on top of her workbench before emptying the bag and contents onto the flat surface. Picking the undergarments up with a pair of tweezers she began her examination.

'Like they had been hidden never to be found!' she suddenly made comment.

'That was my first impression.'

In the natural light the brassiere and pair of ladies knickers looked different to what they had on the landing at the house, softer and more feminine.

'This was a popular style at one time,' Marjorie said 'especially to a young woman.'

Examining the brassiere strap Marjorie unravelled the manufacturer's tag. She placed the tag under the microscope where the washed details were easy to read.

'*Stafford's*' was a well-known clothing outlet in Stockport. I know a lady who still works in their order department. I'll check with her and ask about this set. If anybody knows it will be her.'

'Would the set have been expensive?'

Marjorie nodded. 'Reasonably so and I would imagine that if not a gift from a husband, lover or admirer then a lady would have spent half her weeks wage on such a set such as this. Looking at the logo on the tag I would say that this might have originated in France.'

'Pete Byrne heard a rumour Friday that Arthur Benson might have been the father of a love child.'

Marjorie looked up from the microscope. 'And do you know who that is?'

He shook his head. 'No our informant likes to keep us dangling. She says that she can't remember but we'll go back and give her another try.'

'I'll run this two garments through some tests and see what we can find.'

He was about to thank her when Tom Skerritt called them both over to where he was working.

'I think this might interest you sergeant.'

Throwing the image under his microscope onto the enlarger screen the magnified partial print of a finger filled the screen.

'We retrieved this from the empty cartridge. It's not a full print although from what we can make out it at least sixty five percent.'

Atherton started to smile. 'It's a damn fine sixty five percent Tom and more than we had before. It is our killer?'

Skerritt smiled back 'well we know it doesn't belong to the gamekeeper or either victim!'

Daniel Atherton turned to Marjorie. 'This is a break that we've been waiting for and like you said it would the evidence is trickling in.'

'I'll start running it through fingerprint analysis and see if we get a match.'

Atherton patted tom on the shoulder and congratulated him on the find. It was indeed a break through. If Marjorie could find anything on the lace garment a picture might begin to emerge at last. He didn't ask but knew that fingerprint analysis could take anything from five minutes to five hours to throw up a match, if one existed in the system and that evidentially they would need at least twelve points to be accepted in court. He was about to leave when Marjorie told him that Gregory Tavistock had already been in to CSI to ask how they were getting on with the Edington Hall investigation.

Atherton frowned. 'I wonder what he finds so interesting?' he queried.

'I'm not sure. I got the impression that he was fishing around.'

Atherton pulled Marjorie to one side.

'When he was just a detective, what did you make of Gregory Tavistock?'

She checked that they could not be overheard.

'He made my skin crawl if I'm honest. It was worse when he was made sergeant and he would always ask that I attend any scene that he was investigating even if there were others in the team. Gregory Tavistock had a wandering eye.'

'And now?'

'It's not so bad now, now that he is older. I still would trust his though not as far as I could throw him.'

Atherton nodded 'thanks Marjorie.'

Gabrielle George was passing as they finished, Atherton smiled.

'Hi Gabrielle, how was things over the weekend?'

'Good thanks and if you mean did I see the strange man on the corner then no I don't think so. Friday and Saturday nights tend to be a bit busy round my area so there's always lots of people about and I had a friend stay over Saturday until Sunday afternoon.' She suddenly let out a low sigh. 'I'm not keen on the underground carpark though but that's because there are so many shadows in the corners and near the entrance.'

'Did Marjorie talk to you about installing a pencil camera?'

'She did, but I wasn't keen.'

Atherton didn't pursue why, her private life outside of the station was nothing to do with the police.

'Okay, but if you do want help then you know that you've only got to ask. We will do anything that we can.'

She thanked him and was about to go back to her bench when he noticed the name on the evidence tag that she had in her hand.

'Paddock Mews' isn't that where the estate office is for Edington Hall?'

Marjorie seemed somewhat surprised 'Yes, they had a break-in late Saturday night. Were you not informed?'

Atherton looked unamused 'No, I was not. Somebody in section should have told control to call me.'

'The uniformed patrol who attended put the incident down to local yobs, travellers in the area or a person unknown.'

Of the three potentials Atherton preferred the first and second, the third concerned him more than the other two.

'So why the glass sample?' he asked.

Gabrielle raised the evidence bag so that he was able to see the contents, small pieces of window glass.

'Whoever broke in cut themselves. I was looking at the DNA of the blood left behind!'

134

He felt aggrieved that he had not been told. The break-in would have given him ample reason to go back to Edington Hall and see Mary Thomas. It wasn't until the weekend that he realised just how comfortable he had been with the young woman in the kitchen. He had made up his mind too that he could not wait until after the investigation to see her.

'Did you get anything back on the footprints you found?'

'Only that they match similar models used by the army. The issue that we have there is any good army and navy store will sell similar type boots.'

She went to her desk drawer to retrieve an envelope from which she spread a group of photographs across the bench top. They had been taken at Edington Hall.

'Logically we reason that there was only one perpetrator who engaged Roger and Richard Edington the night that they were killed. We searched around and found other boot marks in the wood nearby but they had been run across by wildlife and too far trodden down for us to lift for analysis. What we did however determine was that Sir Roger had been standing by a tree at one point because we found a torn piece of his jacket in the bark. It matched the jacket that he was wearing the night he was murdered.'

'Fragmentary evidence,' Atherton smiled 'I wonder what he was doing over by the trees?'

'A call of nature maybe,' Marjorie suggested 'men do such things!' Gabrielle grinned as she lowered her eyes.

Atherton studied the photographs taken of the boot prints found at the flume channel. Marjorie was the first to comment.

'If they belong to the killer he went to the flume channel for a reason!'

Atherton suddenly had an idea. 'Yes indeed he did. I need Lady Francesca to agree to me having the flume channel dredged.'

'We are busy but I can spare tom if that would help?'

'No, that's fine Marjorie. If my theory is wrong I'd like to keep it low key and not have Tavistock know. Edington was a friend of his. There was a digger at the farm so I'll get Reg Cullen to help me. At this point he's not under suspicion but any reluctance to help might prove otherwise.'

Keeping an eye on the diminishing number of possibilities that the fingerprint analyser was making Tom called out that the search was down to fifty two.

'We're getting there. Right I'll leave you too it.'

She promised to let him know the minute the machine made a connection. Marjorie also stated that most of the team were in court that afternoon on another case. Going back to his office he collected a pair of sturdy wellington boots and waterproof jacket.

On route to Waxford Hammock he talked to Pete Byrne and told him where he was going and why. Byrne who was still out chasing down enquiries regarding a possible love child was getting nowhere fast.

Beyond the windscreen the nimbus grey clouds overhead were gathering fast and threatened the ground below with rain. Atherton was glad that he had brought along the boots and waterproof jacket. As luck would have it the closer that he got to Waxford Hammock the wind bringing in the clouds changed direction and was now heading south west towards the Irish Sea. Negotiating the bends in the drive up to the house Atherton parked short of the drawbridge.

He tugged hard at the short metal chain which disappeared between the cracks of the masonry going inside to where a brass bell announced the arrival of a visitor. Moments later a member of the house staff answered the door. He was invited in and shown once again to the same study where he and Byrne had shared coffee with Lady Francesca.

Atherton was left alone for almost forty minutes spending the time studying the paintings in the room and either side of the grand fireplace. He was about to go and find Reg Cullen when he heard the door shut quietly behind him. Attired still in her riding outfit Francesca Edington-Forbes looked quite stunning in a brown musto sardinia jacket zipped up to the neck, cream coloured jodhpurs and neoprene half chaps. He

136

noticed too that despite the keen breeze in the air outside her hair was still intact. Once again she came forward and held out her hand for him to take.

'I really am sorry to have kept you waiting sergeant. Had I known that you were here I would not have gone riding. Is this about that infuriating break-in at the weekend?' she asked.

'It's good of you to allow me back so soon. I will investigate the break-in whilst I'm here but I really came to ask if I might be permitted to take another look down at the woods and perhaps with the help of your gamekeeper.'

'Why of course if you think it will help although what you hope to find beats me but please be my guest.'

'Did you enjoy the ride?' he asked quite out of context of his visit.

She gestured that they took a seat opposite one another.

Smiling she replied 'Indeed it's the one enjoyment that I love about Edington Hall. I suppose you might find that interesting and that I am not grieving my loss but I am happy sergeant, happier than I have been for a long time and riding is freedom.'

She pointed to the oil painting of the horses head on the wall beside the door.

'My horse, a beautiful brown mare is named freedom. Roger hated me calling the horse that but I tried to get back at him in every conceivable way possible. In a way my horse helped keep me sane in this madhouse. That and Ginette and Yvette. Would you like some refreshments before you tell me the real reason for your visit?'

As tempting as it was to see Mary deliver the tray of hot coffee he politely declined wanting to get the search under way.

'I have an idea that we'll find the murder weapons beneath the mud!'

'Ah, the shotguns!' she sighed gently 'I myself had wondered about them at the weekend. Before I went riding I had enquired with Reg Cullen to see if he had them. You will need his help sergeant the bottom of the field can

137

be treacherous at the best of times. I never ride *freedom* down near the wood.'

He thanked her for her advice.

'If you will permit me to speak frankly. I see no reason for you to grieve and perhaps the future will make you much happier!'

Francesca nodded and smiled back. 'My future happiness is already assured. 'I will have Mary make you a large flask only it can be very windy down next to the flume channel. That and dark and haunting, I never did like that part of the estate, quite fitting really that he should have been murdered there. Not Richard of course, his death I do mourn.'

'You've been very kind, thank you Lady Edington-Forbes.'

She raised a hand 'Please sergeant, I would much prefer that you called me just plain Francesca. I detested the title and for too long I have suffered that infernal surname. The time has come for me to be plain Francesca Forbes again!'

'Thank you Francesca, you've been very helpful.'

'Oh and when you've done with the mud please call in and see the ladies in the kitchen, I know of one particular young maid that would gladly make you something for lunch.'

'Mary is nobody like I have met before,' he admitted.

Francesca nodded gently. 'She deserves to be happy too sergeant. Edington Hall must have been a terrible place to work when my husband was alive. I had reason to go into the village at the weekend and from the looks on the people's faces you could detect the change that had suddenly taken place. For once they smiled and welcomed me as one of their own and not with guarded indifference. It was as though a great cloud had vanished overnight, simply evaporated.'

'Would you know how often the flume channel received attention?'

Francesca got up from her chair and walked across to the window where Reg Cullen was walking her horse. Atherton thought he saw her wave but couldn't be sure.

'Engineering and estate management never was one of my interests, however I am sure that Reg could help on the matter. Roger had the damn flume put in to gather the excess water and silt. He tried in vain to explain but I was the least interested.

'What I did gather was that with the rotation of crops a certain amount of sediment is left behind at the end of the season. All that waste has to collect somewhere and being a natural hill it accumulates in the dip next to the wood. The cows being the cumbersome beasts that they are broke through the fence last year and regrettably one drowned becoming trapped in the flume channel. It can get very muddy around this time of the year when the rains come.'

Despite her instance that she had not listened, she had and understood its function.

'Your grasp of the countryside Francesca is far more advanced than that of mine. I on the other hand am just a simple policeman dealing with societies misfits.'

They shook hands and she smiled before she accompanied him to the front door.

'Remember Mary will be disappointed if you don't call in after you're done!' with that she closed the door taking herself upstairs to shower and change.

*****

'We had best get underway,' Reg explained firing up the engine of the mechanical excavator 'only those clouds up there were heading west but they look like turning back our way.'

Atherton held on tight as the excavator negotiated the slippery slope of the field. Down near the wood the ground was wetter than it been Friday morning.

Using long wooden planks they laid down a solid surface beside the flume channel to prevent the excavator from sinking in the mud.

139

Reg quickly issued a warning as he jumped back on the excavator 'Watch where you walk sergeant only the ground here can suck you down fast!'

So far he had not detected any reluctance to help. Reg had seemed eager to help as though the double murder had become a personal indignity, a disdainful slur against his professional responsibilities to protect the land, the animals and the people who lived in the big house. Watching Reg work the excavator back and forth depositing large chunks of disgorged mud and slime from the flume channel Atherton was in awe of the gamekeeper's knowledge.

Using a hay rake Atherton he sifted through the mud on the bank. Several bucket loads in he raised his hand and prevented Reg from depositing any more.

'I think you've done it Reg, I've just hit something metal.'

Carefully pulling them from the mud Atherton retrieved one then another shotgun.

'That's them,' said Reg 'I'd know their guns anywhere and if you look on the stock you'll see the crest of Edington Hall.' From the cab of the excavator he laid a plastic sheet on the ground. 'I thought we might need this!'

Daniel Atherton was convinced that Reg Cullen had taken no part in his master's demise. On the sheet lay two very muddy shotguns, caked in grey oozing slime and vegetation.

'I hope that lady forensic examiner that came here the other day is good only they'll take some cleaning!'

Atherton grinned 'Don't worry about Marjorie she has a trick up her sleeve for every occasion.'

Coming down the hill was a young stable lad armed with a flask of coffee. 'Mary told me to tell you sergeant that lunch will be around one.'

He thanked the young lad and asked Reg about his arrangements but he told Atherton that he always took lunch with the stable hands, boys and girls.

Overhead the weather was turning very grey and a slight drizzle was already beginning to fall nothing anything heavy more a misty presence.

'The Atlantic is an unpredictable beast at the best of times,' Reg remarked 'just like a woman!'

As Reg smoothed down the mud so that fresh grass would grow through Daniel Atherton gently washed away the mud from either stock. Sure enough as Reg had implied each had a small round brass logo set into the wood engraved with the face of the devil and a Latin phrase. Switching the engine to idle he came back over to finish his coffee.

'It reads *'superare, ut sine misericordiae'* which means *'conquer all, take without mercy'*. I never did like the implication behind what it stood for and neither many others.

'I tend to agree wholeheartedly Reg,' the inference described the master of the house and his evil ways.

Reg Cullen pointed but did not touch the brass logos.

'Same as it is strange thing to depict the devil. I once asked Sir Roger why and he told me that it served as a warning to his enemies. 'It was his way of saying *'fuck with me, you fuck with the devil'*.

Atherton scoffed 'He danced with him in the end!'

Looking back up at the house he sipped the hot coffee, he wasn't sure but he thought that he saw a figure standing at the attic window watching.

'CSI tell me that you had a break-in the other night at Paddock Mews, isn't that the estate office?'

'Yes, it was the office used by Richard Edington. Odd thing was that whoever broke in looked through the files but as far as I could tell they took nothing.'

'You don't keep any cash on site?'

'A little in my office. I have a petty cash tin for emergencies that's all. Last time I looked there was about a hundred and fifty pounds in the tin.'

'Emergencies?' probed Atherton.

'Leather polish for the livery, a broken dressage whip, that sort of thing.'

They finished their coffee and drove back up the hill with the shotguns safely wrapped in the sheet.

'CSI has some glass shards with blood on them. Was any of the staff injured trying to clear up?'

'No... whoever got in must have snagged their forearm either on entry or upon leaving.'

'How is that possible?' Atherton wanted know why they had tried the door.

'The door is sold oak with a double lock. The window is what serves the front of the office, but the pane is Georgian wired glass and a bugger to break through. It was no wonder the intruder snagged their arm. It would have taken some force to push through, somebody strong, a man I would say.'

Parking the excavator against the side of his office Reg invited Atherton inside.

'You've fifteen minutes before you need to be in the kitchen for lunch. Cook don't like anybody in early only she like to move about without tripping over feet.'

Atherton laid the wrapped shotguns carefully down on the floor. He sat opposite Reg at the desk sensing the need to be up front with the gamekeeper.

'We checked with Leonard Pryce at the Duck and Drake, your alibi holds up for the night of the murders Reg.'

Cullen pulled a bottle of scotch from the top drawer of the metal filing cabinet and offered Atherton a beaker, but he politely declined. 'Thanks, maybe another time!'

Reg poured himself a dram but no more. 'Helps keep the rheumatism down.'

'Old army war wounds?'

142

Reg grinned 'Aye something like that, it's why I left in the end. My old joints couldn't keep up with the pace of a modern army and you have to be ultra-fit.' He looked at Atherton. 'You'd be alright though, it's a young man's profession nowadays.'

'Did you keep any reminders of the good days, like a beret cap badge, the buckle of a belt or a pair of parade boots?'

Reg raised the metal beaker and saluted the regiment.

'No, when I left I wanted a clean break. I gave back everything except my army passport.' He slipped out of his waders and into a comfortable pair of sturdy leather brogues. 'These were a present from the lads, I've had them ever since.'

Reg screwed the lid back on the whiskey bottle and put it back in the metal cabinet.

'Do you play darts sergeant,' he asked 'only we're a member short now, the young master was in the team as a reserve only Sir Roger didn't know.'

Daniel thanked him but quickly excused the offer explaining that his department were constantly in demand working all sort of irregular hours.

'Things will change around here now you know and we'll all feel a lot safer now!'

Atherton was surprised by the gamekeeper sudden admission believing that he had an equal understanding with Sir Roger.

'In what way?' he asked.

'Why even the air feels fresher, untainted with that rancorous taste!'

'Can you elaborate, be more specific?' Atherton prompted.

'Sometimes at night I would hear the odd cry or scream. My lodgings are nearest the house but left over from my days in Northern Ireland I'm a light sleeper and in the dead of night sound can carry a long way.'

'So what you heard did it come from the house and where exactly?'

'The bedrooms of the young maids.'

'Could it not have been a vixen calling her young?' Atherton knew he was playing devil's advocate but he wanted Reg to demonstrate how reviled he was.

'No, not a vixen sergeant but the master. Like a demon he would hunt at night seeking out a virgin maid and threatening the others into submission including my young girls.

'Some nights he come to office knowing that I was working late, we'd have a brandy together only he couldn't hold his liquor. When he left he would seek out a vulnerable stable lass or one working late in the kitchen. Many's the night I could have killed him myself.'

'Why didn't you stop him using your army skills?'

'He threatened me too. Said that if I stopped him or made trouble he would throw me out and tell people that I had been assaulting the young women. As ashamed as I am I had to cower down to his evil.'

'Was he married at the time of the assaults?'

'No. Things settled for a while when he met Francesca but things changed there soon after and she would refuse to lie down with him in the marital bed so he went back to his corrupt ways again.'

Atherton found it strange that he used her name so casually and that Reg knew about her refusing her husband sexual relations.

'Was there any physical signs of violence in the marriage?'

Reg lowered his head and nodded.

'Oh yes, initially they'd argue but sometime after that he would hit her demanding that she be with him. I'd notice the signs only I'd seen similar with army wives with men that had returned from a posting. Army psychologists blamed the stress of combat and the tension of never knowing what to expect as the cause for sudden outbursts of anger. I blamed the men. To me what they did was just a cop-out and a reason to lash out after a night on the lash. It's one of the reasons that I never married Mr Atherton.'

Atherton nodded 'And Lady Francesca, did you ever talk to her?'

Reg kept his head down.

'We would talk when nobody was about or she would go riding. It was dangerous but I felt that I had to help her somehow!'

'Are you lover's?'

It was a gamble to ask and could so easily have backfired and ended the discussion but Reg seemed like he wanted to talk, to unburden himself.

Reg instantly looked up 'Who told you?'

Daniel Atherton shook his head and raised his hands to placate the response.

'Nobody Reg, only you. I see tension in my job and to overcome it some of the men and women find strength being together. There's nothing wrong with it and emotionally they can be as one. I consider myself to be the soul of discretion so your secret is safe with me, I assure you!'

Putting his hands over his eyes Reg Cullen wanted to shut out the daylight.

'It would tear me apart inside when the bedroom light went out. I would stand in the shadows amongst the trees lining the front drive and pray that he didn't hurt Francesca. I am sure that the master knew only he never let on, not to me anyway. It was like he had something over, like a poker player sitting opposite his opponent knowing that that he holds the upper hand.'

'Did you kill him Reg, Roger Edington and then his son Richard because he was in the wrong place at the wrong time?'

Rocking his head from side to side in his hands Reg Cullen denied the accusation. When he looked back up at the detective sergeant his eyes were wet with shame.

'No, I promise you that I was nowhere near the woods that night. I left the Duck and Drake around half midnight. Francesca had been with Ginette and Yvette until around midnight when Ginette told her to go back to her room because I was due back at the house. We spent the night together knowing that her husband and Richard would probably be out all night hunting that damn fox. I left around five just as it was getting light.

'There's an old priest hole in the panel work of Francesca's bedroom. Francesca found it one day whilst she was considering new decoration. She followed the hidden staircase down until it eventually emerged behind a thicket of dense bushes near the main entrance. You have to climb over the drawbridge wall but it's easy when you've worked it out. Sir Roger never knew about the secret entrance so at night Francesca would sneak out and come to me or me to her.'

'You took a big risk Reg.'

The gamekeeper wiped his eyes with the back of his hand. 'When you love someone Mr Atherton you are willing to take any amount of risks.'

'So what happens now?' The question wasn't necessary to the enquiry but Atherton wanted to know in case it did become important.

'We're not entirely sure. When Stuart and Robert arrive things I'm sure will be sorted.'

Daniel Atherton picked up the blanket containing the shotguns.

'Would you mind if I borrowed the sheet it'll ensure that the shotguns get back to the station without being further contaminated?'

'By all means.' Reg Cullen looked at the clock on the wall 'you'd best be getting over to the kitchen they're expecting you!'

'Will you be alright only I can leave lunch until another day?'

Reg Cullen stood and shook Daniel Atherton's hand.

'I promise that although there were times when I could have easily done away with Roger Edington I didn't and I did not kill him or Richard the other night. Richard and I worked extremely well together and we were gradually turning this estate around and making a good profit. I'm going to take a long walk and check on the herd on the far hill. The fresh air will help clear my head.' He let his hand slip away from Atherton's. Thanks for listening. I've never been able to tell anybody about Francesca and me but there's been plenty of times that I wish I had.'

Reg Cullen walked from the office and headed around back of the office towards the farm and the fields beyond.

Daniel Atherton watched until the gamekeeper had disappeared from sight. Like a pair caught in a time warp Francesca Forbes and Reg Cullen were the only two people who could sort their future. Putting the shotguns wrapped in the plastic sheet in the boot of his car he depressed the button on the key fob and activated the central locking.

Waiting at the top of the stairs leading down to the kitchen below he was aware that Mary Thomas was watching. She waved, her smile eager to see him.

Chapter Eleven

Monday Lunchtime

'You saw me coming?' he smiled pleased to see her too.

'I had a feeling that you'd be along soon.'

She stood aside so that he could pass down the stairs.

'Come on let's get you inside you've got wet.'

Atherton shrugged 'It's not much although I'd be grateful to get in the warm.

Mary was right behind him as she guided him through the lobby door but before they reached the kitchen she made him turn around where she pulled him into her and kissed him before he could escape. Atherton responded.

'Am I going to be arrested for assault?' she asked pulling away.

'You'd have to give me time to think about,' he replied, moments later he kissed her.

When they heard Agnes bumbling about in the larder they parted, straightened their clothes and made sure that he had no sign of lipstick on his lips.

'Does this mean that on my day off, providing you have the time to spare we can go for that drink?'

Atherton shook his head grinning 'Do you like Chinese or we can get a takeaway and go back to my flat!'

Mary stole another kiss then pulled him towards the kitchen door 'Takeaway sounds more fun!'

'Thank goodness for that,' Agnes sighed 'since Mary heard that you were on the estate I have been struggling all morning to get her to do things about the kitchen. She's been like a cat on a hot tin roof.'

Agnes Maitland sat Daniel Atherton down at the large rectangular wooden table and laid before him a plate of hot roast beef sandwiches and a side dressing of salad.

'The mistress told me to make sure that you were well fed.'

Removing his jacket having left his waterproof and boots in the car Agnes took a long hard look at him.

'What you need young man is a good woman to take care of you. Look at you, you're a bag of bones!'

Mary wasn't in agreement with Agnes, to her Daniel Atherton felt just right.

He watched as the pair of them fussed around the kitchen whilst tucking into his lunch, the beef was incredibly good the best that he had tasted for ages. When he'd finished Mary took away his plate and left them on the side to be washed later.

'Have you got a few minutes to spare...' she whispered 'only there's something that I think you need to see?'

'Yes of course, although I should be getting back soon!'

She grabbed his hand and guided him to the door.

'I promise that this won't take long and Agnes said I should show you!'

She took him up four flights of stairs arriving at the attic room that she used as a bedroom, it was surprisingly spacious with its own bathroom. Atherton noticed the heavy chair that Mary said she had used to put under the door handle. From under her bed she pulled out a small vintage suitcase crafted in leather with metal studded corners and a rounded sprung clasp lock.

'I decided to change my room around over the weekend. I found the suitcase tucked under the wardrobe, it had been pushed to the back against the skirting board. It was covered in cobwebs so it had been there some time.'

Lying it down on the bed she sat Daniel Atherton.

'Is there a key?'

'No. The lock looks like it's been forced at some point.'

Atherton flicked the clasp and instantly the lid lifted. He pulled it open wide. Inside folded neatly was a nightdress an old creased bible and beside the book a pair of white socks.

'Do you know who it belongs to Mary?'

'There's a name on the inside cover of the bible, it says the owner is Ruth. That's all I know.' She handed it over to Atherton.

He closed the lid and turned the suitcase around on the bed.

'There were many cases like this back in the early part of the last century.'

Pulling open the front cover of the bible he read the inscription inside *'To Ruth, love from Mother and Father'*

It was written in pencil, slightly smudged as though fingered over many times. He read it once more thinking that it lacked empathy, any love or soul. Inside his mind a voice was calling out to him, calling out a single word *'redemption'*.

'What do you make of it Mary?' he asked.

'It made me feel strange when I picked it up as though the soul to whom it had belonged was asking, begging me to do something with the bible. When I mentioned it to Agnes this morning she told me that I should get in touch with you. If you ask my opinion Daniel somebody is reaching out from the grave, asking for help.'

Closing his eyes momentarily a vision appeared in his mind shrouded by a thin veil to protect the face. He thought he saw a woman praying, knelt down by the side of a bed but he could not entirely sure as the vision lasted only seconds. Moments later he opened them again.

'Like whoever was asking the lord for forgiveness!'

'Yes, that's what I felt.' She held his hand 'the energy that passed through me was strong although the message weak as though the person trying to communicate was either scared to speak aloud or wary of who would come through the door!' Mary shivered, he asked if she was alright.

'I will be when you take the case and the contents from the room. It holds bad memories and last night I tossed and turned all night unable to settle. It was as though the owner knew that you would be coming back today. Does that make any sense?'

'All what you've described makes sense.'

He replaced the bible in the case securing the clasp.

'You know I feel how you feel sometimes when I go to a crime scene, especially a bad one. Sometimes it's like looking through a window and watching the scene materialise again only in slow motion. Sometimes it helps other times it can cloud my judgement. We all possess a sixth sense although it's not always so good to have such a strong link with the dead.'

'Do they haunt you, you know in your sleep?'

He smiled 'sometimes, although none of us are the master of what we dream. If I could analyse some of mine they would make more sense.'

He looked beyond the attic window to the wood below.

'The night that they were shot and killed, what kind of night was it?'

'A funny mix, one minute the moon was out with the stars and the next cloudy, overcast as though somebody had pulled down the curtain. Normally at night if the moon is up you can see across the tree tops but not that night. The demons in the woods made sure that it stayed dark.'

'The demons in the woods?'

Reg Cullen reckons that the wood is haunted. Apparently a long time a great battle took place in the field beyond the wood. The men who managed to escape the massacre took to the wood hoping to find shelter and place to hide but when the moon rose high in the sky they were hunted down by the victors and slaughtered as they rested and slept amongst the trees. Agnes told me that on the eve of the twenty third of April each year you can still hear the cries of the men as their assassins came looking for them.'

151

'How many girls have occupied this attic bedroom before you?'

'Lots I would suspect although Agnes would know better than me.'

Taking custody of the suitcase and its contents they went back downstairs to the kitchen. The moment that Agnes saw the case she shook her head from side to side and waved her finger up and down.

'Do you know, I have a feeling that I've seen that case before only for the life of me I cannot remember when and to whom it belonged?'

'It had to be a maid Agnes,' prompted Atherton 'as it was in Mary's room.'

She nodded, searching the annuls of her mind. Opening her eyes wider she remembered.

'There was a young woman maybe eighteen, perhaps a year older who came here as a maid around the same time that I started as a kitchen help. She was a pretty young thing unlike like me.' Agnes laughed at herself 'my dear father would taunt me relentlessly saying that I had been raised by the cows and kicked about by the bull. After a while I stopped worry about what I looked like and used what god give me to my advantage.' The remark made Mary blush.

The kitchen was warm and Agnes wiped the sweat from her brow with the tea towel she was holding 'still beggars can't be choosers and if the good lord designed me this way, then this way I'll stay.'

She winked at Daniel Atherton and he responded with a grin.

'Some nights me and a certain young stable lad would have a romp in the hay. In the shadows it don't harm what you can't see!'

Mary sighed aloud but it only made Vera worse.

'Any port in a storm is better than nowhere to put your boat, you'd do well to remember that my girl.'

Atherton liked the older woman she was straight and didn't beat about the bush.

'Agnes, would the name Ruth ring any bells?'

Agnes stopped stirring what she had in the mixing bowl.

'That was it, her I mean. Now you mention it her name was Ruth.' She shook her head before he asked. 'Damned if I can remember her surname. She was pretty and innocent looking like an angel.'

Agnes suddenly looked down at Atherton's left hand.

'Are you married or engaged?'

'Only to my work!' he replied.

Without realising it she wiped a streak of flour across her forehead. 'Thank the lord for that I don't want her blubbing all over the kitchen!'

Mary Thomas grabbed Daniel Atherton's free hand and pulled him towards the exit before Agnes really got started on him.

'The sergeant's got to go back to work!'

Encouraging Atherton through the door he just about managed to wave good bye and thank Agnes for the lunch before being pushed against the wall where Mary kissed him once again before she asked that he phone her when he was free to which he promised. At the head of the stone stairs she watched him drive around to the front of the house losing sight of his car as he turned the corner.

He did think about ringing the bell again to give Francesca Forbes an update but Reg Cullen would undoubtedly be seeing her later. It would serve no purpose disturbing her once again so he put the drive shaft into gear slowly pulling away. There were some secrets meant to remain within the fabric of an old house.

Chapter Twelve

Monday Mid-afternoon

Francesca Forbes had already dropped the double-barrelled name and wished to carry on with her father's surname and in time Edington Hall itself would be renamed by the brothers wishing to put an end to the terrible history that had long clouded the edifice and estate.

Back at the station Atherton was keen to book the suitcase and shotguns into evidence and leave both in the forensic lab for the attention of Marjorie knowing that they were all in court. He did his best to avoid running into Gregory Tavistock. Using his hip to budge open the door of the lab he was surprised to see Tom Skerritt sat at the bench.

'I thought you were all in court?'

'I was listed although not required. Prosecution accepted my written evidence and besides Marjorie will seal any doubt.'

'She'll do that alright.'

Tom carefully took hold of the folded sheet containing the shotguns laying them down on the workbench.

'This is one hell of a find!'

'Thanks Tom. The credit really needs to go to Reg Cullen.'

'I'd best let them acclimatise in the drying room then tag them later. The conditions will help dry the mud and make it crack which will be easier to remove.'

He returned to the car boot to retrieve the suitcase. Leaving the case intact Atherton filled out three evidence tags and handed two to Tom tying the third to the handle of the case. They put it one side for the attention of Marjorie.

He was pleased to find the CID office empty allowing him some quiet time and the opportunity to think. Slowly the legend was filling although the circle in the centre remained empty, the name of the killer. Voters had thrown up a few possible names, men mainly known to the police intelligence system, small time criminals although none were worth asking in for questioning. Byrne had obtained a copy of the admission record where Roger Edington had attended the emergency department for treatment but he had left with his pride only damaged. Reading down the report Atherton had little sympathy. Heavy bruising to the ribs, concussion, two black eyes and a suspected fractured nose which turned out to be localised swelling. Taking everything into account Edington had got off lightly for his sins.

He was reading other documents left by the team when his mobile rang in his pocket, the call was from Pete Byrne.

'How did it go at Edington Hall?'

'Good… Reg Cullen was a big help and together we recovered both shotguns.'

'Will we get any prints?' Byrne asked.

'We won't know until the morning as both were heavily encased in mud and vegetation. Where are you?'

'Corner of Albert Terrace asking the resident about Arthur's mysterious love child. They either know or won't say or they don't know and still won't say, either way I get the distinct impression that we not very much liked.'

'We could be chasing ghost Pete.'

At the other end of the line Byrne sucked through his teeth.

'At number twelve Albert Terrace, I came across an Archibald Harrington who told me that his daughter used to babysit for the Benson's.'

'Arthur's house or the Rochester Road address?'

'That the daft old sod can't remember. Our next problem is the daughter now lives in Adelaide. I'll go and chase down the mysterious maiden if Tavistock will sign off the expenses sheet!'

Atherton laughed 'And Mr Harrington didn't say whether the baby was a boy or a girl.'

'To be honest he's almost gaga living in the present one minute and the past another. Poor bugger should be in a home!'

Atherton momentarily thought about Agnes Maitland. She could roast beef a treat, but her memory for names was as bad as Archibald Harrington.

Pete Byrne suddenly sighed down the mouthpiece of his mobile.

'I'm on my way back to the station. I've had my basin full of old buggers today.'

Atherton looked at the clock on the wall it was almost three.

'Call it a day Pete, you've earned it. Get home shave, shower and change, then take that family of yours to that new pizza parlour in South Street and grab yourself an early night.'

Pete Byrne said thanks then ended the call before Atherton changed his mind.

Standing at the window of his office where he could see the outline of the city Daniel Atherton had one more task before he also intended leaving off. Heading out towards Hunters Yard he wanted to see for himself where Gabrielle George lived.

Showing his warrant card another resident let him through the gate to the underground carpark where he left his car. Stepping out to the junction opposite the small block of flats he was in awe of what the builders had managed to do to the old warehouse. Stylishly renovated the windows were large and rounded at the top, the cornice work in the brick had been cleaned so that the original moulding was now as clear as the day that it had been set by the original brick layer. Working along the line of flats with his eye line Atherton arrived at Gabrielle George's flat which was on the corner of the first floor, overlooking the junction with Station Road. In the background he could hear the sound of heavy engineering from the railway yard nearby.

Daniel Atherton walked back and forth memorising everything about the flat, the living room balcony to the front, the kitchen at the side and the bedroom beyond that, all noticeable by different curtaining, blinds and opaque glass. Standing at the junction he gauged that the corner flat was a good twenty metres from the nearest street light making it highly probable for a stranger to watch the occupant move about the illuminated apartment. Worse still the living room windows were full size floor to just below the ceiling.

Walking he visited the local shops consisting of a convenience store, coffee bars, estate agents and the odd clothing store. What was surprising and he had expected to find was the lack of a pub. Eventually his walking the pavements brought him to a footbridge.

Standing on top of the crossover section below was the railway engineering works. He watched a wheel-tapper check the rolling stock remembering when as a boy men had performed the same task. Atherton took his mobile from his pocket and selected the details for Pete Byrne.

'I've just got of the shower that was lucky.'

'Pete was one of the victims from the *'wheel man killer'* case found at Hunter's Yard?'

Byrne paused to think.

'Yes, although without looking at the case matrix I can't remember in which order the victim was found. I do recall her being near the engineer workshops not far from Hunter's Yard, why?'

'I'm standing on the footbridge overlooking the engineering works!'

Pete Byrne let out an expletive. 'That's where Gabrielle George lives.'

'That's right. What can you tell me about the victim?'

'She was the landlord's daughter from a local pub called *'The Rolling Stock'*. Pretty young thing about nineteen I think, a brunette. The father and his partner sold the lease on the pub and moved away from the area soon after she was murdered.

'The new owner turned the pub into one of those fancy wine bars with a restaurant on the first floor. Many of the locals however believed the place to be cursed by her death as business always attracted the wrong sort. It closed again a year later and remained empty for years until a group of women took it over and made it into a hairdressers and boutique where you get your nails done.'

'I think that it's a convenience store now and the upstairs in probably the stockroom. It would make sense. The block of flat that Gabrielle George lives is called 'Hunters View'. It's about a quarter of a mile from the engineering works depot for the Southport Railways.

'I know what you're thinking,' said Byrne 'so what do we do about Gabrielle?'

'I'm not sure, if we say the wrong thing we could frighten Gabrielle into not living in the apartment whereas if we don't and heaven forbid our mystery peeping tom strikes then we will be damned either way. I think I'll have a word with Marjorie and see what she advices only she knows her team better than you or me.'

'Do you need me?' Pete Byrne asked.

'No, you go enjoy your meal and say hi to Anne and the girls for me. I'll see you tomorrow.'

From the top of the footbridge Atherton waited for Marjorie to answer but the call went to voicemail. He guessed she was giving evidence in court. He left a message asking her to call.

Chapter Thirteen

Tuesday Morning

With the birds chirping loudly in the branches near his bedroom window Atherton was awoken from his sleep around five thirty, he remembered some parts of the dreams but not all. The last memory that he had was of him standing on a street corner and watching a darkly hooded figure walk by on the opposite pavement. The stranger who had no face looked then disappeared. Looking down on him he saw Mary, she waved then too vanished the moment that he woke.

He arrived at the office just prior to twenty past six having met the early patrols in the station yard making ready their vehicles. Male and females no older than himself they were jovial and talkative.

'Anything interesting happen overnight?' he asked.

'Usual crap,' replied a female officer 'there's a couple in the bin for alleged assault, another for putting in the window down the high street, a drink driver and a young man for distributing drugs.' She scoffed at the idea 'The parents asked the custody sergeant to leave him in overnight to see if it would teach him a lesson.'

'Normal night then,' he replied believing it would be a wasted lesson.

The female officer nodded and smiled at him before closing the boot of her vehicle.

'Oh yes and the fire service attended an incident at the County Records Office around two this morning. So far it's been recorded as suspicious. Fire Service estimate at least sixty five percent was damaged by fire the remainder smoke logged. They're still there damping down.'

Atherton immediately reached for his mobile to call Pete Byrne. His wife Anne answered telling him that Pete was in the shower.

'Thanks Anne, I hope that you and the girls had a good meal out last night. When Pete's done at home will you please give him the message to meet me at the County Records Office.' Swinging his car around Atherton headed for the scene of the fire.

Byrne parked his car behind the last fire appliance on scene. Stepping over an entanglement of charged fire hoses he made his way over to where Atherton was waiting.

'What is this open season for fucking up police investigations?'

He was clearly annoyed having spent most of the previous day tracking down a rumour.

'Just when we seem to be getting somewhere we hit another bloody wall!'

Calmly Atherton asked 'Have you had breakfast?'

'Just coffee. As soon as Anne mentioned the records office I knew something was up.'

They asked to look inside but the senior fire officer informed them that office block was likely to collapse and that until the borough engineer declared it safe nobody was allowed inside, not even his crews. Atherton thanked them for their good work.

'Come on, let's go and get something to eat only like you I've had nothing else but coffee.'

The waitress in the café brought over two rounds of bacon sandwiches to their table quickly followed by mugs of tea.

Pete Byrne talked as he consumed his sandwich. Somebody knows our every move!'

Atherton looked up. 'I'm beginning to agree with you. I had the same feeling when I called you yesterday from the bridge.'

'Somebody in the press. It's been known. Always there first to get the exclusive!'

Atherton shook his head. 'No, I've a feeling that our killer is out there tracking us. Why I don't know?'

'Surely they must know that there'd be back-up data on hard-drives, computer banks. Burning down and office full of records isn't going to prevent our investigation from forging ahead.'

'It all depends if the records were scanned into the system. I reckon that there'd be a good few from the sixties, maybe seventies and prior to those dates now lost forever. Maybe that was what our killer was hoping would happen.'

'Is he forgetting that every family record made up and down the country ends up at the National Archives?'

'That's to our advantage,' replied Atherton. 'Let's hope he doesn't go after the main centre.'

'Did Reg Cullen have anything to say for himself?'

Atherton thought about telling Pete Byrne the truth but he kept the affair between Francesca and Reg to himself as there nothing to be gained by revealing their secret.

'Not a lot. We talked about the victims and how they treated the staff, especially Sir Roger. It would have Tavistock turning in his bed if he knew the truth.'

Byrne shook his head.

'I can't describe it but since we've been involved with these murders there's something nagging me deep inside. Tavistock keeps coming to the fore and yet I don't know why. I know that he's the divisional commander but he seems over interested. Not just because Edington was his friend but something else. I know this sounds daft but I'm sure that it's what's keeping me awake at night. It what like that when I was on the railway murders.'

Atherton told him about the dream that he'd had just before he woke that morning, he ended telling him that it had been surreal.

'Like you were there only you couldn't do anything?'

'That's how I felt. I woke up feeling like I had been walking in the shadow of this hooded figure all night long.'

'There's a lot more to this case than what we realise.'

Atherton agreed. The frustration was knowing what.

'This love child that could be in Australia. I had a bad night too. Anne said it was probably the pizza but I know different, my guts are made of steel. No, for some reason I keep seeing the faces of the victims from the railway murders. I know we all suffer similar every so often but why now, why come back to haunt me just because of this. Oddly enough though I walked past the woman in Australia and I could give an identity artist a mental image although they might think that I'm overdue an appointment with the police shrink.'

'Do it Pete at least we would have a face. It's interesting that you think the child is a woman.'

'Why?'

'There was somebody watching me in my dream as I was chasing this hooded shadow. It was the maid from Edington Hall.' He told her about the suitcase and contents.

'*Fuck* this case gets weirder. I'm beginning to believe in this hocus-pocus stuff.'

'Like a voice from the grave.'

Byrne put down his mug of tea. He lent across the table top.

'Yesterday, walking around knocking on doors I had thoughts going around inside my head. If I'm honest I wondered if they were just thoughts or like you voices!'

Atherton grinned holding up his hands to placate any backlash.

'I'm not mocking you Pete. My Aunt Bessie on my mother's side, she dabbles in the odd medium reading mainly to entertain her oldest friends. She's not a full-blown medium but she's pretty gifted. She believes that I get my feelings from my grandmother, whether that's true or not I can't discount or prove it either way. What my aunt did tell me once was that when we're in tune with the dead, like a police officer would be, we pick up certain vibes, voices or sensations. We call a gut reaction but I believe that we're being guided by the other side!'

Byrne laughed catching the attention of some of the customers nearest their table.

'Right now I'll go along with anything, although if it turns out to be the pizza I'll stick with Chinese in future.'

'Maybe somebody is reaching out and trying to guide us, who knows!'

Byrne's expression changed.

'If that's the case then we should go see your aunt.' He watched as Atherton's jaw dropped. 'I'm serious. After the fire last night and how we're both losing sleep we need to know who it is that's reaching out!'

From their table they finished their breakfast watching the small crowd that had gathered on the cordon side of the tape put in place by the fire service. Every so often a plume of smoke changed from a dirty black to white steam where water had been sprayed over a hot spot. Looking at the crowd Atherton wanted to know how Lucy was doing with collecting photographs from the press.

'Not bad, she's got a decent file together. She and Tim are going through the images looking for known faces.'

Atherton nodded. 'Somebody must have followed you to the records office yesterday.'

'I know, sends a chill down your spine knowing that you're being watched. Did the offenders get anything from the break-in at the estate office?'

'No. Reg Cullen reckons it was only some local kids putting the wind up the farm workers only there was petty cash in the safe and it wasn't touched. CSI have some glass samples with some blood, so our offender cut themselves at some point.'

'I think from now on Pete if we go to a scene or investigate a crime we go anywhere in two cars, one following but far enough back to see if any other vehicle intervenes on route or when we arrive. Let's join this game of cat and mouse. You never know we might strike lucky!'

163

When they left the café they headed back to the cars. Neither Atherton nor Byrne saw the dark blue van which was parked the other end of the fire appliances from where they had parked.

The hooded driver sat behind the steering wheel holding a paper as he kept watch of the rear view mirror. With a sudden loud bang and screech of twisted metal the records building collapsed in a heap of steam, smoke and cloud of dust. The van driver fisted a moment of triumph as he folded the paper placing it on the passenger seat before starting the engine. Along with the ashes and broken brick the Benson family name was now lost forever.

Chapter Fourteen

They found Marjorie alone in her laboratory where Atherton was keen to ensure that Gabrielle was safe. His dream, vision or whatever had been so real.

'She's fine. I'm sorry that I didn't get back to but my mobile battery died on me. I must have left it on during the court hearing. Tom and Gabrielle are on their way to a local school where the administrative office got ransacked overnight.

'Kids probably,' added Byrne. Atherton was less tense knowing that Gabrielle was with someone.

'You still worried about her?' asked Marjorie pleased that he took the time to care.

'Yes. I checked out where she lived yesterday to make sure nothing was amiss. I'm concerned also that she might have a stalker.'

'I did talk with Gabrielle first thing this morning. She would like time to think about having a camera installed knowing where best it could be hidden but I did persuade her to have a panic alarm with a direct link to the station.'

'Fair enough, keep me posted please if we can help. How are the shotguns doing?'

Marjorie went into the airtight room and returned with the shotguns lying on top of a stainless steel trolley. Most of the mud had hardened, cracked and broken away in lumps leaving the firearms almost clean. Marjorie checked close and suggested that they left them another half an hour whereby they'd be ready to examine.

'Any joy with the contents of the case?'

This time she smiled returning with the bag.

'My contact at the lingerie company did a check of their stock ledgers and found that most imports came from France in the late fifties and sixties.

This particular brand was very popular throughout the period and still is to the discerning customer. *Stafford's* sold several hundred according to the sales ledger.' She handed Atherton a print copy of the ledger that had been faxed across.

'I conducted a series of tests and managed to find some interesting results, more so on the panties. Caught in between the fibres were small strands of hair, one belonging to a man the other a woman. Further tests revealed the man's belonged to Arthur Benson, the other a woman although at this point we don't know who. This bit however will blow you away. Gabrielle and I double checked the test results and there was a definite match. Both hair trace had a compatible cross-matched sequence in the chromosomes.'

'Indicating that the underwear belonged to a relative of Arthur Benson.'

'Precisely.'

'Evelyn Benson perhaps?' asked Atherton.

'No. I have the post-mortem results from Matthew Hargreaves and although there are obvious similarities, the chromosomes found on the garment are stronger, suggesting a brother and sister.'

'Possible incest,' Pete Byrne suggested.

'That could well be the case detective.'

Atherton looked at the screen where Marjorie had pulled up the coroner's report.

'No wonder Arthur hid them around back of the hot water cylinder. He was hiding his shame.'

'He could have burnt them!' implied Byrne.

Atherton shook his head. 'Sentimental reasons I would suspect.' He looked at Marjorie 'and not just because of any sexual inference but because they meant something special.' Marjorie nodded in agreement.

'Was any semen present?'

Marjorie checked the analysis printout. 'No, none present although any trace could have been easily washed away.'

'So until we identify the owner we're not really any closer!'

'That's about the size of it Daniel.'

He thanked her anyway.

'Did you hear about the fire at the County Records Office?'

'Yes, control told me about it when I arrived this morning, an odd place to burn down not unless you have something to hide.'

'Like a family history,' added Byrne.

'That was my first thought,' Marjorie responded. 'Like our perpetrator could be disposing of a trail that could lead to his front door!'

She held up the undergarments. 'Well, he obviously didn't know about these. Gabrielle was going through DNA analysis to see if anything threw up another match but so far we've not had the result back. It would be nice if it gave us a name.'

'And if it doesn't,' what next?'

She smiled at Pete Byrne 'Keep remaining optimistic detective.' From her desk drawer she produced another bag very similar to the one containing the underwear. 'If we place an almost identical set of underwear in my bag and replace it around back of the hot water cylinder we can set a trap with cameras and a trip senor to see if anybody comes to collect the bag. It's quite gloomy on the landing in Arthur Benson's house and would easily fool somebody until they examined it in better light, by then we should have the cat in the bag!'

Atherton nodded, he liked it. 'That would work. How soon can you set it up?'

'I'll contact the tech boys and get them to do it as a priority.'

'That's *fucking* brilliant Marjorie.' Pete Byrne realised his outburst and instantly apologised.

'That's okay, it's nice to know that we're on the same wavelength.' She smiled as she looked at Daniel Atherton.

She asked them to wait a few seconds while she went back into the airtight room. A moment later she returned holding the suitcase.

'I have one last surprise before you leave.'

'Blimey, Anne and I had one like that when we went on our honeymoon!'

'You didn't take a lot away with you then?' Atherton said

Byrne grinned 'we didn't need much in the way of clothing!'

Marjorie coughed. 'If we could get back to the matter in hand gentlemen.' She carefully removed the bible, bed socks and the nightdress looking at Pete Byrne.

'I doubt you had any of these on the honeymoon!'

He didn't reply just grinned.

She carefully unfolded the nightdress. 'Another test we performed produced another surprise. The bodily evidence found on the nightdress match the underwear found in the bag from Arthur Benson's hot water cylinder.'

Pete Byrne's jaw dropped. 'The personnel records at Chopping & Sons show that he left school on a Friday and started that Monday at the mill as an apprentice engineer. He was never in service at Edington Hall.'

'That's great work Marjorie,' Atherton congratulated her. 'We're beginning to get a picture. Somebody in the Benson family, a female worked at Edington Hall. The suitcase found in the attic bedroom suggests a maid. The late Roger Edington was a rapist, abusing many of the female staff. It certainly gives us a motive and why our killer went to the wood that night. Richard Edington's death could well have been because he was in the wrong place at the wrong time. The killer just wanted the master of the house.'

With Marjorie's permission Pete Byrne picked up the bible.

'My sister used to own one like this when we were little and sharing a bedroom. At night I would hear her reading. She was the holy one of the family.' He read the inscription written in pencil. 'Doesn't exactly fill you with cheer, does it?'

Marjorie was the first to respond.

'I find it extremely saddening. The bible was her only solace.'

'I've an idea, I'll be back in a minute.'

Atherton got up and left going to his office. He returned a couple of minutes later with the photograph taken in the park.

'I would wager my next month's salary on the girl sitting on the bench as being the sister.'

'Why?' asked Byrne.

'Look at her eyes Pete, they have a similar shape to that of Arthur Benson.'

Putting the photograph on a magnifier screen Marjorie brought up the image as best she could before it became too distorted.

'She looks distracted,' said Marjorie 'as though she is daydreaming.'

'Girls that age do,' added Byrne 'my girls daydream a lot!'

Marjorie nodded but she examined the picture closer. 'I could have photographic enhance this and see if we can get a better image, better than our magnifier.' Atherton was happy to leave the arrangements with Marjorie.

'I wonder where that photograph was taken?' she asked more to herself than them.

'I know somebody who would probably know.'

Atherton caught on fast 'Millicent Watkins.'

They were surprised although happy to see Gabrielle George walk back into the lab, she looked happy and extremely relaxed.

'There's not much to the job at Paston High and Tom said that he could handle it. I thought my time would be better served back here.' She looked at the image of the children playing. 'They look happy!'

'Maybe,' Marjorie replied as she watched Gabrielle go closer to the screen 'we were just wondering where it was taken?'

Gabrielle looked away from the magnifier. 'I played in this park when I was a kid. This is Beacon Heights Park.'

'Gabrielle's right,' exclaimed Pete Byrne 'I should have recognised it. That's not far from where you live now, is it?' he asked her.

Gabrielle frowned 'Not far, why is that important?'

'Not anything that you should be concerned about,' replied Daniel Atherton 'but you have just saved us valuable time on an enquiry and Pete Byrne another embarrassing visit!'

Gabrielle beamed enthusiastically *'really!'*

'You bet you have,' replied Byrne 'and you're now top of my Christmas card list!'

Atherton and Byrne went to Beacon Heights taking a copy of the photograph with them. Much had changed over the years, bushes had grown as had the trees in the background. The skyline looked different too with the introduction of buildings. The one thing that had not changed was children's play area although instead of concrete the surface was a rubberised matting. The slide and the line of swings were new although the roundabout had disappeared considered too dangerous by the authorities.

Pete Byrne pushed open the gate to the play area.

'When the 'wheel man killer' case was at its height we found one of the victim's here in the park. Despite being traumatised and injured she had made out that she was dead eventually walking, staggering and crawling here. A dog walker or more the dog found here next morning lying in the bushes near to one of the exits. She was alive thank god!'

'Could she describe her attacker?' Atherton asked.

'Not as though you could give the papers anything to go on. Lying in a hospital bed she told us that she had been abducted on the way home having spent the evening serving as a waitress in a restaurant over Addleton Street way. Without any warning her attacker had struck from behind before dragging her to the railway sidings where she was clubbed again and raped. By good fortune she was the only victim not to be chained to a carriage wheel.'

Atherton thought that was interesting. Byrne continued.

'She regained consciousness the moment that the perpetrator was rearranging his trousers. Realising what had taken place by the arrangement of her clothes and the pain she felt down below she saw her only option was to feign death until he left. When questioned she told detectives that her attacker was of regular height, white with short dark hair and normal build. The only distinguishing feature however was a tattoo on his right hip.

'The illumination near the engineering works was dimly lit although she was adamant that the tattoo resembled a pair of fish, possibly two snakes or maybe a couple of dolphins. She didn't remember much until she reached the entrance to the park where she heard footsteps coming her way. Hiding herself in the bushes she passed out being woken the next morning by the dog licking her face.'

'Do you remember where she lived?' asked Atherton.

'Crofters Lodge not that far from Hunter's View.'

Atherton watched a young mother arrive, she smiled at them both before letting her young son charge through the gate and head for the slide.

'She was lucky to be alive. Does she still around here?'

'No. She shared a flat with another couple of girls but after the attack they gave up the house that shared and moved back home to live with their parents. I can't blame them as I'd have done the same in their position.'

'I bet the press had a field day with her story?'

'More or less. The Chief Constable at the time was an impatient bugger and wanted results but having little to go on we kept going down a dark alley and hitting a brick wall. Soon the public lost confidence in our abilities and the press hounded us. It's odd, we don't commit the crime and yet we get blamed for what we cannot resolve. Very little blame is apportioned to the perpetrator.'

'The law of the jungle Pete.'

'It's why I don't have a lot of patience with any of their number or our Jasmin Yates.'

From the park they walked to where Atherton had stood on the footbridge the day before, where he had observed the wheel tapper carrying out his checks.

'Did anybody on the task force consider the perpetrator to be a railway worker?' He asked.

'Sure, we checked out every male employee but they all had alibis.'

Atherton seemed pensive as he thought. It was noted by Byrne.

'What are you thinking?'

'I know that this is possibly unrelated to our latest case but your man, he'd be a lot older now wouldn't he?'

'Yes, why?'

'I was just wondering if he's the one watching Gabrielle.'

Byrne suddenly leant over the handrail looking down at the rolling stock below. You could hear the engineers in the shed working but otherwise there was nobody else about.

'At the end of a shift I'd come here and stand on this bridge looking for inspiration, something that would help. I would dread hearing the news that another young girl or woman had been taken overnight and found murdered. I wasn't married back then but the torment that I felt inside was no less easy.'

He turned and looked at Daniel Atherton standing beside him 'Being junior to the team I was one of the fortunate ones as I didn't have to go the door of a mother, father, sister or a brother and deliver the agony message. Thing is, despite my involvement I can still see the anguish in the eyes of the aggrieved as they received the news that one of their loved one's had been viciously taken from them. The public say the police don't feel anything inside when something tragic happens, that we're immune only I know that I do.'

'If it helps Pete, I feel the same. We wouldn't be human if we didn't. Did you tell anybody on the enquiry how you felt?'

He shook his head. 'No, back then you had to be macho and keep your sentiments to yourself, unlike now you can go have a cosy chat, a cup a tea and a biscuit with a psychoanalyst. Back then I would have probably been booted off the investigation.'

Byrne turned around and put his back against the handrail and give his elbows a rest.

'Thing is Daniel,' it was the first time that he had used Atherton's first name 'I had my suspicions. Had I spoken up and said what I thought I might have prevented other victim's from been cruelly assaulted and dying!'

Their conversation was interrupted by a call from Marjorie who told them that the team had eliminated several sets of fingerprints from the stock and barrels of both shotguns, apart from the owners and Reg Cullen there was another set present but they matched nobody in the system. Thanking her he ended the call.

'I suppose that means that were back with an unknown person hiding in the woods, an illegal poacher as Tavistock likes to think.'

Byrne nodded although his thoughts were better focused.

'Gregory Tavistock was my number one suspect!'

Atherton looked amazed and astonished.

'How and why Pete, that's some suspicion!'

'He was a funny bugger, a loner and always going on about women. Most men like to do a bit of window shopping but with Tavistock it's like an obsession. I couldn't explain it only it's why I never said anything but like you said you get a gut feeling for something, until you chase it down it don't go away. Secondly whenever we had another attack Tavistock would be missing, allegedly chasing down a line of enquiry. Lastly, the perp was always one step ahead of us as though they knew what we were thinking.'

'That's a lot of supposition Pete, although I would agree with the gut reaction. My suspicions were heightened when I found out that he was good friends with Sir Roger Edington.'

*****

Millicent was thrilled to see Pete Byrne return so soon although disappointed that he was accompanied by Atherton. Having made coffee she promptly sat herself down alongside the older man purring like a Cheshire cat. They showed her the photograph of the children in the park.

'Is there anything that you can say about the location or the children in the picture?'

Millicent reached for her reading glasses promptly dropping them onto the bridge of her nose.

'This is the park at Beacon Heights, as kids we would go there nearly day after school. I loved that park, we'd spend all summer there.'

With the tip of her fingernail she traced the outline of the slide, the roundabout and long rocking horse.

'The boy on the slide is Jeremy Redding an obnoxious little shit. He would pull the girls hair most days and worse if you had a ponytail. When he was older he'd try and steal kiss when you least expected him to be about, a real pest.'

Byrne wondered just how many men had been in Marjorie's growing up.

'Standing at the bottom of the slide is Margaret Henry she lived next door to Jeremy.' Tapping the side of her nose the names started to materialise again. 'Ah yes, there's Yvette Anderson and Erica Spinksworth, they were both in my class at school.'

Millicent suddenly prodded her fingertip several times on the face of the boy climbing the metal ladder of the slide *'goodness that's Arthur... little Arthur Benson!'*

'And the girl sitting all alone on the bench, do you recognise her Millicent?' asked Atherton.

She shook her head then changed it to a nod. 'I remember her being there, she was Arthur's little sister only she didn't join in with our games. We thought that she was a stuck up little bitch but Arthur told us that she was only shy. As hard as I try I can't remember her name though!'

'And you say that you all went to the same school, including the younger sister?

'That's right, first nursery, then St. Matilda's for junior and finally Havenscroft Senior. Arthur Benson was in my year, only not my class.'

175

She gave the photo back. 'Is there a reward for information only you see it on the television, they're always lobbing tenner's here and there!'

'Only if we catch the culprit,' replied Atherton with a smile.

They finished with Millicent going back to the car.

'Where to now?' asked Byrne sitting in the passenger seat.

'St. Matilda's, they should have a record of Arthur's sibling.'

At the school the secretary asked them to wait in the staff room going to find the head teacher. At first she had been reluctant to give any information unless they had a warrant but Pete Byrne had insisted that it was a matter of urgency in relation to a murder enquiry, several to be precise.

Ten minutes later she produced a school ledger record for the decade that they wanted. There were two entries, made ten years after the Second World War.

Arthur Benson – born: 27th February 1955. Residing at 84 Lincoln Road, Southport; and a Ruth A Benson – born: 12th September 1957. Half-sister to Arthur Benson. Also resident at same address of 84 Lincoln Road.

In brackets there was an additional explanation as to the reason why Arthurs' mother Elizabeth Benson had been killed in the spring of nineteen fifty six, when the bus she had been travelling home on having attended the hospital was involved in a serious road traffic accident with a lorry carrying building bricks. Elizabeth Benson died of her injuries the same night. Mr Stanley Benson, father of Arthur remarried Evelyn Mullins in January nineteen fifty seven whereupon in the September of that year she gave birth to a girl, Ruth Ann Benson.

Despite a second search of the school archives there was no photograph of either pupil.

'Now...' said Atherton we head to St. Cuthbert's at Alton Cross and check out that headstone, I want to see where it ties in with all of this.'

*****

The church and grounds was the same as a good many others in the area that had been ravaged by fierce winds and salt from the Irish Sea. They located the headstone in the picture which was slightly angled as though having been pushed up from the soul in the box beneath the earth. Up close it was easy to read the inscription.

'Sister Sarah, Here lieth an angel of the lord, lost in the cruel challenge of life only not left behind'

'What the hell does that mean?' asked Byrne.

'I have no idea Pete. Let's see if anybody is in the church that can help.'

Arriving at the church door they found it locked. Pinned to the side panel was a laminated notice informing visitors that the inside of the church was undergoing extensive restoration stating that any enquiries should be directed to the Deacon, there was a number which Byrne saved to his phone. He pressed the key and waited for a ringtone. Seconds later the call went to voicemail.

Chapter sixteen

Wednesday Morning

Daniel Atherton sat at his desk studying the photograph. The girl on the bench, Ruth Ann Benson stared back at him her eyes looking directly ahead, at him looking through him. The longer he studied the image the more she became a ghost.

With the thud of a heel to push open the door Pete Byrne walked in carrying two coffees setting them down on the desk top.

'I was thinking as I watched the kettle boil, we seem to have been walking through a smoke screen these past few days!'

Atherton took the coffee and nodded his thanks. 'How and in what way?'

'Dreams, thoughts and having evidence taken from under our feet. I was thinking maybe our killer is playing a game. Psychopaths do play games, leave clues and remove evidence. They want to see how good we are at finding them. I was thinking he knew that photograph of the park would be found so let's say he knew Arthur and Ruth Benson were playing in the park, it was only a matter of time before we made the connection.'

Byrne sat back and drank the coffee, it was too hot to gulp so he sipped at the edge of the mug. Atherton had an idea where Byrne was heading.

'Gabrielle and Tom went to a report of a break-in at Paston High and not St Matilda's. Now let's say that he went to Paston High, so he took his own record not that they would probably know it was missing but he forgot about the records held at St Matilda's, then his smoke screen was flawed. Sooner or later Pete, he will tie himself up in knots. That's when mistakes start to occur.'

Atherton also sipped from the side of his mug.

'We're on the same wavelength.'

Byrne nodded. 'Going back to the footbridge yesterday brought it all back. I've been mulling it over and over in my mind.'

Daniel Atherton sensed that his partner was deep in thought so he let the silence do the thinking, realising that he had relied upon the quiet times himself before. After a few seconds it worked.

'Do you remember those televised portrayals of the Ripper cases, where the cameraman zoomed in and out of a darkened alley as the face of the victim, frozen in horror realised that escape was no longer an option so instead the woman accepted death as a happy release. For the past few nights I have been that camera lens going back and forth. Around four this morning I ended up downstairs by myself crying my eyes out because I had not done more to save them, but when I stopped crying a voice inside my head told me that it was okay and that I was forgiven.'

Atherton listened as Byrne continued.

'The thing is the face that I keep seeing is not from the railway murders but somebody connected to our current investigation, an older version of the child sitting on the bench. It's here that I've been seeing her in my dreams.

'Arthur might have got his jollies hanging onto his sisters knickers doing the unmentionable whenever he felt like it, but I reckon our killer knew about this perverse depravity and that's why Arthur Benson had to die. The parents knew about the incest and that was the reason that he murdered them. This wasn't necessarily a family feud but a revenge attack.'

'But I though the love child was a girl and living in Australia.'

'That's what that old duffer said but he didn't have all his marbles intact most of the time. The child could have been a boy and living in England.'

Byrne lubricated his throat with the coffee. 'Shall I go on?'

'I'm listening, replied Atherton, his index fingers placed either side of his temples as he mentally created a picture in his mind of what Byrne was saying.

'Was the photograph of the gravestone a red-herring or to offer help, I believe the latter. Sister Sarah plays a part in the investigation but as yet we don't know where. My theory however is that she could be the sister, Ruth Benson.'

Atherton grinned over the top of his mug.

'I'm thinking we should go revisit our crime scenes more often and just stand there Pete and have a damn good think. Sister Sarah would make sense.'

There was a rap on the door and Marjorie walked in.

'I'm sorry if I'm interrupting but I thought this was important. I think you'd best come to the lab.'

On the workbench was the vintage suitcase that had been found under the wardrobe in Mary Thomas's attic bedroom.

'I had a strange feeling that I needed to re-examine the case and I'm glad that I did only I found something.'

She flicked open the catch and raised the lid removing the contents that they already knew about. Picking up a pair of tweezers she carefully peeled back the side lining to reveal a folded piece of paper. She left the find in place but instead showed them a photocopy that she had produced moments before coming to find them.

'My sins are known and I shall be damned in hell for all eternity. I am shamed in the eyes of the lord and all who despise me, including those that I love the most. I feel the dread of my being here and I am so desperately alone with nobody to turn to, not even my brother.

What he does with me, he says is right and that we should feel no shame. I know however in my heart that I am wrong and that I have wronged. God will punish me as he sees fit.

I pray with all my heart and soul that my son is safe and that he will grow to be a much better man than I am a mother. God please forgive me!'

Ruth

For several moments the lab remained silent as Atherton and Byrne read through the content of the note again, digesting every word, every punctuation. The meaning of why it had been written piercing their hearts.

'I think that you've just found the mother of our love child, Marjorie.'

Marjorie replaced the items back in the case and closed the lid, gently pressing the clasp into place hearing it click shut.

'I have a theory,' she said.

'And we'd like to hear it!' replied Atherton.

'My gut reaction is that Ruth Benson, sister to Arthur was forced to have sex with him which as a result she conceived a child by his doing and for whatever reason ended up at Edington Hall where she received more abuse.

'As the note explains she was damned and lived out the employment as a living hell. This is a proclamation, an acceptance of her sins in the eyes of the lord and all who have loved her. She herself has damned her soul to eternal darkness and yet she was not to blame.

'I know that we should remain detached from any investigation but the note broke my heart when I read it.'

Quite surprisingly Pete Byrne was the first to place a comforting hand upon Marjorie's shoulder.

'Secrets can be painful sin Marjorie and I know only too well, how painful. We will find the son although I feel that others to whom she refers have already met with their maker!'

'Thank you.'

He let his hand slip away and back down his side.

'You know, I have two young daughters at home and it would destroy me to know of any suffering that would endure. I am at a loss to know how Arthur and the Bensons could have allowed this to happen.'

'In which case we owe it to Ruth Benson to resolve this matter. Is everything set up at the house?' he asked.

Marjorie pulled over a sketch of the interior of seventy two Parkway Drive. She pointed to where a motion sensor had been placed along with two hidden cameras.

'Even a ghost would have trouble find these.' She replied.

'And what about Gabrielle has she agreed to the installation of a camera in her flat?'

'Yes, she has now. When she was about to go to bed last night she pulled back the curtain in her bedroom and caught the glimpse of a stranger watching from the shadows opposite. She's going home this afternoon with the tech boys so that she can advise them as to where it's best to put the cameras without invading her privacy.'

'That's good, at least we can all rest easy now at night knowing that she's safe. Can I have a copy of that note please?'

Marjorie hit the print key on her laptop and instantly produced a copy. They were about to leave when Lucy Fancham poked her head around the lab door.

'Sorry sarge, we've just got word from control of another murder!'

Part Two

Chapter Seventeen

Wednesday Mid-Morning

'Here we go again,' Byrne said 'we didn't have to wait long for his next move!'

Lucy Fancham shrugged her shoulders apologetically. 'It's been a busy couple of weeks and it's not getting any easier.'

'Where are we going?' asked Atherton.

'Seven Wentworth Avenue, the joint home of Hannah Blackburn and a partner. The deceased was found by the female partner, a Judith Venebles.'

Pete Byrne looked at Daniel Atherton but he was looking directly ahead refusing to become involved in a discussion regarding same sex relationships.

'Right,' said Marjorie 'I'll go get my gear and troops together, we'll meet you there!'

Sticking to the original plan Atherton and Lucy went in one car with Pete Byrne teaming up with Tim Robbins following in the car behind. Lucy looked slightly bemused.

'Don't worry, I'll explain why on route.'

Within minutes the two vehicles were speeding away from the rear yard of the station heading towards the call. Watching from his top floor office window Gregory Tavistock wondered where they were going.

'Have we any idea what our hooded man looks like?' asked Lucy as Atherton took a roundabout at speed.

Decelerating to take the third junction Atherton changed gear without indicating.

'No, that's why Pete and Tim have teamed up and are hanging back. We want to see if we can trap our man in between cars only the stills that you got from the press definitely show a figure standing at the back of the crowd wearing a dark coloured hoodie. Although we cannot see the man's face, what we've established so far from evidence we believe that we could be dealing with Arthur Benson's love child.'

By the time that they arrived the crowd of spectators, gawkers and youths had already gathered along with one or two of the press. Atherton and Fancham pushed their way under the cordon.

'It always surprises me how they get to know what's happening often before we do!'

Atherton scoffed 'If it didn't know better I would say that somebody gives them the heads-up, realistically it would only take a text message!'

Fancham was no stranger to adversity. A male colleague with whom she had trained had been sacked for such a misdemeanour divulging sensitive information to a member of the press for cash. At the time all twelve in the squad had been under scrutiny. Even now it had left a bad taste in her mouth.

At the door leading into the address the entrance was guarded by Amanda Jones.

'Have you been inside?' asked Atherton.

Jones shook her head. 'Not this time sarge. Simon Preston is protecting the scene.'

'That's good, keep the hounds at bay for as long as you can, additional help is on its way!'

Crossing the threshold they found Preston waiting inside.

'Back bedroom sarge, you can't miss it!' he smiled at Lucy Fancham.

Pushing open the bottom of the door with his toecap Atherton stood momentarily in the doorway absorbing the scene, feeling the energy in the room.

'Are you okay?' Lucy asked.

'I'm fine Lucy. I like to close my eyes and let the scene tell me what's happening. You should try it sometime you'll be surprised at what else you see.'

She closed her eyes and from behind her eyelids she immediately saw the room upon which they had just arrived. The figure on the bed was a blur but all around she saw other things, colours and lights. When she opened them again Atherton was watching.

'Interesting isn't it.'

'It sure is, it gives a scene a different perspective like a slow moving film.'

He kicked a loose shoe against the door to stop it closing on them. 'The same as I like an escape route in case the dead decide to leave before I do!' He smiled to show that he was jesting.

Beside the dressing table a large document box had been overturned and the contents tipped out haphazardly creating a mess underneath the window. On the bed, representing a crucifixion was a woman, her throat cut and almost naked.

Both wrists had been tied to the corner posts of the headboard and pulled tight. The clothing from the waist up had been shredded with a sharp instrument lying in strips across the bed and floor. More bizarre, disturbing was the crimson message carved into her chest which was made up of one word *'Judas'*.

'Well that about sums up what the killer thought of his victim!' said Fancham as she checked the pulse of the victim.

Under her chin the neck had been cut in one quick slice left to right. The blood splatter was instant covering the breasts and shoulders. Lying beside the bed Lucy found a sharp boning knife. Where it lay had stained the carpet.

'Unlike the other scenes this was calculated, timed to perfection. The victim has a live-in partner so the killer would have struck when the place was only occupied by one person, the victim.'

Atherton was happy to let Lucy record verbally what she saw.

'Interesting that she is about the same age as Arthur Benson, wouldn't you agree?'

Atherton came closer to check. 'About the same,' he agreed 'how's that relevant?'

'I was looking for a connection. Place of work, same school, same youth club or dance hall.'

'That's good, anything else Lucy?'

Fancham was different to Pete Byrne, she voiced everything she noticed as though repeating what she saw so as not to forget. He was pleased to have the opportunity to work with her, she was bright and enthusiastic, eager to progress like he had.

'The strewn papers means he was after something, a document, a photograph maybe?'

Lying underneath the bedroom window were old psychology reports, medical histories, school reports and letters from various legal services.

'It's odd that she should have reports like this at home.' Lucy mentioned as she pushed the aside with the end of a pen.

Downstairs the front door was still open, there was a slight chill in the air which was to their advantage when suddenly lying dead on the bed Hannah Blackburn blew apart her lips and discharge a cloud of stomach gases. At the same time blood poured from her mouth.

'That's not right!'

Atherton checked. He was almost near the end of the bed when he saw something lying on the carpet next to his shoe. It was the woman's tongue.

Lucy Fancham rushed to the bathroom and used the pan flushing a few moments later. She rinsed her face in the sink then came back sheepishly to where Atherton had placed a ceramic dish over the tongue.

'I'm sorry sarge that's never affected me like that before!'

186

'Forget it Lucy, we've all been there and that is unusual.'

'What with the chest and the tongue this is some message.'

Atherton nodded. 'Yes. What I'd like to know is what he was after. Can you have a scout around the room and see what else you can find.'

'Surely somebody must have heard her scream?'

Again he saw the tiny pin prick to the side of her neck.

'No,' he pointed 'a syringe insertion, the killer administers enough pentobarbital to render the victim immobile where without the use of any limbs they are useless to defend themselves. I expect he threatened her with the knife, got what he came for before he cut out her tongue and slit her throat.

'But her tongue,' she stressed 'why that?'

The blood had stopped running from between the deceased lips.

'So that she couldn't tell anybody about her innocence, that's my theory.'

Lying beside the pillow was a thin gold chain and crucifix.

On the stairs behind Marjorie and her team had arrived. Atherton suggested to Lucy that they leave everything to CSI and come back when they had finished. Before they left Atherton told Marjorie about what was under the dish and about the boning knife down the side of the bed.

'When you make your examination I would be interested to know what knot was used to tie the victim's hands to the bedposts only I've a strange notion that it will match the one used to tie the Benson's to the kitchen chairs.'

Marjorie took her digital camera from the side pouch and handed it to Tom Skerritt.

'Start getting everything you can from the front door, up the stairs to the bedroom. I'll check out this room with Gabrielle.'

Atherton and Lucy waited on the landing until they could go back in but when Marjorie came out several minutes later suggesting that they join her again they were surprised having expected the wait to be much longer, once inside she closed the door.

'I know that you'd need to see this...!'

Written in the deceased's blood and on the back of the door panel was a message.

'There are secrets that are meant to be discovered and some that are not. How many more will die before the end of the week'.

Marjorie called Tom back up with his camera and had him photograph the back of the door.

'This was almost certainly done a few hours before the call came in, the blood is almost dry.'

'Done with a finger?' asked Atherton.

'A glove probably.'

Marjorie took a glass slide from her bag of tricks and breathed heavily onto the back creating a misty surface. She pulled the tip of her gloved finger across the glass creating a wide smear. 'The letter case dynamics are too wide for a finger, gloved it gains width. We won't get anything from the smears.'

'Well we have his style of writing. The loops, curves and straight edges. It's better than nothing!'

Checking beneath the bed she was surprised to find a small gathering of blood as it dripped down from the mattress above and in the en-suite Gabrielle George found a pair of eyelash scissors with a trace of blood on the cutting edge. She bagged and tagged them, giving the label a reference. She showed them to Marjorie.

'We need to check her back because I think there's a puncture wound which has seeped through the mattress although I'm inclined to wait until Michael Hargreaves arrives before we move anything.'

'Her lungs?' Atherton asked.

Marjorie nodded 'That's my guess.'

'He was certainly brutal,' remarked Lucy. 'He made sure the victim suffered.'

'He was thorough,' added Atherton. 'And I'd go so far as to say that this all happened before he tied her to the bed. If he administered the pentobarbital as soon as he was inside the front door then brought her upstairs puncturing her lung, the fear of her drowning in her own blood would have been enough to render her submissive to his demands. Tying her to the bed was part of the torture as was the tearing of her clothes, all part of his demonstration of power. I don't consider that there was anything sexual about this attack other than humiliation. Cutting her tongue was out of spite, anger maybe...'

'Or revenge,' Lucy added.

'Yes, revenge and ending her life by cutting her throat the final act of recrimination.'

'And her chest?' asked Marjorie.

'What he believed her to be, a traitor!'

Lucy shuddered as a sudden cold draught entered the room. It hung around in the air refusing to leave. 'That was chilling, macabre.'

'As chilling as our killer,' Marjorie reminded Atherton.

'Indeed, welcome to the world of the psychotic killer.' He looked at Lucy. 'Revenge is a powerful weapon and murder an expression, a purpose to end the confusion. Very often something triggers a memory in the killer's mind, a bad memory that needs to be put right. This whole case is all about retribution.'

'The worrying part of the message,' she said pointing at the back of the door 'is how many more need die!'

Atherton agreed 'Yes that concerns me also. We need to catch this man and soon!'

From the floor below the sound of an agonised wailing commenced coming first as convulsive gasps and then as a whimpering moans, bewilderment, anger and a feeling of being lost.

'The partner who called it in?' asked Atherton.

'Probably,' replied Lucy, 'maybe I'd better help downstairs,' Lucy suggested. Atherton agreed, he suggested that Lucy have Simon Preston call Amanda Jones in to help. The muffled ringtone in his pocket signalled that he had a call.

'How's it going in there?' asked Byrne.

'Pretty much the same as before only with a hint of narcissism attached.'

'That good eh...' Byrne took another look from where he was standing. 'Our hoodies not here!'

'Where's Tim?'

'Still out walking the block. My route was shorter.'

Atherton suggested that Byrne leave Tim wandering for the meantime and for him to them in the house.

When Pete Byrne saw the message on the back of the bedroom door he was less surprised than Atherton had expected.

'We used to get these,' he said 'spray painted down the side of railway carriages. The bastard would taunt us, mock us.'

Byrne went over to the bed taking his time to look at Hannah Blackburn. Her eyes were fixed on the ceiling above as though she had been defiant to the end not heeding the threats given by the killer. He noticed the disarray of records under the window.

'He's looking for something that he knows will bring him down, something he needs to destroy!'

There was not much they could do in the upper floor so Atherton left Byrne with Marjorie to see if a fresh pair of eyes would spot something that he had missed.

Judith Venebles was still wiping the tears from her eyes when Atherton sat next to Lucy as Amanda Jones comforted the stricken woman. The detectives were sympathetic but they needed answers.

190

'We realise what a difficult time this for you Judith however it is imperative that we ask questions to help our investigation. The more that we know the quicker we will apprehend the offender.' He was careful not to say killer.

Wrapping the handkerchief tightly around the end of her finger she subconsciously appeared to be wringing somebody's neck.

'You're confident of catching him then!'

Lucy Fancham replied 'We will if we have all the facts.'

The response was demanding but needed to bring the woman back from her state of shock.

'He could attack somebody Judith and any help that you can give will possibly prevent that from happening!'

Atherton was patient expecting a response. He didn't mind Lucy's approach as long as they got answers. The message on the back of the door had been left as a warning that other attacks would take place.

'Hannah had no enemies. Her whole life all she had ever done is help people.'

'And her occupation?'

'She was a social worker.' Untying the knot a little she allowed the blood to flow to the end of her finger. 'Hannah retired three years ago. So many years in the same office, the same area helping the needy, the sick and the challenging residents of Stockport. Hannah was a highly respected professional, a team leader in the department.'

Lucy nodded acknowledging the dead woman's contribution.

'Outside of the office was there anybody else that she mentioned who might not have thought so highly of your partner, for instance a grieved party where the benefits hadn't arrived or been late?'

Judith Venebles sniffed hard clearing her nose into the handkerchief.

'No, Hannah was a diabetic so they gave her a team leader role and a desk job instead of field work. At first she bucked the idea, but realised her limitations so in time she accepted the change and actually felt that she could contribute as much from behind a desk as she could out in the field. I was happier because not everybody who opens the door can be that friendly, especially on the Babel Fields Estate.

'How long have you been together?' Lucy asked.

'Five years, eleven months. Next month would have been our sixth.' She added a twist to the handkerchief again. 'Why can't people just accept us for who we are and what we are?'

Lucy pushed further feeling that she would have the advantage over Atherton. 'Do you think that somebody amongst the same sex community could be jealous?'

Judith Venebles frowned as she gave the question some thought 'What after almost six years. I doubt it. If anything like that was going to happen then it normally does within the first few months.'

'How did you meet?' Lucy was relentless but thorough.

Holding her head up and straightening her back Venebles replied. 'Hannah was assigned to my case. I was an alcoholic and desperately in need of help and a place to stay. Initially she got me into rehab and then later managed to get me into a women's hostel. Unethical as it was professional, I had only been a resident a week when Hannah invited me around for dinner, after that I never went back to the hostel.'

'Do you work?'

'I'm employed behind the counter at Stafford Place, Green's the Turf Accountants. The way that I see it the job has a dual role, keeps me away from the bottle and being a predominantly all male environment prevents jealous arguments.' Venebles looked at Flemming as though she had just scored an emotional victory.

'Did you argue, is that what today was about?' asked Atherton quite out of the blue.

Judith Venebles had her mouth open, astonished that he would have the affront to ask such a question.

192

'Are you *fucking* me around detective?' She replied but Atherton didn't flinch just stared back demanding a response.

'After doing a bit of mid-morning shopping I got back home just before lunch leaving Hannah to sleep off a migraine that she'd had from the night before. When I opened the door there was no reply so I headed straight for the bedroom where I expected her to still be sleeping. What I saw was Hannah tied to the bed and mutilated. Whoever did this to my lovely Hannah should be strung up by his balls and left for the birds!'

Venebles realised how one sided her reply had sounded, she breathed in deep accepting that the question had, had to be asked. Trying to calm herself she continued.

'No we never argued. Hannah and I had a very good easy-go-lucky relationship. We enjoyed one another's company and shared the same bed. We were like any other couple and did not need to try, experiment in anything sordid or lewd.'

Atherton thanked her, allowing Lucy to intervene.

'How about neighbours, any long term disputes, gripes only they happen?'

She shook her head. 'No. We regularly see and speak with our neighbours. No doubt at first they were as surprised as many are to see two elderly women get together, but once the initial bombshell had settled we all got along fine.

'And professionally in the office, was anybody jealous of Hannah's promotion?'

'None that had come to Hannah's notice. Being in the profession the others in the office understood her health issues so accepted the change realising that Hannah could be just as helpful in whatever role she was given.'

'And as a couple, how do you think she took being retired. Some people find the transition difficult clambering to find something else to occupy their day, their mind?'

Venebles gave a shrug of her shoulders, reliving the vision in her mind of when they had sat in the sun together listening to the birds sing, sharing a coffee and planning the day.

'Hannah adapted well to the sudden change in her routine. Every morning except of course today she would rise around six, shower then dress. She would eat a small breakfast and by the time that I had done with my shower we would make fresh coffee and listen to the radio discussing anything that was topical. Every day was magical and relaxing. Together we enjoyed and celebrated her freedom and the time we shared with one another. Now I don't know how I will cope without here!'

Once again the tears began to well up producing large clear streaks as they ran down her cheeks, real tears full of pain, anguish and heartache.

'What kind of a monster does this sort of thing detective?' she looked accusingly at Atherton the only man in the room.

'The kind that we need to arrest.' He replied.

On one side of the mantelpiece he noticed an orange coloured bottle containing prescription medication.

'Which one of you was on tablets?'

Venebles turned to look at the bottle.

'Hannah. She'd only been on them a few days. She went to the doctors because she said that she felt menopausal albeit that she had already gone through the change, it can happen in older women. The doctor prescribed a low dosage antidepressant.'

'In the bedroom that you share there is a document box, did you notice it when you found Hannah?'

She nodded but did not reply.

'The box had been turned out and the papers looked through. Was there anything in the box of any specific interest?'

'Not that I was aware of although I did find it odd that Hannah kept the documents at home. Only last weekend I caught her going through the box. When I asked why she showed me a newspaper cutting where the parents of an Arthur Benson had been murdered around the same time that he had also met with an unfortunate end.'

'And you've no idea what she was looking for in relation to those murders?'

Again Judith Venebles shook her head wiping the damp from her cheeks.

'I tried to leave Hannah to her memories. She was very attached to some of her clients, that's all I can tell you sergeant.'

Judith Venebles sucked in air through her nostrils expanding her lungs accepting that, that was all she had left, memories.

'The box was a mystery,' she went on 'Hannah told me that every record was about somebody that had died. I found it a little macabre.'

'Did she keep any other records at home, secreted about the place?'

'No only the one document box.'

'One last question for now,' began Atherton 'has there been any strange callers lately, door-to-door salesmen and charity collectors, anybody wearing a hoodie?'

'None, although I cannot vouch for the hours spent at work. Why in particular a hoodie?' she looked puzzled.

'Just a hunch. We've had reports of a person matching a similar description in the area, it's one way of eliminating that person from the enquiry.'

Atherton excused himself from the room stating that Flemming and Jones would explain the procedure regarding the coroner and registration of the death. He took himself back upstairs to see if Byrne and Marjorie had made any progress.

'The knots used to tie her wrists and ankles, they're identical to the one used on Stanley and Evelyn Benson.'

'I thought that they would be.'

He told them about the conversation that he had been party to with Judith Venebles and how she had made the connection to the Benson murders.

'This web gets more entangled with each crime scene we attend.' Marjorie nodded. 'And the live-in lover,' asked Byrne 'what's her story?'

'I think she's innocent.' Replied Atherton. 'She came back around lunchtime and walked in to find her partner butchered. Not what you would expect after a trip to the shops.'

Atherton looked down at the document box then the papers that were now neatly piled. 'Did you find anything?'

'Only that the case files are stamped deceased. They're all dead people!'

'I know, that was what Judith Venebles told us. Seems a bit odd to keep such records?'

'Like she was expecting their ghosts to come calling?' Marjorie added.

Atherton was deep in thought.

'That was what I was thinking Marjorie only we're back to somebody reaching out from the grave. And Hannah Blackburn was going through the records over the weekend which seems almost pre-ominous.'

Marjorie showed him the evidence bag containing the cosmetic scissors.

'Gabrielle found a small hair in the ride of the scissors. We won't know to whom it belongs until we get it back to the laboratory.'

Byrne and Atherton checked the back service alley where the residents had their rubbish bins noting that the narrow passageway was awash with discarded cigarette packets, used condoms and fast-food cartons. Keeping step with one another they walked a circuit of the immediate block.

Both scanned the faces of the crowd out front but there was no hoodie in sight.

'How come he doesn't show today and yet he's been around every other crime scene? Again it's as though he's one step ahead of us, fuck it annoys me!'

'I know it's strange.' Replied Atherton, calmer but no less frustrated.

Standing at the corner where they had a commanding view of the press and crowd they saw a car pull up outside of the address and moments later Jasmin Yates emerge. She straightened her suit jacket before immediately taking her place in front of the press. They noticed that nobody was smiling an indicator that an individual was pleased about what had taken place inside.

A short distance from where they stood the occupant of a dark blue van adjusted his rear view mirror and watched the two detectives as they surveyed the street ahead. He smiled to himself. Not once did they look his way, not until he started the engine and slowly pulled away from the kerb heading in the opposite direction but even then their attention seemed focused elsewhere.

Walking back to the house Atherton was pensive.

'Maybe we've been going about this all wrong Pete, maybe we need to get inside the killer's head and read his thoughts, maybe then we can get ahead.'

Byrne shrugged his shoulders.

'Believe me I've been trying to do that ever since I joined the police force!'

Atherton smiled 'I think I know somebody who might be able to help.'

Chapter Eighteen

Late Wednesday Evening

When the man emerged from beneath the amber light of the partially enclosed porch the occupant of the van which had been parked in the shadows watched as the stranger lit a match, attached it to the end of the cigarette then promptly ignited the end into a red glow before discarding the wooden splinter aside.

There were some meetings of the grand lodge that could be tediously boring, the same inane speeches, balls in the black bag and endless chanting until another fool was admitted into the order. There were times when the smoker wondered why he had joined. Admittedly there were advantages where members in high places, members of the council, businessmen and dignitaries could help promote his building business and get it off the ground but everything he soon realised came at a price. Advocates of charitable support the men ruthlessly passionate about their secret order. Puffing away towards the end of his cigarette he was joined by another member attired in the same black suit, white shirt and black tie, the cloak draped down the back of their jacket.

'It won't be long now Terry,' said the other man as he encouragingly patted his friend on the shoulder 'then we will know if the committee finds your latest venture in favour. I'm sure they will as long as you are prepared to give something back!'

'I need this Bill I really do,' he replied stamping out the end of the cigarette on the stone step 'without the committee to back me I could go under!'

Encouragingly his comrade patted his shoulder 'Come on let's get back in and hear your fate.'

The occupant of the van chuckled. Fate, what a word. It held the world in the grip of fear, the unknown. Hope would have sounded better but very few believed in hope. He alone had given up long ago.

For a good two hours he had sat watching the driver in the four by four read his paper from cover to cover, consume a sandwich and drink from a flask but when the side door of the town hall suddenly clicked shut and he heard the latch drop into place, he rubbed his hands together, it was time to move. Using the rear door of the van where the light above the panel had been removed he exited unobserved.

Like a cat on the prowl looking for mice he made his way between the parked vehicles that had filled every available space. When he reached the rear of the 4x4 he lay down and slowly released the air from the nearside tyre. Pushing the end of a small flathead screwdriver against the valve the air from within hissed out. Slowly the tyre deflated bringing down the nearside corner not that the driver would notice.

With the interior of the driving compartment nicely warmed the occupant had settled himself into the leather upholstery. It would be at least be another half an hour before they concluded their business inside the grand chamber.

With a sharp rap on the front passenger window the driver responded with a start having had his eyes shut. The hooded stranger was pointing at the rear of the vehicle. Through the toughened glass the driver could just about make out the man's explanation.

'You've got a flat, down this side mate!'

Alf Barrett straightened up and depressed the button on the dashboard that had secured the central door locking device. He yawned as he pushed open the driver's door. It was nippy outside and a shame to leave the warm interior. He looked about but the stranger had melted into the night, simply gone. Standing at the rear of the vehicle he scratched the irritation on the back of his neck.

'This is all I bloody need tonight!'

He never saw the piece of wood that hit him coming from behind but instantly his world went black as he slumped against the rear door. Dropping the small wooden post the hooded man prevented the policeman from falling using his own weight to hold the unconscious man and at the same time open the rear hatch. Minutes later Alf Barrett was bound and gagged with gaffa tape not that he knew and bundled into the boot. Shutting the rear door the attacker warmed his hands by rubbing them together, the air was keen and maybe frosty later.

It had gone exactly to plan and been executed just as he thought it would. The thing was that when the victim least expected the unexpected, it was inevitable that it would happen. It had been the same when he had gone calling on Santa last December. Not of course that the police would ever connect the crimes. Santa had pleaded, begged for his life, even given up the address of the taller elf but in the end there were just some things in life that were unavoidable.

He walked back to the van and waited patiently, waiting for the members of the freemasons order to begin drifting out. One by one they departed the hall going to their respective cars waving goodbye at other members before heading for the entrance to the car park. With a free space alongside the four by four the hooded man drove the van across and parked next to the highly polished BMW. The second part of the plan had been as easy. Watching the side door the third would soon be executed.

Inside the grand chamber Gregory Tavistock was still revelling in the pomp and ceremony of the occasion. He had just been accepted into the lodge. Despite his police rank he was at the lowest level of the order but in time he would rise up and achieve greater things, it was just a matter of time. As far as he knew David Cherrington was not a member.

'Bad press of late Gregory,' announced the worshipful master of the lodge as he held out his hand and shook that of the police commander.

'Good to see you again Geoffrey.' Tavistock knew that this was the man who could take him places. 'A minor hiccup,' he replied with a smile 'we'll soon nip it in the bud and I assure you that as and when the offender is caught the newspapers will print the story and have the public know that it's all been domestic related.'

Geoffrey Jenkyns let his hand slip away and down to his side straightening his lodge robe.

'I knew of Sir Roger Edington-Forbes and his son Richard. They were invited to join the lodge last year but unfortunately the father was a suspicious old bugger. All the same they did not deserve to die in the manner that they did.'

'No, it was very tragic a lone poacher we believe.'

'Oh well these things happen I suppose. Give my regards to David Cherrington when you next speak to him. Did you know that we attended the same school?'

Jenkyns walked away to retrieve his papers leaving Tavistock to check the time. It was still early and time enough to cross town and visit the clubhouse at the golf club, perhaps grab a couple of whiskies. Tavistock would see Alf Barrett alright and grant the additional overtime maybe let him have a drink too.

Using the gentlemen's bathroom Gregory Tavistock dried his hands under the automatic blower before combing his hair. He caught sight of himself in the mirror. Life had so far been kind to him and with a bit of luck the next three years would see him become an assistant chief constable then who knows. Straightening his tie, the lodge could help achieve his greatest goal. David Cherrington was bound to retire soon and then the chair would be vacant.

Stepping out through the side door he noticed that the air was slightly fresh although no different than you would expect for a September night. Inhaling additional oxygen he saw the BMW. Walking towards where Barrett had parked the vehicle Tavistock did not remember seeing the blue van when they had arrived. He scoffed, some of the lodge members were common builders all vying for contracts through more influential members.

The police commander was surprised not to see Alf waiting by the passenger door. In fact the closer he got the more irritated he became unable to see the driver anywhere.

'What a time to go for a piss,' he muttered looking at his watch.

Tavistock was about to turn and remonstrate having heard a sound from somewhere behind when from his left he caught sight of an object

201

descending fast towards the side of his head. Instantly the lights of the hall entrance went black as the ground came rushing up to meet him.

Climbing into the front seat of the van the hooded attacker inserted the key in the ignition firing up the engine. Moments later he too was heading towards the exit. Taking a glance back at the lone BMW the driver laughed, it had all been so easy.

Every so often the reflection of a passing street light passed through the inside panel of the van momentarily illuminating the motionless figure that lay on the metal floor. Blood was trickling down the side of Gregory Tavistock's neck staining the collar of his dress shirt but rocking with the motion of the moving vehicle he was none the wiser.

Turning the corner heading towards the beach front the driver looked back around to speak.

'I have waited a very long time for this night to happen. First however we need to take a little drive and then we arrive at our destination we will have ourselves a nice long chat. I hope by then that you'll listen intently because when I ask the questions I will expect answers!'

Chapter Nineteen

Thursday Morning

'Daniel,' the woman said joyfully as she pulled him in close to her chest and hugged him tight 'it has been such a long time.' When she did finally let go of her nephew she stepped back to admire how he had grown. 'My look at you, all handsome and a man too boot!'

Kissing her on the cheek he introduced Pete Byrne room then closed the front door.

'Head through to the conservatory and I will put the kettle on.'

Shuffling about the kitchen she filled the kettle and searched the cupboard for a pack of new digestives.

'Make yourselves at home,' she called out 'I'll be there in a jiffy.'

Atherton put his elbows on the round wooden table and leant closer to where Pete Byrne sat opposite.

'As you gather this is my aunt, the older sibling of my mother. She might across as slightly eccentric but trust me Pete what she doesn't know isn't worth worrying about.'

'And this aunt, she's the one that can tell my future?'

He grinned wryly 'Well that's one of her many talents!'

Aunt Bessie came into the conservatory carrying a large tray with a teapot, three cups and saucers, a plate of digestive biscuits and bowl of sugar.

'Daniel wouldn't come visiting when he was a little boy unless he was assured that there would be biscuits!'

Byrne raised his eyebrows but he knew that anything said in response would fall on deaf ears not that there was anything wrong with her hearing. Aunt Bessie sat herself down on the vacant chair and poured. She looked at Pete Byrne as she gave him his tea.

'I should begin by explaining that I have exceptional hearing Mr Byrne. I've not yet told the future to anyone that I did not trust and being labelled a clairvoyant is too limited in my opinion to express the wonders of what we don't always understand, me included. I consider myself a transmitter between worlds. Do you follow my meaning?'

He smiled as he picked up a biscuit 'Pete, please call me Pete and yes, I understand. I didn't mean to offend you.'

It was the first time that Atherton had ever heard Pete Byrne apologise.

'Right, I'm glad that we got that sorted.'

'I'm afraid that our visit today is to explore what the future holds,' explained Atherton 'only we've a baffling case and we need to see if you can help.'

Stirring the air bubbles from the top of her tea she saw Pete Byrne watching, mischievously she gave him a wink.

'I know I had notification that you would be visiting before I took a shower this morning.' She stopped stirring the bubbles in her cup.

She asked that they each place their hands upon the wooden table top.

'This is no parlour trick Mr Byrne... Pete, the same as there no mysterious voices, knocks from beneath the table or moving objects on the window cill. The table has been constructed from oak a good old English tree and thus remains a living organism. Just because the trunk was felled, cut and shaped the wood continues to thrive breathing in the air as we do. This table has the energy of life and through the table I am able to see things.'

She looked at her nephew.

'The help that you seek is it in relation to the recent murders?'

'Yes.'

'Thankfully I do not see them in my dreams although I hear the voices as they pass across. They tell me things, ask many things, some that I cannot always understand.'

Aunt Bessie suddenly turned her attention towards Pete Byrne.

'You possess a strong energy field only you don't realise it. I see a pain inside that disturbs your sleep, is this right?'

Pete Byrne wanted to lift his hands from the table but he felt that if he did it would interfere with what she could see.

'I've never really thought about not until your nephew joined the department.'

She placed her hand over his and the other on Daniel Atherton's.

'Close your eyes, let your mind clear for a moment. Keep them closed until I say open them again.'

Pete Byrne instantly sensed that he was elsewhere and not in the conservatory, but he was, it just his thoughts travelling, going back to when he has been a junior detective. He saw young women some he knew smiling at him. None said anything but he knew who they were and why they were there. Standing on the bridge looking down at the railway shunting sheds he saw a man running a man that he recognised from the back. That was when he opened his eyes again.

Aunt Bessie took her hand away from his.

'You don't have to tell me what you saw, that is for you to work out. I only acted as the transmitter remember.'

When Daniel Atherton opened his Aunt Bessie was smiling.

'Now yours I did take a peek at but only a small peek. You know where you are heading so don't delay is all that I will say.'

Atherton looked across at Byrne.

'Are you alright?' he asked.

'Yes, strangely enough I feel... I'm not quite sure how to describe it, cleansed is what I was going to say although that sounds too holy for somebody like me!'

'Then maybe that is how you do feel,' added Aunt Bessie. 'The souls that latch onto my thoughts come because they have a purpose not because I call them. I did not know who would come today until we sat at the table.

What you saw or what you was told was for you alone. If that makes you feel better then it was believing in!'

She took a long drink of her tea, then sighed as a wave of exhaustion passed through her body.

'Aunt Bessie, are you alright?' asked Atherton the concern evident in his voice.

'A man just walked through me Daniel, a bad man. He had no face not that I could see. I felt pain although I could tell whether it was his or it belonged to somebody else.'

Atherton looked at Byrne.

'You say that you couldn't see his face, was that because he had a hood up?'

She nodded not wanting to see the man again, but he was still there lingering in the background.

'He watches you both. Has seen you at work, not the station but at crime scenes, places where he has done terrible things. The voice that calls to me I do not believe to be his but another's, somebody that has gone ahead. A woman perhaps. Like the man she does not smile and her eyes are shielded in shame.' Aunt Bessie paused. 'Although the blame is not hers to own!'

They looked at one another and nodded. Arthur Benson was the name on both their lips.

'This man, do you know where he will go next?'

She shook her head. 'That I cannot tell Daniel. I only see a shadow and water, lots of water.' She suddenly pulled back from the table as though needing to find dry land.

Sitting either side they supported Aunt Bessie before she fell from the chair.

She blew out then calmed herself.

'Thank you, I felt like I was drowning, it wasn't nice.' She noticed that Pete Byrne had almost finished his tea 'would you like some more Pete?'

'No, I'm fine... thank you, are you alright that was some fall you almost took?'

She patted the back of his forearm.

'I'm alright. Sometimes the occasion can be a little overwhelming. It did feel like I was drowning only it wasn't me but the man. The water was very black, oily black although I got the impression that we weren't in water but travelling through the decades of his life going from when he was very young to now. The drowning could represent the pin that he feels. I sensed a journey, a long journey where he has had to claw his way up to free himself of pain, not just physical pain but mental anguish. The feeling in my throat was because the end of the journey was almost in sight.'

Aunt Bessie took a biscuit, dunked it in her tea then devoured it almost one piece.

'I need sugar.'

Atherton poured more tea into her cup as Byrne added two sugars.

'Thank you boys, I needed that,' she drank her sugary tea accepting the change in her body as the glucose surged through her bloodstream. She held their hand in hers. 'I'm afraid the voices have all gone.

'Don't worry Aunt Bessie they'll be back for either you or us!'

'What I will say is that there was much sadness when they went as though they had been crying. I heard the name Ruth before they disappeared, does that mean anything to you?'

Byrne nodded 'It sure does!'

They sat around the large oak table that had been sculptured not planned flat. There were several knots that looked back up like eyes. Byrne thought that if you looked at it long enough you'd see a face appear. Oddly enough he liked the table and sitting there he felt at peace with the world, at peace with himself.

Without being asked she refilled their cups. The tea had stewed was stronger but with a splash of extra milk it was still as good as the first.

'You need to relax Pete and not take the troubles of the day home with you. Sleep has been a problem of late?'

'Yes it has, although I think I know the reason why. I didn't until I came here.'

She raised her hand.

'Please don't tell me. That was for you to find know. I am just Daniel's aunt, nothing else.'

'There's a peace here that doesn't exist elsewhere.'

Atherton agreed 'As a boy, I always thought of this place as paradise, a small piece of heaven. With my sister we would spend many happy summers here. I have some of my happiest memories here Pete.' He held his aunt's hand and smiled at her. 'Nothing's changed, it is still that little bit of heaven only better.'

She touched her heart.

'This is where heaven exists, beyond that you make paradise what it is.' She was still concerned with how Pete Byrne was feeling as it was he who she sensed needed the most help.

'The young women that haunt your dreams, let them go and let them sleep. They accept that it was not your fault. They are together Pete and happy.'

Pete Byrne had never thought of any victims as being happy but then again he had never thought beyond the grave.

'Would you mind if I took a walk down your beautiful garden?'

'No, please do and go to the end there's a stream. It's peaceful down there and there is a bench upon which to sit and hear the birds chatter.'

Pete Byrne took himself off wanting to clear his head. Although he didn't feel it physically, he sensed a calm sweeping through his mind.

Sitting watching Daniel Atherton realised that the day would come when with Sandra, his older sister they would have to deal with the estate and divide *Beeches*. Looking down the garden to the stream he vowed that whatever the decision he would buy her out. There was no way that the bungalow, the garden or the stream could be lost.

'When I woke this morning all that I could see in front of my eyes was red, which I took to be blood Daniel. At first I thought it belonged to you but I soon realised that it belonged to a woman instead. You came from a murder scene to come here didn't you?'

'Yes. The murders they're all connected and we think because of a dark family secret.'

'Don't tell me about it. I can tell you because I am being told however the other way around their souls could haunt my sleep as they have your colleague.'

She looked to where Pete Byrne had sat himself down on the garden bench.

'You have always been a gentle soul Daniel, Sandra was always the stronger and yet here you are dealing with death. Somehow it doesn't seem right. There are times that I worry about you.'

'It's not that bad most of the time, just moments like now but this will pass soon.'

He also looked down the garden seeing the sun dance across the ripples in the water. 'Pete Byrne is a good colleague and a very experienced detective.'

She nodded. Like you he has a gentle soul and yet he displays a tough exterior. It shields him from the pain and sadness of your profession.'

She suddenly focused back on the vision that had made her so tired and in need of a glucose fix.

'The man that you seek has a terrible secret to tell Daniel. When you do find him, I ask that you give him the opportunity to explain and try not to be too judgemental.'

They saw Pete Byrne coming back up the garden.

'The things that this man has done are wicked but in that hate and rage there is also love.'

Before he returned to the conservatory she had one last message.

'There is a soul that has come into your life a gentle soul such as your own. Do not pass up the chance to be with that person because she will enrich your life and you hers.'

She placed a finger over his lips.

'There is no need to tell me her name, I would rather find that out for myself when you introduce me to her. You should bear in mind that I never married nor had a family of my own and there are many times that I crave what I have missed out on. Find a balance in your life and let someone help you find it!'

'One day soon I promise to bring her to *Beeches* to meet you.

She smiled 'One day *Beeches* will be an ideal place to raise a family.

Before they pulled the gate shut Byrne looked at the name plaque screwed next to the front door. 'I can see why you enjoyed your summer holidays here, mine was spent knocking around a council estate. There's a peace here that you don't find anywhere else. Sitting down at the stream I was able to put a lot of things into perspective.'

'I used to come back here whenever I had a problem Pete. Somehow Aunt Bessie and *'Beeches'* always had the answer.'

'Before I met you and Aunt Bessie I had always kept my feelings to myself, some even from Anne and the girls. Before today I had never known such peace. What just happened in there?'

Atherton grinned.

'Nothing special, you just found yourself Pete and it's been long overdue. I found myself a long time back but only because I spent so much time here. *Beeches* has a certain magic about it that I have never questioned. You'd be wise to do the same and just accept it.'

Pete Byrne walked back to the car a much different person. He could think straight and had a clear vision about his future.

Atherton was about to ring the station and tell Lucy Fancham that they were heading back when instead she called him.

Chapter Twenty

Late Thursday morning

The briefing was set for twenty minutes past the hour giving time for the mobile patrols to complete their current assignment and return to the station. Atherton and Byrne got back in ten.

Pulling together his team Daniel Atherton wanted to give them the heads up on where they were with the investigation including the murder of Hannah Blackburn.

'I need one of you to go to social services and start foraging around.' He picked Lucy believing that she had the right approach to get inside and dig deep without suspicious eyes prying in the background.

He said nothing of where he and Pete Byrne had just been.

'This is like chasing a ghost,' George Gunn implied.

'That's what this case is about George.' Atherton agreed with a wry grin. 'A ghost left over from the past that has come back to haunt the victims. Our killer seemingly has a list and is eliminating his victims one by one.

'The one thing that has become apparent is that he's also been watching us work. He attends our crime scenes, watches and observes us out and about on enquiries. The records office fire proved that. He might even be watching Gabrielle George, why we don't know but we must be vigilant. So for now we work in pairs. George you accompany Lucy today. This killer is dangerous and he will stop at nothing to achieve an end result.'

Atherton pointed to the legend board.

'There are some new names that we've added so familiarise yourselves with them and when we get this briefing out of the way we'll start turning over stones until we locate the right one.' One of the names that he pointed to was Ruth Benson. 'I don't care how we do it, let's get out there and find out everything we can about them.'

Tim Robbins went across to the board and highlighted the photo of the headstone in the graveyard.

'Sister Sarah. One of my cousins joined the order and adopted a new name. It could be that this Sarah did the same!'

Atherton grinned encouragingly 'this is what I am talking about, let's get inside the mind of our killer and let us see how he is putting together his chess pieces. He has a head start so let's see if we can't catch him up. Tim go to Alton Cross and locate the curator of St Cuthbert's, there has to be a record somewhere relating to that headstone.'

'The suitcase that you were given, does it hinge around what happened at Edington Hall?'

'It's certainly a piece of the jigsaw George. I have a contact at the hall so I'm hopeful that soon we'll unravel all the secrets!'

He thought about what Aunt Bessie had advised, finding a work and life balance and how Mary Thomas could and would help. It would be good to see her again and soon.

'A lot of people just sat by and watched it all happen, that is probably what this is all about. Had they stepped in and helped we might not have had so many murders to deal with!'

The remark came out of the blue from Pete Byrne who had sat in the corner listening.

'A lot of people did sit by and watch Pete, you're damn right they did.'

He went back over to the legend on the wall and stabbed at the people that they knew about.

'Arthur Benson had a love child, quite possibly with his sister. Stanley and Evelyn Benson did little to support their daughter. Somehow she ended up employed as a maid at Edington Hall where the master of the house sexually abused her. I'll wager that Hannah Blackburn was involved through social services.'

Atherton checked the photographs and names of the board. 'It's beginning to form a pattern. We need that information about the

213

headstone Tim and Lucy everything that you can dig up down at social services. Right does anybody have any idea why the inspector has called us all back for a briefing?'

The phone in the office rang and was answered by Tim Robbins.

'You won't believe this but Pauline Tavistock has reported her husband as missing. Apparently he didn't come home last night!'

Daniel Atherton cussed under his breath but George Gunn was the first to react. 'Probably shacked up overnight with some young lady golf pro.'

Tim Robbins gave a shake of his head not as convinced as his older colleague. 'I think it's a bit more complicated than that George. Gregory Tavistock was at a meeting of the Freemasons last night. A uniform patrol have just located the commander's vehicle in the car park outside Coronation Hall and in the boot bound and gagged was Alf Barrett.'

Atherton pushed himself clear of the desk. 'Right let's get down to the parade room and see what this is all about. Tim and Lucy you cut away and deal with your enquiries only Tavistock doesn't warrant all of our attention. We still have murders to solve!'

Accompanied by his chief inspector the uniformed inspector walked into the briefing room and called for silence beginning with a short account of the last known movements obtained from Alf Barrett who though feeling cold, tired and hungry was no worse for his ordeal except for the bump on the back on the back of his head. Temporarily pinned to the wall was a map of the immediate area including the locality of Coronation Hall and surrounding streets most of which those in the room already knew.

'The last sighting of the commander was around five to eight last night when he entered the side door of Coronation Hall. From what Alf Barrett has managed to remember the meeting inside was due to finish around eleven so we have a three hour window people in which Gregory Tavistock could have gone missing. Local hospitals have already been checked and so has the gold club where he was a member. The commander attended neither. Before we organise a full-scale manhunt has anybody any suggestions?'

As expected there were none and nobody in the room was fool hardy enough to make any. Professional reputations could be severely damaged or lost through the action of another person's mischief. The inspector and duty sergeant split the mobile patrols giving them a section each of the map that they were to cover whilst Atherton said that his team would take the beach and nearby docks.

'I'm still inclined to agree with George,' said Byrne as they followed the older detective out of the rear station yard.

'And Alf Barrett?' asked Atherton 'he was gagged and bound, it's extreme to say the least, just so that he can slip over the side!'

Byrne scoffed 'I wouldn't put it past Alf to be in on the plan only he can be a devious old bugger and his pension is just around the corner. Tavistock would see to it that Alf's last three months were spent behind a desk as an acting sergeant pushing files around all day to help boost the coffers and commutation.'

'I could have done this alone,' Byrne suggested 'and given you time to get things together back at the office!'

Atherton indicated then slowed behind a queue of cars waiting at a set of lights.

'I at least owe Gregory Tavistock for my promotion board Pete. I suppose in a way I'll look at it as giving something back!'

'Have they got anybody going to interview Pauline Tavistock?'

'Bill Holden and Jasmin Yates. When word gets out about what happened to Alf Barrett the press won't take long to see a story evolving.'

As they approached Coronation Hall, Atherton swung the car hard left and parked alongside the mobile patrol who were speaking to the caretaker. Next to the side door was an ambulance.

'I know him,' Atherton said to Byrne as they were about to get out of the car 'he's ex-army and not exactly pro-police. I reckon in his time he's either had a running with us when he was on leave or he's done time in a military punishment block.'

'He has a mean look about him, I'll give you that!'

Joining their uniformed colleagues they listened to what Joseph Charles had to say for himself.

'We get a lot of men pass through here,' he replied when questioned 'they all look the same to me. They turn up looking like stuffed penguins do a bit of chanting then bugger off home, I don't go in for all that kind of stuff so generally I sit in my office until the meetings over.'

'And what time did you closer the side door last night?'

'Last one was out by twenty past eleven. I saw that the BMW had a flat tyre but I didn't pay it any real attention as the owner couldn't be bothered to change the tyre so why should it concern me!' Surly as well thought Byrne.

'And you've checked all the toilets, offices and other meeting rooms?'

216

Joseph Charles was fast becoming agitated by the endless questions. 'Yeah, twice and I'm satisfied that he ain't in any of them!'

Byrne took over where uniform had done with their questions. 'Don't I know you?'

The caretaker felt the hackles rise suspicious of the new arrivee. Atherton he recognised but the other man in the suit he did not.

'I don't think so!'

'You were in the army,' Byrne added 'only you got...?'

'Kicked out,' Joseph ended the sentence 'only it was all a misunderstanding between me and a jumped-up corporeal.'

'I was going to say fed up with the same old food!'

Joseph frowned 'yeah that as well.'

'Did you check the vehicle?' asked Atherton.

'No, only it ain't in my job description, I just put the chain across the gate and secure the padlock end of the day.'

'What about minicabs, taxis or pickups, were there any hanging about waiting for their fare?'

'Not when I come out of the side door, place was empty except for that flash looking BMW.'

Byrne and Atherton found Alf Barrett inside the small reception area talking to the ambulance crew who were trying to persuade him to go to hospital and have his head medically examined.

'Don't be a stubborn old git Alf and do as the lady asks.' Suggested Byrne.

Alf Barrett looked up recognised a friendly faced gave a smile before wincing as the ambulance attendant applied an ointment to his bump.

'Bugger me Pete Byrne,' he held out his hand. 'I ain't seen you for donkey's years.'

Byrne introduced Daniel Atherton to his old working partner.

'Alf showed me the ropes when I joined the job. We were at South Homerton together.'

'Cor those were the days,' Alf replied 'when law and order meant respect, nowadays they just take the piss!'

'The man who attacked you last night Alf, can you describe him?' asked Atherton.

'Not that well only the lighting from the inside of the hall was poor.' He gave it some thought holding the back of his head.

'However, he was about Pete's height and build, white male could be about forty I suppose. Local accent and wore one of them hoodies that the kids all wear nowadays. I reckon it was him that let the tyre down to attract my attention.'

'Nothing distinguishing that stood out, like a tattoo, scar or piercing?'

'Alf went to shake his head but didn't as the ache was moving down his neck. He looked at the female paramedic and conceded. 'Perhaps I had best go and get my bonce checked out!'

'One more question Alf,' asked Pete Byrne 'where was Tavistock going when he left here?'

Alf Barrett looked at them both and realised they guessed the commander had other plans rather than just returning home. 'Sometimes after the funny handshake brigade he asks me to drive him to the golf club where we have a drink together.'

'I've one Alf,' prompted Atherton 'was Mrs Tavistock at home when you picked up the commander?'

'Yes, she waved at me from the lounge window. Nice lady, very reserved although she always has a kind word to say when I'm around.'

They thanked the ambulance crew for their attention and let them take Alf to hospital.

'This could be like looking for a needle in a haystack. In the distance they heard the distinctive sound of a claxon indicting that the lifeboat crew was required. Instinct had Atherton and Byrne getting back in the car.

'That bloody thing is always going off at the end of the season when day-trippers don't realise how cold or lethal the water can be.'

Atherton ignored the red light and jumped the junction.

'Gut feeling say's that we might be interested in their shout Pete.'

He brought that car to a halt at the beginning of the pier and pointed at the launch which was making its way towards the head of the pier. With total disregard for the signs stating no vehicles were to use the pier Atherton drove to the end where a waiting fisherman was leant over the metal balustrade looking at something down below.

'What's up?' asked Byrne as he approached the fisherman.

'Down there,' he pointed 'there's a bloke lashed to the leg of the pier!'

Atherton and Byrne rushed to the balustrade and looked down. What was left of Gregory Tavistock was washing back and forth in the swell around the cylindrical support.

Before Byrne could prevent him Daniel Atherton was over the other side of the metal barrier and climbing down. When he reached the divisional commander he had already been dead for some time. Lashed around the leg of the pier and around his over indulgent waistline Tavistock was held in place by a length of barbed wire which stopped him from toppling in the water. His head lay heavily down on his chest and his arms dangled at the sides like a pair of redundant octopus tentacles. He could not see below Tavistock's knees as the water was vortexing heavily around the metalwork.

'Is he alive?' Pete Byrne called down.'

Atherton fought off the extreme cold as it clamped his jaw in a deadly lock knocking his teeth together. The water was probably about four degrees above zero. Other than the puncture wounds made by the barbed wire he could see no other obvious injuries on Gregory Tavistock. Looking back up

219

at Pete Byrne, Atherton gave a shake of his head. Feeling a lapping around his calves he saw the lifeboat coming closer.

'Stay where you are,' a crewmember shouted 'we'll soon have you aboard!'

With difficulty Atherton explained that he was a detective on a murder enquiry and that the man lashed to the metalwork of the pier was a victim. He asked if they had a camera on board. The crew searched the coxswains boot locker and found an instamatic.

'Will this do?'

'Yes. Take as many photographs as you can and get as close as you can. Then keep the camera safe for developing, it might be all that we have as evidence.'

When the crewman had finished shooting they helped Atherton on board getting ready to cut the dead man free. With a pair of bolt croppers Gregory Tavistock fell forward and went head first onto the deck of the boat.'

'Something's keeping his feet tied to the pier leg,' yelled Atherton as a woman crew member passed over a blanket.

The coxswain brought the boat in as close as he dare whilst another of the crew lay on the deck with his upper body hanging over the side. Another prevented him colleague from going into the water by straddling his legs. Feeling his way down with his hands he came across more wire wrapped around both ankles. Using a pair or wire cutters he managed to cut Tavistock free. At last with Atherton's help they dragged him on board and turned him over.

'He's been there some time,' remarked the coxswain, 'livor mortis had set in and most of the blood has settled at the lowest point.' He pushed the throttle down hard and headed back to shore. 'We need to get you a hot drink friend.'

On the decking of the pier head Pete Byrne turned the car around and sped back to await the arrival of the emergency launch. As marked units began arriving he organised a perimeter tape and wanted to know when CSI would attend, he was told that they were already on their way.

On the quayside they laid Tavistock on a tarpaulin although neither detective imagined that forensics would get anything of evidential value from the body. Tavistock was more bloated than ever, his bulging eyes staring straight ahead in terror with his lips a funny shade of blue as though they had been injected with antifreeze. He still had on his dress trousers but everything else, jacket, shirt, tie, socks and shoes had been removed.

'I had a bad feeling when we heard the claxon that this is what we would find!' Pete Byrne handed Atherton a hot chocolate that the lifeboat crew had made.

'I can't say that I'm surprised. There was always something odd about Gregory Tavistock, only you could never quite put your finger on it and I thought that he would met with a sticky end one day. He had used up many of his nine lives down the years!'

Byrne sipped the side of his Styrofoam mug.

'A random killing or do we connect this as well?'

Atherton looked up. 'I can't quite decide which, not until I get the feeling back in my feet they are like blocks of ice.'

'What's with the puncture wounds?' asked Byrne.

'He was lashed to the metal supports by barbed wire.'

Byrne sucked in hard. 'I bet that *fucking* hurt.' He sipped again. 'So it wasn't just meant to keep him upright but to torture as well.'

'That abouts sum it up I would say, although my theory is that he was tortured on the end of the pier then lowered over the side where he was lashed to the metalwork. If you look under the hems of the trousers you'll see that both ankles were also secured by wire. Tavistock had his hands free but in the icy water it probably dropped a few degrees last night, he would have thrashed about trying to free his bonds only his efforts would have sapped whatever little energy he had left. Eventually he was fallen forward and accepted his fate as the tide came in. He probably died of hypothermia before he drowned.'

'From the look in his eyes, the tide came in fast!'

'It does this part of the coast.'

Atherton took off his shoes and then his socks ringing them out as best he could. Coming down the quayside he saw Marjorie and another forensic van weaving between the fishing equipment and the small boats awaiting repair.

'You were right, he did come for one of us only why Gregory Tavistock, that is a mystery.'

'Because he was the commander of the division?'

'No,' replied Atherton 'that's too loose an assumption. Tavistock knew something that he never let on about only now we might never know.'

Close behind Marjorie was the inspector and chief inspector, followed by David Cherrington, the chief constable.

'It's time that I made myself scarce,' remarked Byrne 'I can't be doing with all the crap that goes with high and mighty rank.'

'You might need them one day Pete, when you go for your sergeants!'

Byrne laughed 'I like what I do being a detective. My life is uncomplicated which means I turn up for work every day do my bit then go home to Anne and the girls. Besides my mouth would kill my chances on a promotion board.'

Neither detective noticed the dark van parked alongside the repair shop. To anybody even curious it blended in nicely and looked the sort of van that would be associated with the area.

Chapter Twenty Two

Thursday afternoon

With the death of one of their own a detective superintendent arrived from headquarters to head the investigation. Daniel Atherton saw the immediate advantage of having Harry Lane along for the ride was that Lane had been on his promotion board.

With Pete Byrne in tow the three of them met at the examination room where Michael Hargreaves had side-lined another post-mortem until later. Hargreaves was about to begin when Marjorie walked in, she took her place alongside Daniel Atherton. From where they all stood they could only see the left side of Tavistock's naked body.

Hargreaves switched on the overhead microphone to begin his preliminary physical examination.

'The deceased is Gregory Ian Tavistock, born on the third of May, nineteen fifty three. A white Caucasian male, weighing a hundred and eight kilogrammes with height measured at one hundred and seventy two centimetres.

'Death was caused by drowning with the possibility of hypothermia affecting body temperature, blood pressure and heart rate.

'There are puncture wounds around the abdomen and ankles where the deceased was secured to the metal framework of the pier head. There appears to be surgical scarring at the side of the patella of the right leg possibly indicating a cartilage repair. On the right shoulder there is a small round tattoo of a sporting motive, although unfortunately the slogan is blurred due to ink run. On the right thigh there is a larger tattoo of two blue dragons, they appear to be squaring up to one another.'

Daniel Atherton was the first to react. In an instant he was around the table followed closely by Pete Byrne. He repeated what Byrne had told him when talking about the railway murder victim that had survived. 'The suspect was of regular height, white with short dark hair and he had a tattoo on his right hip. Like a pair of fish, two snakes or maybe even dolphins.'

'What's going on?' asked Hargreaves as he switched off the microphone, slightly irritated at the interruption. Harry Lane and Marjorie also walked forward to join them.

'We're sorry sir, we didn't mean to impose.' Byrne pointed at the tattoo on Tavistock's hip. 'I was part of an investigation shortly before the turn of the century. Do you remember the case of the *wheel man killer* and of the victim that survived the ordeal?'

Hargreaves pushed his hair from his left eye with his gloved hand.

'Yes, I remember them. The victims were sexually assaulted then murdered having been left tied or chained to the wheels of rolling stock.'

Byrne continued 'Well one of the victims managed to escape and during interview she described her attacker as having a large tattoo on his right hip. She couldn't quite make it out but said that it looked like two large fish, snakes or dolphins. What she saw could easily have been two blue dragons!'

Harry Lane jumped in on the conversation see in where it was heading.

'Gregory Tavistock was a respected divisional commander amongst the staff and Chief Constable's office at headquarters Pete, there are probably a lot of male Caucasians walking around with a similar tattoo on the right side of their body. I would seriously consider thinking about what you're saying here only this is some accusation that you're making!'

'With respect Sir the *wheel man killer* was never caught and a good many victims family suffered because of his atrocities. Like any good detective would I was only looking at the possibility factor.'

Harry Lane had been around long enough to know that Pete Byrne was right, in similar circumstances he too would be adding up the numbers. He looked over at Michael Hargreaves.

'Anything that occurs in this county comes through this office, is that right sir?'

Hargreaves agreed that it did.

'Then forensically for the sake of argument DNA would have been taken at the crime scene and from that of the young woman who survived the attack.'

Hargreaves agreed again 'And you would like me to see if we can make a match superintendent?'

Harry Lane looked at his colleagues wanting his first day on the case to count. 'It would certainly be useful to know either way!'

Michael Hargreaves carried on with the post-mortem although the thoughts of each person in the room already elsewhere and not just with the dead man undergoing the examination. Eleven years back a lot of innocent young women had suffered terrible, terrifying ordeal ending in their death bar one the lucky one.

The coroner concluded that Gregory Tavistock had met with his untimely death in circumstances that could only be described as unusual. He recorded a verdict of murder and promised to check DNA records.

Standing to one side Pete Byrne looked at the naked cadaver despising everything about the dead man. For hours, days and weeks he and many others in the investigation team had been searching relentlessly for a rapist and murderer and all the time the perpetrator had been under their noses, gloating and using the correlation of information to his advantage. Turning around he walked out of the room unable to suffer the indigence of being in the presence of a monster.

Chapter Twenty Three

Late Thursday afternoon

Harry Lane suggested that the four of them go for a drink after the post-mortem. Now in charge he could easily say that they were already on enquiries in relation to Gregory Tavistock's death, which in light of what Pete Byrne had said wasn't strictly untrue.

In a private members club the four sat in the snook where they could talk in private. In less than half an hour Daniel Atherton appraised the senior detective on the progress that they had made with the murders. Lane listened intently picturing each scene in his mind.

'On paper it doesn't look much but given the time frame that these incidents have occurred and with what you've had to cope with it is hardly surprising. However what you have got is a damn good start. Take it from me that I think you done a great job getting to where you are. Soon this will all drop into place.' He specifically looked at Pete Byrne.' And I take it that you're linking Gregory Tavistock's murder to the others, how?'

Byrne replied. 'According to Alf Barrett the commander's driver, the bloke that slugged him was wearing a hoodie. We believe that our killer uses the same style of clothing to get in and out of the victims addresses without being recognised. We also think that he's been watching us!'

'That's a lot of 'if's' and speculation there Pete, although I agree that we work best on our hunches. Did Barrett give us a description?' he asked.

'Nothing that would hold up in court!'

Harry Lane raised his glass pleased to be drinking with his new colleagues. 'Well for my first day on the job I cannot deny that you people don't make it interesting, here's to us working together.'

He especially chinked the glass of Marjorie Matthew's. 'And I hear from Daniel and Pete here that you are the best forensic investigator in the county!' Marjorie blushed.

'Right then,' he put down his glass 'what say you that we go get this bastard!'

They walked into the office where George Gunn, Tim Robbins and Lucy Fancham was waiting to greet Harry Lane. He closed the door and systematically shook each of their hands.

'Okay that's the formalities out of the way, what's new?' He started with Tim.

'I went to St Cuthbert's and with the help of the deacon we went through countless parish records, there was very little on Sister Sarah other than her body was brought down by a funeral company from the Lake District. She had been a nun at the Lady of the Shrine Convent at Deacon Head, three miles east of the village of Windermere. The date of the funeral was registered as July twenty third, nineteen ninety one.'

Atherton wrote the details on the legend. 'That made her twenty four!'

Lane had been studying the expressions on their faces as he went around the room, he stopped at Pete Byrne.

'Is there something that you want to add Pete only you have the floor?'

Byrne adjusted the chair to his liking before he began. 'This case is all about a family. Putting aside what took place overnight the rest of the killings are we believe linked. What if Sister Sarah joined the convent because she had too, because she had no other option.'

Atherton was on his wavelength, when Pete paused he took over 'and because she had a love child by Arthur Benson she was forced to give up the child, taking employment at Edington Hall where she was sexually abused.'

'Running away because she was so ashamed of her own part in this sad affair, only to be then abused and badly ill-treated by Edington the only place that she believed she would find solace and have her might be a convent. If she was turned away by Arthur, Stanley and Evelyn Benson she would have been desperate.'

Harry Lane caught on fast 'And because of everything, illness in one form or another took hold ending her days as Sister Sarah. It certainly fits.'

Atherton tapped the legend with the end of his pen attracting their attention.

'Let's say that she was between fifteen and seventeen when she had a son. He would be around my age, thirty five, maybe six. Athletic and strong enough to handle Gregory Tavistock and haul him over the pier balustrade in the dark before lashing him to the pier support. Fit enough to tackle both Sir Roger and Richard Edington.'

'You're throwing Tavistock into the equation this early Daniel, suggesting that he was murdered by our hoodie?'

'Yes sir, I am. Ignoring his past for the moment my gut tells me that our commander was murdered in an act of retribution.'

Lane got up from his chair going across to the legend board, in the centre of the board he drew the picture of a hood, including a large question mark where the face should be.

'In the meantime we continue with our enquiries...'

Harry Lane's closing line was interrupted by the phone ringing on Lucy Fancham's desk. She answered the call and with a pen in her hand began writing. When the call ended she thanked the caller and put down her pen.

'That was a call that I had been expecting from a Geraldine Fisher at Social Services. She worked alongside our dead Hannah Blackburn in the early seventies through to the mid-eighties. She says that she cannot remember the boy's name connected with a case that Blackburn was interested in but when she searched the file is missing. Hannah Blackburn was the lead social worker in the Ruth Benson case.'

She paused to let the impact settle.

'However, what she can recall was Hannah Blackburn was making arrangements to have the boy sent away to live and be adopted by relatives north of the border and that the mother, Ruth Benson was to be employed at a big house somewhere near Waxford Hammock.'

Banging his fist down on the desk top Pete Byrne was the first to salute the information.

'At last progress and we have our motive. Ruth Benson is abused by her brother. They have a child that Arthur wants nothing to do with. The boy is sent away to be brought up by family members he doesn't know. His grandparents probably set up the meeting with social services where low and behold unwittingly Hannah Blackburn comes into the picture. For her sins she sends the boy north and dispatches Ruth Benson to a waiting Roger Edington-Forbes where we know what took place there. Eventually the boy becomes a man. It's a past full of torment, disappointment and pain, enough to send any sane individual over the edge. With no mother to love and hold him, a father and grandparents who despise him, and lastly a social worker who steals his mother away sealing her fate. He seeks revenge. If I were not a police detective I think that I too would seeking revenge!'

Lucy Fancham had noticed a sudden change in Pete Byrne. He was different, much calmer and more open. She liked it.

'Just out of interest Lucy,' asked Harry Lane, 'do we know when the boy was sent north of the border?'

'Geraldine Fisher thought it was around December time, just before Christmas!'

Pete Byrne lowered his head and shook it incredulously. He wanted to call Anne and talk to her but knew that he couldn't not just yet.

When Lane suggested that Lucy show him where the kitchen and the gents toilets were Atherton took the opportunity to get Pete Byrne alone.

'I think I'll take you to see Aunt Bessie more often!'

Byrne had a tinge of sadness in his eyes as he looked back up. 'Cases like this can tear you up inside, especially when you've got family. I feel different and since this morning sitting in the garden at Aunt Bessie's I see things differently.'

He chuckled and patted Atherton's arm 'You know you should go see that maid back at Edington Hall, life really is too short Daniel.'

Atherton was about to ask how he knew when Lane and Lucy came back in with a tray of coffee's. Harry Lane called them over to the tray. 'This doesn't happen often I assure you, so take advantage of what's on offer today!'

As a team they discussed strategy, who should go where and deal with follow-up enquiries. Harry Lane suggested Byrne and Atherton revisit Edington Hall and turn over a few more stones. Lucy to head back to social services, Tim to contact the funeral directors in Windermere and George to discretely go up to the commander's office and have a sniff around.

'I'm not asking you to look for anything in particular George, but you will know what I'm getting at when you find it.' Harry Lane winked at Pete Byrne. A gesture to show that he believed in him.

When the moment presented itself he called Atherton outside into the corridor.

'This is a good team you have here Daniel and you've all done a damn good job in a very short space of time. David Cherrington himself asked that I come and give you some help so don't go looking upon my being here as you being incapable because we both know different.

'It doesn't do to have senior police officers being bumped off in the middle of the night and basically it's bad for moral and a sends a shiver up the spine of the crime commission figures. Regardless of me being here you and your team would have started to unravel this mystery with or without my help, although I am lucky to be on board.'

Harry Lane checked the time.

'I know that I have only just arrived but I've been summoned to the big house to see Cherrington, I can only surmise that it has something to do with Gregory Tavistock!'

Lane smiled as the expression on Daniel Atherton's face change.

'You're a smart detective sergeant and good team leader, think about it for a moment alone and you'll arrive at the answer why before I get there. I promise that you'll be the first to know when I do, oh and for the time being do me a favour though don't mention any of this to Pete Byrne. He's a bloody good detective and without his knowing I've read his file on a number of occasions in the past. He should have gone for promotion years back only his mouth and ideals got in the way.'

Atherton assured Lane that he wouldn't say a word.

'I think you will find that Pete is a changed man. Before today he would tried to solve the mystery alone but he's become a team player from which we have all benefitted, me also.'

From the office window he watched Harry Lane get in his car and drive away from the station heading east. Sensing that someone was in the doorway to the office he turned.

'So did he give you a gold star like at school?'

Atherton smiled 'Not me Pete, just you!'

Chapter Twenty Four

Thursday evening

Daniel Atherton was at home when Harry Lane called. He had thought about staying late at the office, but the atmosphere inside the station was one of melancholy and Atherton had no intention of being drawn into endless discussions that kept going around in circles. He recognised the number calling.

'Hello Daniel, I thought you'd be wise enough to slip away when you could.'

'I'm not into all that gloomy temerity. Nothing can change what's happened, we can just catch the offender and move on!'

Harry Lane smiled although it was obviously unseen by Atherton. The young sergeant had a similar approach to an investigation and it why he had got his vote on the promotion board.

'As you gathered earlier I was called back to headquarters to see David Cherrington. He had an hour before I arrived taken a call from Michael Hargreaves, the coroner to say that Tavistock's DNA had been run through the system and it made a match which evidence left at scenes of the *wheel man killer* case. The evidence is conclusive without any doubt and that Tavistock was our man.'

'Obviously, however none of this will ever get to the media,' remarked Atherton his tone calm and understanding

'Probably not. I know it might seem as though we're sticking our heads in the sand and ignoring the fact that he was a rapist and murder but as Cherrington put it, we have others to be thinking about and should the facts ever be disclosed the past would be racked up by the press. Families of the murdered women and the young woman who survived would go through hell all over again. Lastly, he is sympathetic to Penelope Tavistock and the reputation of the force and of the men and women who serve today. They don't deserve to be dragged through the mud because of one vile creature.

'What Gregory Tavistock did, sinks lower than any man I have ever despised. I know Penelope Tavistock personally and if she knew what her husband had done to other women while she and their two daughters slept soundly in their beds, it would surely destroy them as individuals.

'Lastly and this might choke a little. If we let the press know the facts the lawyers representing the families of the dead and the woman who survived will seek compensation. Any such compensation could cripple the force budget with long term implications. Not only would moral go into decline but so would the opportunity to invite new officers to be part of our force. We would lose so much prestige that it would take years to recoup, if ever.'

'I understand. What matters is catching our hooded killer.'

'Good man Daniel.' Atherton could tell that Lane was relieved.

'Do you want me to tell Pete Byrne?'

'Thanks but no thanks. Any other caser than the railway murders and I might have said yes but I know how it affected Pete. I will get him to one side tomorrow and have a word, he'll understand.'

Atherton was happy not to have the conversation with Pete Byrne. He had no dealings with the railway murders and only newly promoted it might have seemed derisive to be offering advice on something so sensitive.

'He will appreciate you telling him Sir.'

Lane laughed 'I'll take that as a compliment!'

'Did George find anything of interest?'

Harry Lane had been waiting for him to ask.

'I asked George to do it rather than Lucy or Tim because he's old school and would know what I meant without me spelling it out.'

There was a pause in the line as Harry Lane rubbed his temples, it had been a long day.

'George did find things and what he found conclusively put Tavistock in the frame for the murders. Like a lot of serial killers he took a trophy from each victim, a necklace, chain even a pair of knickers. Tavistock had them under lock and key but George had spent time of a burglary squad back in the old days, he knows how to pick a lock or two!

'Tavistock was a fool for keeping them but the man was a pompous bastard at the best of times and he probably got a buzz every time he opened the drawer, also knowing that Pete Byrne was working only two floors below. I told George to reseal the envelope and place it in lost property for the meantime until I decide how best to deal with it. I'll probably have the lot burnt in time, it'll save a lot of heartache.'

Atherton agreed nodding.

'I would not want to be the one taking back anything and handing it over to a relative.'

'Me neither,' replied Lane.

'George won't say anything, I can vouch for him.' Said Atherton.

'I know,' replied Harry Lane 'don't worry neither, me and George go back a long way so I'll take him for a drink one evening to make it up to him.'

Watching a marked car bring a prisoner to the station Harry Lane looked up at the wall clock of the CID office, it was almost seven and time that his thoughts turned to food.

'I hope that you have a good woman at home Daniel, somebody that you can talk too when you go home. Keeping it bottled up inside doesn't do anybody any good!'

'I have sir, believe me and I appreciate you keeping me in the loop.'

'I am just here to help remember.'

Lane ended the call leaving Daniel Atherton checking the time. He scrolled through his list of contacts and hit the listing for Mary Thomas. She answered almost immediately.

'Wow, this is unexpected only I thought it might be weeks before I heard from you again.'

'Are you busy?' he asked.

'When?'

'This evening?'

There was a brief pause as she discussed the evening off with Agnes Maitland.

'Agnes say's that I should go for it!'

He laughed. 'Say thanks from me, shall I pick you up in about half an hour?'

Mary Thomas fisted the air to the delight of Agnes.

'That will give me time to get out of my working clothes. By the way Agnes is asking if you've eaten anything today!'

He shook his head Agnes reminded him of his Aunt Bessie, always concerned with his health and well-being.'

'Not yet although I was going to get us something on the way back!'

He could hear the opening and shutting of cupboard doors and drawers as the cook pulled out what she had been looking for.

'Agnes say's to remind you that eating all that unhealthy stuff will only stunt your growth. A man needs wholesome food so if you like game pie, then we can have that for supper and she will get together a hamper while I get changed.'

'Is there any point in my rejecting the offer?'

'None!'

'Then thank her again and tell her that she's top of my Christmas card list, after you!'

By the time that he covered the long drive up to the house and down to the side where the kitchen was located Mary was already waiting with a small wicker basket. Atherton swung the car around so that she could get in and he could wave at Agnes watching from the window.

Placing the basket in the rear footwell he made sure that Mary was buckled up before he leant across and kissed her. Moments later he pulled away and looked her in the eye.

'I needed to be with you and all day people have been telling me that I should be acquainted with a good woman.

She pulled him back, kissing him for longer. 'Only acquainted sergeant!'

Atherton laughed, he really did like Mary Thomas, her engaging smile, her eyes and how on the gloomiest of days she could make everything seem like the sun was out.

'More than that!' he replied much to her delight.

In the kitchen Agnes stood watching remembering when she had sneaked off to the stables to have a romp in the hay with one of the stable lads, good times that left happy memories.

As they passed the front of Edington Hall, Francesca Forbes still dressed in her bath robe watched the red Saab negotiate the drive. She smiled placing a hand to her heart happy that Mary had found a man worthy of having.

Allowing the robe to drop from her shoulders she stared back at the reflection in the dressing mirror, turning left then right she admired her figure which had somehow managed to remain untainted by her late husband. Soon Edington Hall would rejoice his passing and romance, guests and parties would fill the landings and rooms. She had plans for the big house but she needed to discuss them with Robert and Stuart first.

Picking up the robe she spun the garment around and high above her shoulders twirling like an angel in the breeze. Francesca Forbes felt free and happy, happier than she had for a long time. It was time to make plans, time for change. It was still early but when Agnes had retired to her room and Reg Cullen had returned home from the Duck and Drake she would once again leave the door open so that he could emerge from the priest hole. Tonight she wanted him in her bed, inside her and to make her feel whole again. Together they would see the dawn rise from above the cill of her bedroom window.

On the journey back to his place they talked about their families, parents and siblings with Atherton including into the conversation *Beeches* and Aunt Bessie. He avoided anything to do with work wanting to keep the evening just for them only. Pushing open the front door he took the basket and put it down on the worktop in the kitchen before pulling her in close.

'Agnes did say to put the pie in an oven so that they would stay warm!'

Finding her lips he kissed her not wanting to let go, but when they were spent with air Mary gently pulled back.

'Maybe it'll stay warm in the warming tins!'

He smiled. 'Good.'

Unbuttoning his shirt he lifted the tee-shirt up and over her head revealing the rounded swell of her breasts as she kissed his bare chest slowly moving up to his neck. Moving his hands around back he undid her bra only before it fell away she held the cups in place.

'Can we go in the bedroom,' she asked 'I want this moment to last forever?'

Daniel Atherton scooped her up in arms carrying her through to the room at the end of the hallway where with just a trickle of the sunset wafting through the gap in the curtains he laid her gently on the bed. Moments later they were under the duvet cover.

'You really are beautiful,' he murmured as he caressed her, touching where her senses flinched, tickled and caused her to sigh.

'I look better because of the sunset on the bed,' she replied feeling his erection stabbing hard at her thigh.

Gently easing her onto her back he began kissing and sucking at her nipples arousing her inner senses until the mounds on her breasts could go no harder. Letting his tongue slide down the side of her ribs he went lower until he reached her nether regions. Mary gasped holding the back of his head and pulling his hair through her fingers, she wanted him, needed him.

With the tip of his tongue he began to explore licking aside her soft wet lips before changing position and letting his erection disappear between her legs. Mary gasped as he entered instantly accepting and feeling the heat rise within her groin, surging rising up through her abdomen like a fire. Gently at first he tenderly rocked back and forth wanting her to enjoy, savour the experience but when she dug her nails into his back feeling herself giving in to his need she felt him go harder still. Soon they bucked in rhythm becoming as one kissing, gasping and touching.

When the juices of their lovemaking exploded it was like an eruption. Mary closed her eyes as Daniel kissed the underside of her neck making his lips eventually find hers. He stayed inside her not wanting the moment to end and she was just as happy that he stayed there holding him tight. When they made love for a second time she begged that she just let him do whatever he wanted.

Lying in one another's arms the sun had finally disappeared from the room leaving in its wake a blue hue. In the distance if you were keen to listen you could just hear the traffic.

With her head resting on his chest where she could hear his heartbeat Mary looked up and into his eyes. 'Was that your idea of us getting acquainted?'

He looked back down. She was beautiful, incredibly beautiful. Stroking his fingers through her hair he watched as the loose strands fell back into place.

'I was never any good at choosing the right words for the occasion.'

Mary grinned to herself as she puckered at his chest.

'If you only ever talk through your actions then I promise that you will get everything just right!'

They had a late supper in the front room sharing the duvet and one end of the settee, leaving room for a bottle of wine. He had started out by watering down his wine but Mary had quickly added more wine whispering in his ear that she had no intention of sleeping in her attic bedroom that night.

Later they watched the stars flicker into life until sleep became a necessity. Wishing that he didn't have the need Atherton set the alarm for five forty five.

'That should give us enough time to shower have breakfast together and then get you back to Edington Hall.'

Reaching across him she turned the clock away so that they couldn't see it, it was only just gone three.

'Make love to again,' she asked 'only I want you inside of me as I need you to know that, that's where I will always want you Daniel Atherton!'

They had only been asleep for under an hour when the alarm started to buzz.

Chapter Twenty Five

Friday morning

Kissing her affectionately at the bottom of the stairwell leading into the kitchen Daniel promised enthusiastically that he would be in touch with Mary again over the weekend. On the journey back to Edington Hall he had briefly told her about Tavistock explaining that a senior officer had passed away the night before last in suspicious circumstances and that for the next twenty four hours he was likely to be kept busy by others wanting answers. Mary Thomas understood although she was eager that they be together again and soon.

Armed with the empty containers and wicker basket she waved and waited until she could no longer see his car before placing her free hand on the lower part of her abdomen, she ached but it was a good ache. Minutes later she descended the stone staircase.

With her back resting against the door leading into the kitchen she sighed and closed her eyes momentarily *'soon Daniel,'* she murmured reliving the night *'I will need you again soon'.*

Idling at the junction he was about to negotiate the left turn when he braked to retrieve his mobile which was ringing.

'You're early?' he responded looking at the time on the dashboard clock.

'I thought you'd still be at home, I did try calling!'

Atherton looked left then right but the traffic was steady without the opportunity of a gap to slip into.

'I had to drop off a friend!'

'About bloody time, I was beginning to worry about you.' said Byrne.

Atherton didn't mind Pete Byrne knowing. 'We're just taking it one step at a time!'

Byrne sniffed 'and that was taking it one step at a time, you must let me know what comes next and I'll try it with Anne tonight!'

'I would but it's private.'

'Well I'm glad that you got laid at last but I'm sorry to ruin your day. We have just received a tip-off from the police at Windermere that the Mother Superior at the Lady of the Shrine Convent was found dead in the chapel this morning when the nuns began arriving for early prayers.'

'And how would that involve us other than we have an ongoing enquiry at the convent?'

'One of the nuns who was dressing prior to prayers thought she saw a monk leave the chapel twenty minutes before the mother superior was discovered. One they don't have monks in a convent and two he had a hooded garment covering his face.'

Atherton killed the engine.

'Do they say who's in charge of the investigation?'

'Detective Inspector Bob Gambitt. Ironically enough he was the cross-border liaison officer when we were running the *wheel man killer* investigation. He's a nice bloke, decent and approachable.'

'How did she die?'

Byrne sighed. 'She had been crucified on the chapel cross.'

'Tom was going there today as arranged, if Harry Lane's alright with the arrangement we should tag as well.'

'I can't only I've been called to headquarters with Lane. We're off to see David Cherrington.'

'About Tavistock?'

At the other end of the line he heard Pete Byrne exhale loudly.

'That bastard should burn in hell and have his *fucking* precious reputation left in tatters but you and I both know that cannot happen. Public opinion would crucify us.'

'That and other considerations Pete.'

Byrne let out a low sigh of resignation. 'Yeah and I can imagine what. Did you know that at the time we had a temporary female detective on the investigative team?'

'No.' replied Atherton.

'Her name was Alison Dyne, a bright young enthusiastic chirpy thing with high ambition to go far. Dyne dealt with the agony messages and the one victim that did survive the attack.' He paused. 'Nobody on the team saw the pain that she absorbed nor any of the psychological cracks until it was too late. One night after an alleged drinking session Alison drove her car along the marine road and veered sharp right where the carriageway is closest to the sea. Her car and body was recovered the next day.'

Atherton was beginning to understand how Pete Byrne's nightmares had tortured him for so long. 'Go on.'

'There was an official investigation, but the chief constable at the time marked up her file as death due a road traffic accident caused through intoxication.'

Atherton could see the warning signs in his mind.

'When you see Cherrington later Pete please just watch what you say. Think of Anne and the girls. I have had it on good authority that you can still further your career with a little help.'

Atherton suddenly realised what Byrne had said.

'You just said alleged.'

'That's right I did. When nobody else seemed to care or have the time to care I did some discreet background checks on Alison Dyne before the official party line stepped up to be applauded by headquarters. Dyne was born over here but her father was a strict Muslim. Alison had used her mother's maiden name on the police application believing that had she kept her Islamic surname of Bukhari, sooner or later prejudices would started creeping under the carpet and created certain barriers. I said alleged because away from the police she practised her faith religiously and abstained from drinking any alcohol.'

'Toxicology would have shown her to have been drinking!'

'Yeah that and along with half of the *fucking* Irish Sea in her lungs. It was a set up!'

'Alison Dyne was murdered?' Atherton took an intake of air having guessed where the conversation had been heading.

'Somebody had plied Alison with drink, how I wasn't sure but my guess is by force. They then drove her to the spot where she was found. There's a sharp bend at the exact point where her car left the jetty.' He paused. 'Are you with me so far?'

'I've not gone anywhere Pete.'

'The ace card in the pack was that her partner on the investigation was none other than Gregory *'I'm a fucking rapist and murderer'* Tavistock, who had just made DS. My guess is that she saw through what he was up too but before she could tell anyone on the team he killed her.'

Atherton lowered his forehead onto the top of the steering wheel to think.

'That's one hell of a secret to have shelved inside of you Pete. Does Harry Lane know?'

'No.'

'Look. Please do me a favour, tread carefully this morning Pete, that's all I ask. You are far too valuable an asset to loose. I will keep you posted as to what I find at the lady of the shrine.'

Accompanied by Tim Robbins the pair headed into the next county where at the convent they were met by Bob Gambitt. They were surprised although pleasantly pleased to see Marjorie Matthews waiting as well.

'Harry Lane asked that I come along as an impartial observer. I have already spoken to DI Gambit and assured him that I will not interfere with anything that his own team have under control.'

Atherton was especially pleased that she was there.

Gambitt took them straight to the chapel where the body of Mother Theresa was still hanging from the wooden cross. Her night robe had been torn down to her waist leaving her breasts exposed. Hanging limply from the underside of her right ribcage was a long metal shaft. It had pierced the skin, the liver and punctured the heart causing as much pain as possible before ending her life and the torture. To the unenlightened the length of iron rod resembled the spear of destiny. Outspread on either end of the crossbeam her wrists had been attached to the wood using ordinary fencing nails and the same went for her feet where they were nailed side by side.

'Just like Jesus,' said Marjorie taking a photograph with Gambitt's permission 'she has been crucified.'

'I understand that you had already arranged an enquiry for today at the convent,' asked Gambitt.

'As part of a murder enquiry we came across a headstone at St Cuthbert's at Alton Cross. We were enquiring about a Sister Sarah who is named on the stone and we think she might be the reason for our murders taking place.'

Bob Gambitt reckoned that he would have his hands full with the investigation at the convent without confusing the issue, he was however happy to hear how the two cases overlapped. Atherton and Gambitt took a walk to discuss the details. Taking themselves to a bench in the courtyard they sat under a black chokecherry tree where the bees were still searching for late nectar.

Gambitt was a keen gardener.

'Did you know Daniel that the chokecherry is a deciduous and that the fruit has a variety of uses, baking, jams, jellies, syrups, teas, juices and wine. You cannot eat the fruit raw as it will affect the acids in your stomach. Birds and wildlife, bees included like the fruit as well.'

He suddenly grinned looking across to a heavy locked door, 'not that were here to go exploring but I reckon that if we did and went down into the vaults we would find ourselves a store full of wine vats. I bet these old girls know how to spend a good evening together!'

Gambitt was nothing like what Atherton had imagined. Roughly the same age as Harry Lane there were similarities. Going by what he had been told and saw there was little that he had not seen in his years of experience in the force.

'Like the bees some bugger was busy here either last night or the early hours of this morning. What's your take on that scene inside?' he looked at Atherton studying him, recognising particular characteristics that he had heard about from Pete Byrne. He especially liked that Atherton didn't jump in with the first idea but gave his answer some thought.

Picking up a fallen cluster of chokeberries Atherton gently caressed the fruit.

'At times we've found ourselves floundering. Our killer has always been a step ahead of us not that we could have predicted his next victim, not without finding every family member going back at least three generations. We believe the name on the headstone is the mother, Sister Sarah or as we know her Ruth Anne Benson. She was sent to the convent in an act of contrition by a social worker who met with her fate this week. What I hope to find here was some answers which would help resolve our case and point us in the right direction of our murderer.'

Atherton went on to tell Bob Gambitt about the abuse, torment and hell that she suffered at the hands of Sir Roger Edington-Forbes.

'That name rings a bell,' he said as he racked his memory cells as to where and when. With a click of his fingers he suddenly remembered 'he was a friend of Gregory Tavistock.

Bob Gambitt watched as Daniel Atherton held the berries between his fingers.

'Watch that you don't puncture one or several of those buggers they'll stain your suit something rotten. My missus is always berating me when I've been down the fruit patch end of the garden. I know that Tavistock was your commander but I never trusted the bugger. He had a funny look about him and he was always watching the young women. It unnerved them and several complained about it but political correctness was still in its infancy back then. The men were the dominant force and many were still in charge. A show of leg or a bosom around the station helped boost morale and the hierarchy turned a blind eye. Men like Gregory Tavistock believed that they were infallible. I wasn't surprised when I heard that he had died.'

Atherton liked Bob Gambitt, liked his easy manner and how he kept his reality in check.

'Strictly off the record Tavistock's DNA matched that of the victims from the *wheel man killer* investigation.'

Gambitt kept staring straight ahead remembering his involvement 'and on record?' he asked.

'Too many considerations will come into play should it ever be made public!'

The detective inspector scoffed 'that's how the system works. It stinks but then do we for allowing it to happen. What we hope is that in time the players will hang themselves!'

'May I suggest Sir that you give Pete Byrne a call this afternoon, I think that you could both benefit from arranging a drink together soon!'

Gambitt was as shrewd as much as he was intelligent. Right there and then he was angry, angry that Tavistock had got away with it for so long.

'Please call me Bob you bugger, I have never liked the formality of rank. There are those whose ego compromises who they really are. Gregory Tavistock revelled in the glory better than anybody I have come across in the corridors of power. He abused everything that he touched. I'm glad that you told me Daniel and don't worry I won't say where or who I heard it from. I'll give Pete a call later. I take it that because he's not here, he's having coffee with the chief constable?'

Atherton nodded.

'If Pete could hold his opinions in check, he will go places. Perhaps you could remind him of that when you meet up.'

Gambitt took the chokecherry berries from Atherton before they ruined his suit. He considered it was time that they went back inside.

'So where do you suggest we start?' he asked watching Marjorie assist his CSI team in removing the dead woman from the cross.

Atherton looked around, there was no obvious CCTV and witnesses if any would have been in the residential quarter of the convent which was on the far side beyond the garden where he and Bob Gambitt had just sat. The chapel was the ideal place to murder somebody without being disturbed.

'Speaking with the sister's.'

Waiting in the wings was a woman in her fifties, she had on her work clothes as morning prayers had been cancelled. Atherton noticed that she clutched a bible to her chest where all prayers were being recited in memory of the soul of Mother Theresa. Gambitt went over and invited her to join Atherton, Tim Robbin and himself in the dining room leaving the forensic examiners to go about their work unhindered.

'Can you tell us about Sister Sarah, starting with when she arrived?'

'To relate what I have to tell you gentlemen will once again cause me pain.' Sister Monique laid her bible to the side of the table. 'And I would not want the lord to hear. Ruth came to us a few days after her twentieth birthday. When I laid eyes on that poor child she reminded me of the walking dead. Her eyes were trapped inside a soul that had been so badly treated that she had retreated within herself. We knew then that she had been badly treated and sexually abused. It was later that she told me about her baby son.

'What neither of us knew was that our conversation had been overheard by Mother Theresa. Now mother superior was a kindly woman and could accept most sins but having a child out of wedlock was something that she could not bear. In private she would verbally abuse Sister Sarah never letting the girl forget her sins. She would call her terrible names, referring to her as the sinner of the devil. Before the lord came to take Sister Sarah she was a broken shell, a husk without love or hope. She believed that the lord had turned his back on her for the second time.

'The day before she slipped into eternal sleep she could barely talk and yet talk she did despite feeling great pain. She told me that the lord had come down during the night and told her that she was to be punished. He said that she had been responsible for what happened between her and her brother and then at the place called Edington Hall she was again a sinner and that the master of the house was working for the good lord. What he did to her was cleansing her soul of any unrighteous sin. I could not believe what I was hearing but Ruth or Sister Sarah was already lost to us. She told me that she had left a suitcase hidden beneath an attic bedroom wardrobe of which inside was a bible, a nightdress and a pair of bed socks. She had left it there hoping that one day it would be found and that somehow the truth would be known.' Holding her head in her hands she started to weep. 'I am sinned for not helping her!'

Bob Gambitt gave the nun his handkerchief, he was unlike other detectives that Atherton knew.

'Why is Sister Sarah not buried in the garden with the other nuns?' he asked.

'Mother Theresa refused to have her buried here citing that a disciple of Satan had no place in the convent. She contacted the social worker who had made the previous arrangement and together with the help of the brother they had her interned at St. Cuthbert's at Alton Cross.'

'During Ruth's stay at the convent did Arthur, her brother ever visit or get in touch with his sister or the mother superior?'

'He came once but was he refused entry by Mother Theresa so he never came back. I never did find out what she had said to him but I saw from his reaction that he was shocked.'

Atherton could only guess that it was about the love child.

'Sister Monique, did Ruth ever mention the boy?'

'Yes, frequently when we were alone. We would go the garden together to turn the vegetable patch one of the few places where you could converse without being overheard. Sister Sarah would enthusiastically describe the boy, his blue eyes, the brown waves in his hair and the birth mark on his right shoulder. She had one similar.'

'Anything else?'

'She told me that he had been sent to an aunt north of the border.'

'Scotland?

'Yes.'

She crossed herself and picked up her bible.

'The lord will forgive me I know but without the mother superior knowing I used the excuse that I was heading north to aid an ailing uncle who did not have long to live. I travelled to a small village called Lochfallen where with the help of the local priest I found a young boy living with his aunt. At first sighting I knew that the boy he was undeniably her son, he had his mother's face, her eyes.'

Sister Monique carefully folded the handkerchief and gave it back to Bob Gambitt.

'Little Jack was an adorable child although it was quite evident that his life had been harsh and he was with sorrow. It broke my heart when he asked when I was going to bring his mother to visit.'

'So even at that age he knew that she was a nun?'

She nodded 'Yes. I told his aunt that I was doing a treatise on children living in the Trossachs National Park. She gave her permission for me to write to Jack. It was the only way in which I keep communication going between his mother and Jack. I tried to think of other ways to help but this convent has many eyes that pry. We might not speak a lot but many watch.'

'What you did was a courageous and very risky!' Gambitt suddenly added, it made her smile although weakly.

'I don't suppose there were any photographs of young Jack in the exchange of letters?'

Sister Monique shook her head.

'After a while the letters stopped coming back and that's when I noticed the change in Sarah. Almost overnight she had lost everything including the will to live. Jack was her world. A month later the lord put her to sleep and the angels collected her soul. I was there when she died. I will never forget her dying breath as she uttered the words *'please ask Jack to forgive me and tell him that I love him'*.

Tim Robbins went with her to collect the correspondence that had been sent. Sister Monique who had found Mother Theresa that morning in the chapel did not return to say goodbye to Gambitt and Atherton instead she knelt at her bed and asked the lord for his mercy.

When they went back to the chapel the body of mother superior had been shrouded with a black sheet. Marjorie showed them a digital image that she had taken when the dead woman had been lowered to the ground. Inscribed into the skin across her shoulder blades was the word *'Satan'*. Lying near the cross was a bloodied screwdriver.

'Some might say poetic justice.'

Bob Gambitt sat himself down on a wooden pew.

'I never really understood a *crime of passion* or the plea of a defence lawyer who pleads for temporary insanity of a client, perhaps not until today. If Jack is our killer and it sounds like he is then he has a reason to kill. Any love that he had was stolen not once, not twice but three times and if that wasn't a good enough reason for his revenge attacks then I am in the wrong profession.'

He looked down at the black shroud. 'Just because you wear a penguin suit doesn't give you right to judge others. First off she should have judged herself.' Gambitt stood up again.

'Mens rea could be argued that the killings were premeditated but that the killer acted out of temporary insanity. It would be hard to prove either way. And was a young boy of Jacks age living in Scotland capable of thinking up such crimes of hatred. I'm glad that I am not a lawyer.'

'Thank goodness then for judges and juries.' Atherton added.

Bob Gambitt looked up at the stained glass window behind where the cross had stood. Looking back down in an assortment of colour was an angel resting on the branch of an olive tree.

'I suppose we should give Harry Lane a call to see if he will release you and Pete Byrne only I've a feeling that we're all heading north of the border.'

Chapter Twenty Six

Late Friday Evening

They travelled in two cars with Harry Lane and Daniel Atherton leading, closely followed by Bob Gambitt and Pete Byrne giving the two men behind time to discuss and vent their frustrations concerning the late Gregory Tavistock and how he had single handily corrupted the investigation. It had been Lane's idea as to which pair travelled in which vehicle.

Harry Lane had agreed with Bob Gambitt and wanted to be part of the team covering the two hundred miles to the outlying village of Lochfallen sensing that the end was in sight. With Atherton driving he would have liked a few moments alone with Pete Byrne before the start of the journey to ask about the meeting with David Cherrington but perhaps an opportunity would present itself when they stopped. An hour in and sixty miles later Lane turned his head Atherton's way.

'Is your silence because you're thinking Daniel.' Lane asked.

'I'm sorry I was just concentrating. The M6 is a tedious motorway at the best of times.'

Lane smiled to himself.

'You can stop worrying about Pete Byrne he did good with Cherrington today and I believe that it helped the two of them getting together. From what I gather it helped clear the air.'

Atherton looked straight ahead as three columns of brake lights activated, slowed then moved ahead as if nothing had taken place to cause the slowing down.

'I was concerned that he would blow his chances for the future.'

'Who Cherrington. No, I think he'd weather most storms!' replied Lane with a wry smile.

Atherton joined in pulling out to the fast lane. Byrne had successfully left headquarters with his career still intact. Had it not been the case he would not have been in the car behind.

'Are we certain that Jack Benson is going to be at the address?' asked Lane.

'There's always that distinct possibility that he might not be. I did consider asking a local unit to pay a visit and if there apprehend him, but I didn't want anybody else getting hurt on our behalf. Call it pride if you like but this is the break that we've been working on, so it's best we handle it our way!'

Lane watched as the motorway signboards flashed by his window.

'This is one hell of a revenge vendetta!'

Atherton shook his head wondering. 'All because Arthur Benson got into bed with his younger sister from which they produced a boy child. I wonder why he waited so many years later to begin the reprisals.'

'Maybe other things got in the way. We'll soon know when he take him into custody.' He read the information on the next signboard which had the symbol for a motorway stop. 'Hopefully the nun was the last casualty in this unhappy affair!'

Atherton nodded having seen the sign too. 'There can't be many left who would be involved.'

He turned off and slowed taking the service road of a motorway stop-over just beyond Carlisle so that they could take a welfare break, grab a coffee and stretch their legs. Harry Lane took the opportunity to speak with his opposite number in the Scottish Constabulary politely explaining why they were travelling north into his territory. Superintendent McTavish offered the use of a local fire arms unit aware that the body count had been stacking up and wanting no adverse publicity for his own part in the operation. Harry Lane gratefully accepted the offer.

Returning to where the others were enjoying the break, coffee and a pastry he told them about the firearms backup.

'I've a feeling that he won't cause us any trouble!' suggested Atherton.

'How come' asked Gambitt.

'Jack's been on a mission to avenge the wrongs of his mother. I believe that he will accept his fate quietly knowing that he laid her to rest, peacefully at last.'

'An interesting thought,' admitted Lane, all the same I'll be happy to have the shooters there just in case.'

Bob Gambitt having spent time in the convent garden with Atherton was inclined to agree. 'I'm also in favour of back-up although I'm with Daniel on this one. I reckon our boys done what he set out to do and now that it's over he will rollover peacefully wanting this to come to an end.'

'He'll certainly get that in prison,' said Byrne as he finished his pastry and washed it down with the last of his coffee.

Having left Cherrington's headquarters office he had managed a quick call to Anne to tell her that everything went well and that at last he had been given the opportunity to have his say and have it heard by somebody that was in agreement. The moment he had stepped out of the building he had been met by Harry Lane who told him that they were travelling up the M6.

Just shy of two hours later the two cars dropped down the long winding road where in the distance beside a small loch they saw the village rooftops shrouded in a watery mist. At the side of the road the longhorn cattle looked up as they passed but took no further notice chewing on the rich vein of grass beside the hedgerow.

'I've never fancied a holiday here,' lane admitted 'too much bloody fog for my liking!'

Getting closer to their destination they saw a marked police unit parked outside of the bungalow. Harry Lane was unimpressed.

'I specifically asked that they wait until we had arrived.'

Lochfallen was a small community with no more than two dozen properties scattered about the undulating land and hills, sitting beside the loch surrounded by woods and farms. Passing a house that was part pub, part grocery store Atherton applied the brake and brought the car to a halt. Stretched between the posts of the garden gate was a length of blue and white crime scene tape.

'Now what?' Lane said as he pushed open the door.

A lone officer guarding the entrance guided them down the side of the property and around to the back where they were met by a Scottish firearms officer. Having seen their warrant cards he stood aside to let them pass.

'Our inspector told to look out for a Jack Benson.'

'That's right,' said Atherton getting in first before Harry Lane asked why they had not waited 'but why the crime scene tape?'

'If you follow me, you'll see why.'

He escorted them inside the detached property arriving at a side bedroom where he introduced his female colleague. Pointing at the bed they saw the lifeless body of a partially decomposing elderly woman.

'At first we thought that this was your man, until we checked closer.'

With her head denting the middle of the pillow the woman was in her late seventies perhaps early eighties. There were no clear signs of any injury to suggest that she had been attacked. Atherton stepped closer. The air in the room was dank and heavy with death although he sensed an unusual peace in the bungalow. Decomposition had started immediately after death. Gently pulling back the bed covers he uncovered her hands.

'At a guess I'd say that she's been dead around three weeks.'

'How do you know?' asked Harry Lane.

'Because the woman has already gone through the first and second stage of decomposition and she's entering the third stage.' He pointed at the ends of her hands. 'The finger nails have come away. Another couple of days and she'll begin to liquefy.'

Pete Byrne came in and stood beside Atherton having heard the evaluation 'you have definitely been hanging around Marjorie far too long.' He looked around the room 'why no flies,' he asked.

'Somebody left the window open,' suggested the female officer pulling back the curtain. 'Although I would say from the damp in the room that the window was only opened in the last couple of days. It can get a wee bit nippy around these parts overnight,' she pointed to the outside 'and we've normally a mist down in Lochfallen coming in from the water only it never lasts this long but there's little sun today.'

Around the bottom of the metal window frames the condensation was dirty where the windows had not been cleaned for some time. Down by the side of the bed Harry Lane found an empty pill bottle.

'Suicide?' said Byrne.

'It would seem that way.' Replied Lane as he read the name on the label.

Bob Gambitt who had checked the adjoining bedroom informed the occupants of the room that the bed had been unused and was distinctly cold. He had also noticed that nearly all the cupboards were bare.

'And the milk in the fridge is growing hairs!'

Harry Lane asked the Scottish officers how they had forced a way into the property.

'We didn't have to Sir, the back door had been left unlocked, although again that's not uncommon in these parts.'

Lane continued. 'You said that you thought somebody had been here recently, what made you think that?'

She took Lane and Gambitt into the front room where the windows were closed shut. Down on the carpet there were damp spots where somebody had trodden into the thin weave blades of broken grass.

'Any moisture on the soles of our feet would have already been absorbed and possibly vanished. However these damp spots are significant and suggest that somebody quite heavy stood here thinking.' To prove her point she knelt down and touched the damp with the ends of her fingers. Bob Gambitt did the same.

'You know young lady you're wasted in firearms, you'd make a damn fine detective!'

She smiled at them both.

'Too much paperwork Sir and I like the open air!'

Pete Byrne took himself next door to enquire with the neighbour. He was greeted by an old gentleman still dressed in his pyjamas. Byrne produced his warrant and asked if he could be invited in.

'Aye,' said the old timer as read the details on the card wondering why it did not have the badge of the thistle at the top. Cupping his right ear he warned 'only you'll need to speak up young man as I'm a little deaf.'

He was offered a chair beside the meagre fire which he gratefully took, the air inside the cottage was no better than that of outside. 'Do you remember a man living next door?' he asked.

The old man closed one eye before leaning forward. 'What's that you say, that the man next door was poor?'

Pete Byrne muttered something under his breath then tried again. *'No. The man from next door have you seen him lately?'* he added extra volume.

Rolling his dentures around the soft mounds of his gums the pensioner eyed Byrne suspiciously. 'Aye, although not lately. Jack took his van to go south a couple of weeks back and I haven't seen him since. When I asked why, he said he was paying some relatives a visit. I told him that they were a rum lot down south and not to be trusted. Never did like the Sassenachs, do you?'

Byrne sighed, ignoring the smear 'You said a van, what colour?' he shouted again to be heard.

'Ranger's blue of course like the colour of my lad's shirts. Who do you support?' the old man suddenly asked.

'The wife and kids.' Byrne replied.

Pulling the door shut he was happy to leave Rory MacGregor to his memories when as a younger man he had stood proudly amongst the home supporters of Glasgow Rangers cheering the loudest when his hero John Greg had just put another in the net. Byrne was almost at the garden gate when he heard the old timer call out.

'Did you hear about that bad accident over at Glen Arran earlier, it was on the midday news and said that a blue van had been involved?'

The firearm's officer checked with her control and they confirmed that there had been a road traffic accident about the time that the four detectives had stopped at Carlisle for refreshments.

Several minutes later they came back with more information transmitting the information through her ear piece.

'Control say that our traffic units are still at the scene and that the road between Glen Arran and towards Kinlocharderie is still shut. It's unlikely to open for a few more hours. The van is a write-off and there's trees strewn all over the highway. Traffic say that the van jumped the junction colliding with an articulated lorry transporting felled trees on the way to the lumber yard. Apparently the lorry driver told our units that the van just sat at the side of the junction then suddenly jumped into his path. He had no chance to avoid the collision.'

'That sounds like a death wish,' exclaimed Atherton 'is the van driver alive?'

She checked again and was told that the van driver's injuries were extensive. He had been airlifted to The Royal Firth Medical Centre at Ambleton Deer.

Thanking the officers for their help they ran to the cars knowing that every second counted.

Chapter Twenty Seven

Early hours of Saturday Morning

Because of the road closure and diversions the journey was longer by thirty five miles and in the dark the fog had refused to lift all day shrouding the night in an eerie grey blanket. By the time that the two cars arrived at The Royal Firth Medical Centre at Ambleton Deer it was already gone past midnight.

They explained their visit to a duty sister who asked them to wait in her office while she made enquiries as to whether Jack Benson was well enough to receive them.

'Was his injuries that bad?' asked Daniel Atherton.

'Aye sergeant, they were indeed. When the poor man arrived by air ambulance his internal injuries were extremely extensive, he went straight to surgery. He was fortunate to have Mr Grahame here. I will see if the surgeon is still about.'

'What are his chances?' Asked Pete Byrne.

'Slim,' replied the sister 'gravely slim.'

They had been disappointed although not surprised not to have found any photographs at the bungalow belonging to Shelley McDuff, the dead woman, expecting to find at least one of Jack Benson and that of his mother Ruth.

When they heard the soft footfalls returning they stood anticipating the worst news. She was accompanied by a man who looked physically and emotionally drained of all energy.

'This gentlemen is Mr Thomas Grahame, our principal consultant surgeon!'

The nursing sister stepped aside to give the surgeon room to shake their hands. Atherton offered his chair so that the surgeon could rest a minute.

'We are very grateful for your time Mr Grahame, especially knowing the hour and we promise not to detain you long.' Harry Lane respected a dedicated professional. He outlined the reason for their visit.

The surgeon nodded accepting why they had come in numbers.

'Before I start gentlemen might I explain something ethical, first and foremost I am a doctor and as such I am bound by my Hippocratic Oath to value the privacy and life of my patient, however in the circumstances I appreciate the urgency to deal with this matter.

'However, whatever atrocities this man might allegedly be responsible for I am here employed to patch and heal where I can. When Mr Benson was delivered to my table today his injuries were so extensive that I had little option but to do the best I could knowing that his chances of surviving the next twenty four hours were very limited.

'Jack Benson has suffered numerous structural fractures, a swollen brain, facial cuts and a broken jaw. He has cracked vertebrae, a damaged spleen, torn liver and internal bleeding which I have cauterised but there is every possibility that my patient will continue to bleed from another as yet identified injury. On impact with the lorry he suffered a punctured lung although the attending doctor and paramedic on board the air ambulance did an amazing job. Besides the obvious he will need god's help to pull through. To be brutally blunt our patient is dying.'

'Can we see him?' asked Harry Lane.

Thomas Grahame looked at Jessie MacFarlaine where together they approved the visit 'as long as you do not exact my patient's health and that you are mindful that he has not long been out of surgery.'

They agreed.

'And I can only permit two of you in to be at his bedside as I have to consider the other patients.'

With Sister MacFarlaine leading the way they slipped quietly through the ward where most of the four bedded bays were occupied. Pushing aside a door into a side ward she advised Atherton and Gambitt that they could have ten minutes but no more. Sitting either side of the bed they were amazed at how many monitors and tubes were keeping him alive. Jack Benson was indeed badly cut, smashed up, battered and bruised. Bandaged almost from head to foot.

Sensing a presence in the room he slowly opened his eyes, surprisingly smiling through the pain at Daniel Atherton.

'I thought that we would meet one day sergeant.' He turned his head across the pillow to look at Bob Gambitt. With the tube still sucking blood from his lungs, taped awkwardly to the side of his mouth his words were punctuated by a gargling sound. 'You I don't know although if I had to guess I would say that you were here because of a certain dead convent nun.'

Bob Gambitt introduced himself, his manner was calm and remarkably sympathetic.

'I guess you killed here because of the way that she treated your mother?'

Jack Benson tried to smile but it hurt. He felt the morphine flow through his veins to help. *'Ah, the lovely Sister Monique, my loyal and faithful angel?'* Benson whispered.

'She said to say that she was sorry Jack but she had to tell the truth!'

He moved his head very slightly to indicate that it did not matter. 'Sister Monique was the only nun to care for my mother. Without her my mother would have suffered more!'

His eyes went to where Atherton was sitting. 'Did you find the clues that I left you?'

Atherton grinned 'Most Jack, I just hope that we didn't miss any.'

He grimaced but dealt with the pain. 'I wanted you to find them. I would have left more but I'd guess that you would set up cameras and perhaps a motion sensor in my father's house. I watched the police technical van leave.'

'Why Gregory Tavistock?' Atherton asked.

'Because he was a sinner, a Judas. My mother in desperation had gone to him for help.'

Although it hurt to move he managed looking first as Gambitt then Atherton.

'As children we are always told that if you needed help to find a policeman. My mother found one that she thought would help only he double crossed her. She confided everything with Tavistock, told him about the rape and the abuse, the malevolence that went on in Edington Hall. She trusted him because he was a police officer. What she didn't know was that Tavistock went straight to that bastard Roger Edington. His betrayal made things a lot worse. He died the way that he deserved.'

Through the eye glass of the door Jessie MacFarlaine indicated that they had five minutes left.

'And the social worker, Hannah Blackburn, why kill her?'

'She too was supposed to have helped only she didn't. All that she succeeded in doing was make my mother's life a living hell at Edington Hall then from there she put her in the convent at The Lady of the Shrine.' He coughed up blood but wiped it from his lips using the back of his bandaged hand. 'Did you know Mr Atherton that Sister Theresa and Hannah Blackburn were cousins?'

It was all beginning to fall into place. The corrupt web of evil that had existed before the turn of the century was slowly being put together again by a dying man. Despite the agonising pain he felt and the extent of his injuries Jack Benson appeared remarkably calm for a man knowing that the end would be soon. He smiled, recognising Jessie MacFarlaine as she slipped through the door to stand at the end of the bed.

'Please sister, let them hear what I have to say. I won't be long!'

Sister MacFarlaine nodded, smiling back.

'As a young constable Gregory Tavistock had dated Hannah Blackburn. I can only image that when he found out that she was a lesbian it somewhat tainted the relationship!' he tried to laugh but it hurt and the tube at the side of his mouth gurgled loudly.

262

'Gentlemen...' MacFarlaine said 'I think Mr Benson would benefit from some peace and sleep.'

Lifting his good arm Jack Benson gestured that he was okay to continue.

'Okay, I will allow a couple more minutes then I will be back, if needs be with Mr Grahame only the monitor is too erratic for my liking.'

'My last question,' asked Atherton realising that they and Jack Benson were running out of time 'do you know what happened to your aunt?'

He coughed, brought up specks of blood then moments later settled back down again.

'How she chose to die was of her own choosing not mine as long as she did die. Before this matter became the interest of you and Mr Byrne I went back to Lochfallen where I told my aunt everything that I had found out. She listened, realising that she was as much to blame as all the others, her only saving grace and why I did not kill her was that she had raised me from a young boy, clothed and fed me. Her undoing however was her wicked side.'

Jack tried to sit up but his injuries forced him back down. 'Easy Jack,' Atherton reminded him.

'Many of the letters addressed to me ended up on the fire although cleaning the dying grate later that day I would find the remnants in the ash. They were the times that I suffered most. The hopelessness of my existence was worse than the terrible weather beyond the bungalow door. The not knowing would rip through my soul. I had so many times asked for a photograph of my mother and yet I had none. She would only exist in here.' He gently touched his heart.

Taking a small black and white photograph from the inside of his jacket Atherton handed it across to Jack Benson. He pointed to the young girl sitting on the park bench.

'That's your mother Jack, that's Ruth Ann Benson. You look like her and nobody can deny that. That's for you to keep.'

Jack Benson stared at the photograph, felt a tear appear and fall from the side of his eye as he clutched the image to his chest. Suddenly the blood pressure alarm sounded as the monitor began throwing up erratic numbers. Jessie MacFarlaine burst into the room closely followed by Thomas Grahame.

'He's bleeding out,' Grahame said as he whipped off his jacket and rolled up his sleeves.

Almost instantly the monitor recording his heartbeat flat lined. MacFarlaine ordered Atherton and Gambitt out of the room.

Standing to one side of the corridor wall they observed the trolley being pushed into the room as the crash team pumped and massaged Jack's heart and even when they added extra voltage to the defibrillator pads, their best went unrewarded. Jack Benson had finally got what he wanted from Daniel Atherton and at last he was at peace with himself and the world. At last his soul would join that of his beloved mother.

By the time Harry Lane and Pete Byrne ran down the corridor to join Gambitt and Atherton it was all over. In the side ward the nurses were beginning to remove the various tubes from the mouth and nasal passage of the late Jack Benson.

With a gentle pat on the back Bob Gambitt was glad that he had been present to have seen Jack Benson's passing 'That was a noble gesture you did in there Daniel giving him the photograph. You sent him on his way a happy man.'

'Jack Benson deserved some kind of peace in his final minutes.' He looked across at Lane and Pete Byrne 'It is not our place to be seen as judge and jury.

The four men respectfully bowed their heads forward as a nurse covered the face of the deceased with a white sheet. Ruth and Jack Benson had been through so much together, united at first they had soon been torn apart to live alone in a world full of fear, humiliation and dark evil.

Later Atherton and Lane would draft a report together for David Cherrington, as would Gambitt for his part in the investigation.

And what of Jack Benson. The four detectives saw to the arrangements themselves making sure that he was laid to rest beside that of his mother where at last they could be together, joined in eternal love. Atherton had one large headstone made to cover both graves, removing the older and damaged stone that had sat lonely above the body of Ruth Benson.

Under the names and dates etched into the headstone there was a small inscription, penned by Daniel Atherton.

'For some sons and mothers the love never dies, whereas for others the road is never long enough!'

Chapter Twenty Eight

Sometime Christmas

Outside of the jeweller's window Mary Thomas was unable to contain the excitement in awe of the many trays of diamond rings, unable to decide which she liked the best.

'I just don't know,' she said 'they are all so beautiful!'

'Then the only way to make the right choice is to go inside.'

With his arm clamped through hers he guided her inside and over to the waiting sales assistant.

'Good afternoon and how may we help today?' the assistant asked.

With her heart doing somersaults inside her chest Mary Thomas sighed as she smiled. 'We would like to look at some engagement rings please.'

An hour later they walked from the jewellers with Mary holding on tight to a small ribbon tied bag.

'So what happens now?' she asked as she kissed him in full view of everyone going by.

'Well, I guess that I find us a mysterious but magical place where I need to propose, after which we to contact DS Byrne and ask him to be our best man!'

Printed in Poland
by Amazon Fulfillment
Poland Sp. z o.o., Wrocław

57571795R00157